CHECKMATE
Ty Drago

Books

Pennsville, NJ

PUBLISHED BY
eSpec Books LLC
Danielle McPhail, Publisher
PO Box 242,
Pennsville, New Jersey 08070
www.especbooks.com

ISBN: 978-1-956463-69-9
ISBN (eBook): 978-1-956463-68-2

Copyediting: Greg Schauer, John L. French, and Ef Deal
Interior Design: Danielle McPhail
Cover Art and Design: Mike McPhail, McP Digital Graphics

FOR CHERYL, THE REAL ONE...

CHAPTER ONE

DRUMTHWACKET

WHITE PAWN TO KING'S BISHOP FOUR

Friday, July 4, 2048

"LADIES AND GENTLEMEN, HONORED GUESTS, MADAM GOVERNOR. Checkmate here."

New Jersey State Police Trooper Jake Merryman snapped to full alert as, around him, all conversation in the crowded conservatory stopped with an almost audible thud. At least twenty VIPs, with dozens more pouring in through the open door leading to the tented veranda, all gaped as a Wizard of Oz-sized head appeared above the round hors-d'oeuvres-laden table in the center of the fancy room.

Not surprisingly, the mansion's holoprojector was state-of-the-art, the image it cast filling fully a quarter of the room. Jake had always wanted one of those, if only to watch football in glorious 3D. Smaller units had become fairly commonplace, mostly with government and corporate types. But one of these big systems, even refurbished, would cost him more than a year's rent. Maybe the side gig he'd recently landed would help with that.

We'll see...

Meanwhile, the face now captivating the assembly of state politicos, portrayed in glorious detail, was instantly recognizable.

A skintight black hood and a weird checkerboard mask concealed the entire head. Not an inch of skin showed. The visage was one that had become hugely famous over the last year, having been repeatedly displayed and discussed on every news outlet in the country. Everyone knew it. Everyone talked about it. Some kids had even worn homemade knock-offs last Halloween.

According to analysis, the voice behind that mask was that of a young, college-educated male, definitely Jersey. Whatever his identity, it seemed Checkmate was a local boy.

"Sorry for interrupting the party, but I'm afraid we've got a serious matter to attend to."

Jake caught the eye of Sarah Burke, the trooper closest to him. After a few seconds, she tapped her ear, looking confused. And he could understand why. By now their earpieces should have been buzzing with chatter. There were at least twenty troopers stationed in and around the mansion. Somebody, whether a sergeant, one of the higher-ups, or even Colonel Rhona Johnson herself, should have been barking orders.

But there was nothing.

Jake pressed the transmit contact on his Cuff. "Merryman in the Conservatory requesting orders."

For a second, he heard nothing. No static. No background chatter.

Without warning, music began to play in his ear.

It sounded like—the Beatles.

"I'd like to be under the sea in an octopus's garden in the shade..."

What the holy hell...?

This was the Annual Gubernatorial July Fourth Gala, the social event of the state's political season, held here at Drumthwacket, the governor's mansion in the ritziest part of Princeton, one of the ritziest towns in the state. Only the crème de la crème of New Jersey's political elite got invited—which was why Jake had welcomed the chance to fill in at the last minute. After all, how many bus driver's sons got an opportunity to hobnob with the governor?

Not that he'd been "hobnobbing" with anybody.

The state troopers' role here tonight was strictly security. He wasn't allowed to eat or drink anything, much less "fraternize" with the guests. It stuck in his craw, making him all the more optimistic about his burgeoning side gig.

"Merryman," said Burke, sidling up to him. She looked nervous. "What's happening?"

"Comms are down," he replied.

"You think?" she asked. Burke was a wiseass. But Jake didn't mind that since she was also good-looking. He might even have considered asking her out except she was a bit too by-the-book for him. Sarah Burke lacked Jake's "street smarts" as well as his keen understanding of how the world worked. "But that doesn't explain the music!"

"Nope," he admitted. He scanned the room again. "Where's the governor?"

"Right there," Burke replied. "She and her husband just came in from the veranda."

Jake looked where she pointed. New Jersey's governor, the Honorable Susan Lapidus, stood beside her husband and the state's first gentleman, Dr. Joel Lapidus, Chair of the Philosophy Department at Princeton University. They were a handsome couple, tall and slender — young-looking despite being in their early fifties. Nestled in with them stood Gordon Neary, the Lieutenant Governor; Edgar Portermann, the state's Attorney General; and Victor Cardellini, the Speaker of the Assembly. Add to that the chief justice of the New Jersey Supreme Court, Sally Cooker, and you had what were probably the six most powerful people in the state, all closed in on one another, weirdly reminding Jake of a football team at huddle.

Everyone else was staring up at Checkmate.

Where the hell's the colonel?

Jake almost asked Burke, but the big floating head started talking again.

"Government is, or ought to be, a contract with the governed, a promise made by the electees to electors. For the most part, everybody here shares that responsibility. Some of you do so honorably. But some of you don't, and that's where I come in."

"Somebody shut that off!" the attorney general demanded. Portermann had a deep voice, one that carried.

At that moment Colonel Rhona Johnson, Superintendent of the State Police, pushed her way through the crowd and into the huddle. She was a small, fit woman near sixty. Jake figured she might have been pretty once, but now either age or the job had turned her grim. He didn't think he'd ever seen her smile.

She started talking quietly into the governor's ear.

Checkmate said, "Somebody in this room is guilty of accepting over two million in bribes over the last ten months, all of it from Vladimir Antonov. I'm betting most of you have heard of him."

Jake certainly had. Antonov was a Russian gangster who operated a number of import/export and civic construction businesses out of New Brunswick. Though Antonov kept a low profile, in law enforcement circles he was widely rumored to be the king of New Jersey's underworld — not that anyone, from the state troopers to the FBI, had ever been able to prove that. No indictments. Not even a subpoena. But in the past two decades, whenever something shady went down in the state, fingers pointed at Antonov.

Though he would never say so, Jake admired the guy.

Antonov was someone else who understood how the world worked.

At the mention of Antonov's name, the quiet in the drawing room got even quieter. Weirdly, it reminded Jake of elementary school—the silence that fell whenever a kid was called out by the teacher for screwing around in class.

"For God's sake, governor!" Speaker Cardellini exclaimed. "Ed's right. Can't we shut this off? How's he even doing this?"

But before anyone could answer, the floating head continued, "I've managed to secure records of funds transferred to an account in the Cayman Islands that's registered to a phony corporation with only one shareholder. Every dollar of those funds came directly from a holding company owned by Antonov. I also have backups of Cuff messages passed between Antonov and this person, in which the terms of the bribery are spelled out. Basically, Antonov wanted certain business deals to be fast-tracked through the state assembly. Favors for cash."

"You two!" someone barked.

Jake and Burke snapped to attention as a sergeant marched up to them. Jake, being a last-minute addition to this detail, didn't know the man. But Burke clearly did.

"Sergeant Staunton!" she said.

Staunton was in his forties, average height, and with narrow shoulders. His dark hair was cut military short, half his face hidden behind a thick beard. He wore, as they all did, a formal trooper's uniform, complete with billed cap. He stood in front of them, glowering, with Checkmate's oversized head at his back. "We've been trying to reach you both."

"Our earpieces are on the fritz, sergeant," Burke said.

"How so?"

"Well, they're playing music," Burke replied.

"Music?"

"Yes, sergeant."

"They don't play music."

"They do, now," Jake said, offering his earpiece to the sergeant. "Oldies."

In the middle of the room, Checkmate said, "The proof of these crimes has been compiled and sent to every major news outlet in the state. A full copy can be found on a nanocard in the right breast pocket of the perpetrator, Assembly Speaker Victor Cardellini."

Murmurs swept through the crowd like a shockwave. Several of the VIPs actually staggered a step.

"That's a lie!" Cardellini declared.

Every head turned toward him.

When the governor spoke, Jake expected her to say something like, "These serious charges will need to be fully investigated," or "Speaker Cardellini, let's talk in private." But instead, she turned to the red-faced speaker and said in a loud, clear voice, "Vic, would you please empty your pockets?"

Cardellini tried for "outraged" but only managed "desperate." "What? No! I'm telling you, this is a lie!"

"That's easy enough to prove," the governor pressed. "Just show us."

"I won't give in to this... terrorist's false accusations!"

Governor Lapidus' expression hardened. "Victor Cardellini, I am ordering you to empty your pockets."

Cardellini went so pale that Jake wondered how he didn't faint. "I need to make a call," he said.

"Later." The governor nodded to Attorney General Portermann, who turned to Colonel Johnson and said, "Rhona, would you please assist the speaker? I'm afraid he may have lost something."

Expressionlessly, Johnson stepped up to Cardellini. "Please raise your arms, Mr. Speaker."

"I will not!" Cardellini exclaimed. "Don't touch me!"

"Don't make it necessary for me to call over a trooper."

"You won't find anything!"

"Then you've got nothing to worry about, do you?" said the lieutenant governor.

Hovering above the table, Checkmate had gone still, almost as if he, too, were watching the drama unfold. But that couldn't be right. This holoprojection had to be a recording, didn't it?

Checkmate can't be here, can he?

Looking like a trapped animal, Vic Cardellini let the colonel pat him down. She did so respectfully but thoroughly, finally pulling something out of his tuxedo's breast pocket. Even though he stood twenty feet away with a crowd between them, Jake could see perfectly well what it was.

A bishop, a black chess bishop.

Cardellini stared at it in utter, speechless disbelief.

Johnson locked eyes with the governor who said, "Turn it over."

Nodding, Colonel Johnson examined the bottom of the chess piece. "There's a nanocard taped here."

Cardellini seemed to shrivel. His hands shook and he was visibly sweating. "It's a lie," he said again, but the fire behind it was gone.

"Arrest him," the A.G. told Johnson.

The colonel flagged a nearby trooper, who wordlessly shackled the speaker's hands behind his back.

"This is crazy!" Cardellini exclaimed.

Johnson ignored him, instead instructing the trooper, "Escort the speaker to the barracks. Nobody books or even questions him until I get there."

"Yes, ma'am," the trooper replied smartly.

As Cardellini was marched out, he screamed for a lawyer, the sound becoming ever shriller as he disappeared through the conservatory doors.

Still filling the room's center, the masked holo spoke one final word. "Checkmate."

The projection ended.

Meanwhile, Staunton, with Jake's earpiece to his ear, said, "I don't hear anything."

Jake almost told him, *Who cares? Did you see what just friggin' happened?*

Then, without warning, a figure burst out from under the serving table, knocking the skirted tablecloth aside and overturning the shrimp tower in the process. Food went flying. People screamed.

"What the hell?" Staunton exclaimed, whirling around.

Jake stared, not quite believing his eyes.

The figure wore all black, his face covered by a checkerboard mask. He pushed through the crowd, knocking down at least four people on his way to the veranda exit. As he neared it, two troopers converged on him, their hands on the butts of their guns.

Checkmate threw something at the floor.

Jake recoiled, covering his mouth as thick white smoke filled half the conservatory.

The VIPs went into full panic, falling over each other to escape the spreading billows. With the door to the veranda blocked by smoke, they instead started pouring out through the two interior exits, fleeing deeper into the mansion.

As they did, however, Jake noticed that nobody seemed to be coughing or clawing their eyes. Whatever this stuff was, it didn't seem to be in any way toxic.

"Come on!" Staunton ordered. "This way."

"Wait!" Burke exclaimed. "We can get him!"

"And we will!" the sergeant replied. "Follow me!" He plowed a path through the panicked crowd.

Burke and Jake swapped glances. Then they did as ordered.

The three departed the conservatory through a side door, navigating through an ornate library and down a short corridor that ran past the governor's private office, before spilling through an exit that put them on the south lawn. Their timing proved perfect. Just as Jake got his bearings, Checkmate sprinted past them, no more than ten feet away, having cut around the rear of the big house. Nobody else seemed in pursuit; likely, he'd lost them in what Jake supposed amounted to a good old-fashioned smoke screen.

With a cry, Staunton took up the pursuit, running full tilt.

Somewhere behind them, Jake heard Colonel Johnson command, "Full lockdown! Full lockdown! Nobody leaves!"

He and Burke took up the chase as well.

"We gotta call for backup!" Burke exclaimed.

"I'm trying!" the sergeant replied. "Comms are down! Hey, you! This is the state police! Stop where you are!"

This did nothing, of course, as Checkmate made a beeline across the manicured lawn. He was maybe fifty feet ahead of them, neither gaining nor losing ground, running with his arms flailing, like a panicked child.

Ahead, the lawn gave way to a curved drive that led from the mansion to the security gate. The latter stood wide open, and Jake could only guess that whoever was stationed there hadn't heard the lockdown call.

But at least the guy wasn't blind.

As they all neared the gate, a trooper stepped into view from inside the security booth. To his credit, he instantly blocked Checkmate's path, his gun drawn.

Perp's going to throw another smoke bomb, Jake figured.

But that didn't happen. Instead, the masked fugitive collided with the trooper and they both went down hard on the tarmac.

Staunton, Jake, and Burke reached them moments later. By then, the trooper had Checkmate on his stomach and was shackling him.

"We got him!" Jake exclaimed. He was breathless, but still laughing like a kid at Christmas. "I don't believe it!"

"Pull off his mask," Staunton said. "Let's get a look at this guy." He tapped on his Cufflight and shone it down on the captured — what? Jake wondered. Domestic terrorist? Not really. Criminal? Sure, kind of. Vigilante? That was probably closest to the truth.

But that was for the brass to figure out. All that mattered now was that he, Jacob Merryman, would be getting an "assist" in the capture of the most wanted man in the state.

With Checkmate trussed up, the gate guard, whose name Jake didn't know, rolled the perp over. Then, with a nod from Staunton, Burke reached down and pulled off the mask.

The face underneath blinked up at them.

He was older than Jake had figured, forty, at least. He had several days stubble on his chin and eyes that looked more wild than calculating.

"He paid me!" the man declared. He sounded lucid enough, but nothing like the holoimage. "A thousand bucks!" He grinned, showing yellow teeth.

Staunton blew out a sigh. He moved his Cufflight across each of their faces, one after another. "Well, troopers," he said. "Any of you been drinking tonight?"

It was a weird question.

"What?" Burke asked.

"Yes or no. Drinking?"

"No," she said.

"No," said the gate guard.

"Of course not," said Jake.

"Good," Staunton replied. There came a faint *whoosh* from the sleeve of his raised arm, barely a sound at all.

Something sweet hit Jake's nose. Still a bit breathless from the run, he inhaled it without thinking, and the world immediately started spinning. He didn't fall. Instead, he felt himself kind of float down to the tarmac beside the shackled man, the Checkmate who definitely wasn't Checkmate.

The last thing he saw before everything went black was both Burke and the gate guard collapsing beside him on the governor's driveway while Staunton looked grimly down at them.

The last thing he heard was Sergeant Staunton saying a word. Just one word.

"Checkmate."

CHAPTER TWO

THE ASSIGNMENT

BLACK PAWN TO KING THREE

Saturday, July 5, 2048

"I DON'T GET IT. WHY BOTHER WITH THE HOMELESS GUY AS A DECOY at all? Why not just use the uniform and walk right past the gate guard?"

Cheryl Walker looked up from her Cuff. Around her, the open-concept offices of the New Century 22 Media Cooperative buzzed with activity. There were at least twenty-five journalists on hand, most under thirty years old, busily producing content to fill NC22's demanding twenty-four-hour news cycle.

At twenty-three years old, Cheryl was the newbie, hired one month after finally finishing her scholastic career with a 4.0 GPA, two prestigious awards, a Bachelor's Degree in Communications from The College of New Jersey, and a Master's of Journalism and Media from Princeton University.

"Better than mediocre," her father had quipped at her graduation.

But despite her pedigree, Cheryl had been unpleasantly surprised by the differences between academic and real-world journalism. Since joining NC22 five weeks ago, she'd worked twelve hours, six or seven days a week, to not just meet the stringent content quotas but blow past them.

Her editor wanted six thousand "quality" words a week, minimum. Cheryl routinely doubled that.

It was a lot of writing, so much that she often awoke to find her fingers tapping on her Cuff, with the actual device sitting on its nightstand charger. Not that "Cuff tapping" was unusual. In the last twenty years, Cufflink, the company behind the world-changing invention, had turned one-handed typing into the absolute norm in the U.S. and most of Western Europe. By middle school, Cheryl had learned to type on her wrist by activating the small gadget's virtual keyboard and running the fingers of her right hand across it. These days, it was as natural as breathing — the most common muscle memory of the mid-twenty-first century.

Of course, her determination to produce content for her employer didn't mean she shouldn't engage with her colleagues. She was supposed to be a journalist, after all.

Which was why she said, "Because he did that at Barnaby's back in April."

The clique by the coffee bar were full-timers like herself, but with experience measured in years, not weeks. In their late twenties, each was young enough to manage the workload, while being apparently old enough to look down on rookies. Cheryl had discovered on day one that engaging without being spoken to first earned her condescension, if not outright ridicule. Her awards and her GPA were all well and good, but with this lot at least, she remained a kid in a room full of adults.

It also didn't help that, despite her newbie status, Cheryl kept landing choice assignments.

"What's that?" Omar Polat asked. With his almond skin and sharp brown eyes, Omar had the good looks to be a politician himself but had opted instead to write about them. Cheryl liked his work, though she could count on one hand the number of times he'd even glanced her way.

Cheryl regarded his vaguely interested expression, as well as the smirks worn by his entourage. Then, steeling herself, she explained, "Checkmate disguised himself as a Trenton cop when he exposed Bradley's extortion at that fundraiser at Barnaby's, remember? Afterward, he walked out the door and right past the cops in the street. He even chatted briefly with them. When it all hit the fan, Trenton P.D. had egg on its face. After everything exploded at Drumthwacket last night, Checkmate probably figured the staties would be on the lookout for the same trick, so he used a decoy instead, which he then pretended to chase and catch, all to get him close enough to the gate to use anesthetic gas and escape."

"Quite a mouthful, sweetie," one of the guys said. Cheryl thought his name was either Mark or Mike. In any event, his calling her "sweetie" landed him firmly on her Asshole List.

That list was getting long these days.

"How do you know all that?" demanded Edwina, a late-twenties redhead with a perpetually sour expression.

"I'm writing the noon piece on it," Cheryl said.

That made the entire clique groan. "Again?" Edwina exclaimed, throwing up her hands. It made her look like a cartoon villain.

Cheryl didn't respond.

"Didn't you tell Dag you wanted the next Checkmate story?" Mark/Mike said to Omar.

"That, I did," Omar replied, looking more confused than angry. He asked Cheryl, "Are you doing it on your own, on spec?"

Cheryl replied, "Dag assigned it to me."

"When?"

"A little over an hour ago."

"You got here at nine?" another clique member asked. "On a freakin' Saturday?"

"Eight-thirty," Cheryl corrected.

"Brown nose much?" Mark/Mike asked.

Cheryl ignored him.

"Dag must be losing it," Edwina declared. "Omar, you should—"

"Walker!" someone yelled.

Everyone looked toward the row of doors that occupied the open layout's only interior wall. The editorial offices.

Dag Roman, NC22's State and Local Politics Editor, stood outside the corner office. He was a big, balding, pale-skinned man of Norwegian descent who insisted on wearing a tie, the only person in the office, maybe the only person in the cooperative, who did so.

Dag scanned the room. When his eyes settled on Cheryl, he waggled a finger. "In here."

Cheryl tapped off her Cuff. Nearby, a Sports and Leisure full-timer named Felicia, less cliquey than the politicos, asked loudly, "Wait a sec. Hey, Edwina, didn't you say he was in there with Senator Bourbon?"

Edwina didn't reply, opting instead to continue glaring at Cheryl. Beside her, Mark/Mike had gone red-faced with consternation. The rest of the entourage just gaped, as though at an alien in their midst.

Except for Omar, who just looked thoughtful.

Finally, someone else answered. "Yeah. I saw him go in. There's another guy too. In a state trooper's uniform."

"What the hell do they want with you?" Edwina demanded as Cheryl walked past them, icicles forming on her every word.

Cheryl looked blandly at the group. Lately, she'd been practicing "blandly" in the mirror. It was a subtle thing, a calculated mix of bored, dismissive, and insanely confident that came in handy around here. "Maybe the senator needs to talk to a journalist."

As she turned her back, she heard Felicia laugh and say, "Okay, now that was a nice burn!"

Cheryl hid her smile.

Dag's office wasn't big, but it had floor-to-ceiling windows and a great view of the New Jersey State House. Cheryl liked it. She also liked the man who worked here. Dag Roman pretended to be hard as nails, a real "Perry White" kind of old-school newspaperman. But in the month and change that Cheryl had worked for him, she'd seen him celebrate three staffer birthdays with cakes, noisemakers, and full-throated singing. He'd even worn the pointy hat without a trace of irony.

You kind of had to admire that.

But right now he was all business.

"Sit," he instructed, motioning to the only empty chair. The other two were currently occupied by a dapperly dressed man of about fifty and a much younger guy with a bandaged head in the aforementioned trooper's uniform. The first man was easily recognizable: Michael Bourbon, President of the New Jersey Senate and one of the most powerful people in Trenton. He was also the founder and CEO of Cufflink, the New Jersey-based tech company that had created the Cuff, the invention that had ultimately supplanted the smartphone. Since its introduction two decades back, the Cuff had become the single most ubiquitous piece of gadgetry in the country and had made Bourbon a billionaire. But what had he done with that wealth? Aside from investing millions in poor urban schools and neighborhoods throughout the state from Newark to Salem, he'd decided to run for state senator, winning the seat on his first try and rising steadily through the ranks until he was now the president of that august body. His face routinely appeared in print and online, and he was often called the "Father of Modern Privacy."

On the flip side, his critics and political opponents labeled him an elitist .01 percenter who thought every problem could be solved by throwing money at it.

Either way — Bourbon was a very interesting person to be occupying one of Dag's cheap plastic guest chairs.

As to who the other man was—well, Cheryl could make a good guess.

"Senator Bourbon," she said. Then, rolling the dice, she addressed the other man. "And you must be Trooper Merryman."

The only surprise Bourbon showed was a Spockesque raising of one eyebrow. Merryman, on the other hand, looked like she'd just pulled a live dove out of her sleeve.

Meanwhile, Dag laughed and settled into his desk chair. "Told you. Smart."

Senator Bourbon stood and, with genteel politeness that Cheryl supposed was meant to be old-world charming, offered his hand and said, "A pleasure, Ms. Walker."

Cheryl shook the hand. Then she shook Merryman's, who presented his a bit gruffly and without making eye contact.

"Nice to meet you both," she replied. She took the proffered chair—and waited.

Finally, Bourbon said, "Your credentials are impressive."

"Thanks. Yours, too."

Dag smiled a little, though Bourbon didn't seem to notice. Instead, he rattled off her curriculum vitae as if having spent some time memorizing it. "You grew up in Flemington. High school valedictorian. National Honor Society. Dean's List. Editor-in-Chief of the school newspaper. Earned your bachelor's at The College of New Jersey where, I understand, you won the Pinnacle College Media Award."

Cheryl nodded, just once. Supposedly, single, decisive nods conveyed confidence without seeming boastful. It was an interview technique her father had taught her.

And she felt suddenly sure that this was exactly that—an interview. *Except... what am I interviewing for?*

"But you were at Princeton, getting your master's when you wrote the article that really got you noticed."

Cheryl asked, "Senator, where's all this going?"

Instead of answering, Bourbon said, "First tell me how you knew this gentleman is Trooper Merryman?"

"An educated guess," Cheryl replied.

"Based on... "

Cheryl held the man's eyes, another interview technique. "When I came in this morning, Dag asked me to write up two thousand words on last night's arrest of Speaker Cardellini at Drumthwacket. Now, just an hour later, he calls me into his office and here you are, sitting alongside a uniformed trooper with a bandaged forehead and... no offense... a hangdog look."

Merryman said nothing.

So she plowed on. "Not a big jump to figure the two things are connected. Now according to the official press release, four people were incapacitated by Checkmate during his escape. One was a homeless man. Another was a female officer. The other two were male troopers. The press release said only one, Jacob Merryman, suffered a minor injury when he struck the tarmac while losing consciousness." She nodded at Merryman's bandage. "That seems pretty minor to me."

Merryman grimaced.

Dag chuckled.

Senator Bourbon nodded. "Very good, Ms. Walker. A+"

Cheryl didn't reply.

Bourbon asked, "Why do you suppose Mr. Roman picked you over more seasoned staffers, both for today's assignment and this meeting?"

Cheryl said, "I have experience reporting on Checkmate."

"Experience," Bourbon echoed. "In fact, last year you wrote an article on Checkmate for the Daily Princetonian that was picked up by Reuters and The Associated Press and ultimately made you the youngest-ever recipient of the National Press Club's Sandy Hume Memorial Award for Excellence in Political Journalism."

Cheryl offered another of those single nods, as if this man weren't recounting the proudest moment of her life.

Senator Bourbon said, "I read the piece. You're an excellent writer."

"Thank you."

"You were the first to suggest a motive behind Checkmate's activities that wasn't political. At the time, the media and even the governor's office were calling him a partisan 'hit man' with a flair for the dramatic, a hatchet for the opposition party."

"All I did was go where logic took me," Cheryl said. "Checkmate's crusade against corruption in New Jersey is altruistic. He's a vigilante with a moral compass."

"*And* a flair for the dramatic," Dag added.

Bourbon said, "Your story was brilliantly written and ground-breaking. You deserved the accolades."

"Thank you."

"Not to mention this job," Dag added, smiling. "She beat out no less than fifty applicants."

This time, Cheryl had to fight a blush.

Bourbon said, "But tell me, Ms. Walker, how much do you know about the details of Checkmate's... crusade."

Cheryl shrugged, trying not to let on that they were now discussing her favorite subject. "He first appeared about two years ago, when he exposed a Casino Control Commission official for taking kickbacks. As always, he made his case with enough spectacle to force an arrest and enough evidence to make it stick. The CCC person, Angela Pierce, got seven to ten years for fraud and conspiracy."

Bourbon nodded. "Correct. And his second victim?"

"A freeholder from Middlesex County named Chester LaRoy. He was convicted on four counts of sexual assault against staffers. He received fifteen years. Checkmate, himself, convinced the women to testify and obliterated the 'he said/she said' defense with video taken from inside LaRoy's own office. Apparently, Checkmate had been surveilling the freeholder for weeks."

"Quite illegally," the senator pointed out.

"Their legality is a matter for law enforcement. Checkmate's a vigilante, not a cop."

"He's a criminal." The senator said this flatly, his eyes never leaving Cheryl's face. Sitting beside him, Merryman offered a bitter smile while, across his desk, Dag's face remained carefully neutral.

Another test.

Cheryl replied, "I'm a journalist, not a juror."

"Yet, in your article, I couldn't help but detect a certain subtext. Not explicit approval, of course, nothing that anyone could call bias. Just an impression, a gentle lean in favor of Checkmate's behavior."

Cheryl had heard that before. Her own father had thought the article a bit slanted. At the time, Cheryl had argued the point. But then, arguing with her father was an old habit.

This, however, was Michael Bourbon.

So she said nothing.

If the senator was non-plussed by her silence, it didn't show. "What about his third and fourth victims?" he asked. "What do you know about them?"

The man's repeated use of the word "victim" wasn't lost on her. "Um... I'm sorry. I'm still not sure where any of this is going."

"Indulge me," Bourbon replied.

Just what the hell was this?

Cheryl considered a moment before replying, "The third person Checkmate exposed was the husband of Assemblywoman Eleanor Brumhall. The guy quietly embezzled over a quarter million from the school fund that his wife had been championing for a decade. When Checkmate laid it all bare, he was indicted, and she was forced to resign."

Bourbon nodded. "And the fourth?"

"Senator Nathan Bradley, just last April. He'd been ready to run for reelection this fall. But Checkmate revealed that he's been quietly taking illegal campaign contributions. From whom, exactly, is yet to be announced, though Vladimir Antonov's name has been kicked around. Bradley's also been indicted."

Bourbon said, "Five public servants. All either in prison or awaiting trial. That's including Victor Cardellini, who'll be arraigned on Monday. Quite a record for a 'vigilante with a moral compass,' wouldn't you say?"

"Sure," she replied.

"Tell me about his methods," Bourbon suggested.

"Why?"

"Again... indulge me."

"He's quiet, at first. He can't hack Cuffs, of course. No one can. But he can and does hack into older backup systems. He also burgles his targets, sneaking into places that are supposed to be... well... unsneakable, and often leaves behind very high-tech surveillance equipment, audio and video. Usually, no one finds out he was there until after the arrest. By all accounts, he's an expert pickpocket, a master of disguise, good at appearing and disappearing when he needs to, and especially good at creating a spectacle when it's time for his 'big reveal.' In that regard, he loves to put on a show."

"Has he ever used violence?"

"That depends on how you define it. During the Bradley business, he used an inhalable anesthetic on one of the private security people. Then, just last night, he sedated three state troopers, including Officer Merryman here, with the same substance."

Merryman remarked, "Whatever it was, I was down before I knew what was happening. I thought 'knockout gas' was just stuff in novels."

"Checkmate's made it a reality," Cheryl replied. "He uses a custom derivative of something called sevoflurane. It works by briefly stifling the central nervous system, causing a loss of sensation followed by unconsciousness. It's been around for ages, but Checkmate's flavor of it is much more potent than the standard formulation they use in hospitals."

Merryman seemed to consider this. "Right before he did it, he asked if any of us had been drinking."

"Sevoflurane and alcohol don't play well together. He didn't want to risk seriously hurting you."

"Nice of him," the cop groused.

"How do you know all that, Ms. Walker?" Bourbon asked.

She shrugged. "It shouldn't surprise you that Checkmate's a special interest of mine."

"Fair enough. Well, given the drug's obvious effectiveness, I suppose we should include 'chemist' in his list of talents."

"And tech stuff," Merryman added. "The son of a bitch managed to pump Beatles music into our earpieces last night."

"How?" Cheryl asked, surprised. That much hadn't been in the official reports. "Don't the state police issue Cuffs?"

"They do." Bourbon replied. "But their earpieces still use old-fashioned Bluetooth. Checkmate found a way to replace their current pairing with one of his own, thereby cutting the Cuff out of the equation and effectively foiling the troopers' short-range communications."

Cheryl said, "He also hacked into Drumthwacket's holosystem. So I think Trooper Merryman's right. Whoever he is, Checkmate's a 'tech wizard,' too."

"You admire him," Bourbon said, somewhat accusingly. "This vigilante."

"Checkmate isn't Batman, senator. He doesn't go around beating up the 'bad guys' and leaving them in back alleys. He seeks out corruption in state and local politics and exposes it. He's a watchdog for our political system."

"We *have* a watchdog for our political system, Ms. Walker. It's called 'elections.'"

That statement struck Cheryl as ridiculously naïve.

In fact, it was more like deliberately naïve.

"You don't believe that," she said.

"Excuse me?"

She glanced at Dag and found him smiling thinly, which told her she'd guessed right. To Bourbon, she said, "What's going on here, senator?"

"What do you mean?"

"I mean that all this smacks of some kind of test or interview. In attacking Checkmate, I think you're fishing... trying to gauge my reaction."

"Is that right?" Bourbon's face gave away nothing. Merryman, however, fidgeted in his chair, looking annoyed.

Cheryl said, "I think so. I also think you're sizing me up for something, though you're taking your sweet time getting around to it."

Bourbon nodded and gently clapped his hands.

"Told you," Dag remarked.

"I'm so sorry, Cheryl," Bourbon said. "May I call you Cheryl?"

"May I call you Mike?"

He blinked, momentarily taken aback. Cheryl knew she'd crossed a bit of a line. This man was a billionaire, old enough to be her father, and the state's highest-ranking senator to boot. Never mind that, by long-standing if unwritten agreement, journalists didn't get on a first-name basis with politicians. Simple etiquette insisted that the brunt of respect be on her side of their relationship.

But right now, she didn't care. These men were playing games with her, and she was tired of it.

Dag cleared his throat and said, "I think maybe—"

But Bourbon held up a hand. "It's okay. Yes, Cheryl. You can call me Mike if you'd like to. Especially since I hope we'll be working together over the next week or so."

"Doing what?" Cheryl asked.

"You're not the only one who's been watching Checkmate's crusade. Let me put my cards on the table. I need someone, specifically you, to help me deliver a message."

"To whom?"

"To Checkmate."

"I don't understand."

"It may seem to you that Checkmate works alone. And for the most part, perhaps he does. But there's also evidence of a loose network of... associates, people who help him in small but important ways. They funnel him key information, provide bits of intel, smooth his path to the evidence he needs."

Cheryl, who'd never heard any such thing, asked, "How do you know?"

"A few of them have been caught on security cameras around town. Men and women of different ages. Very grainy and very brief. But the context suggests that each was digging up something for Checkmate."

"That's not in any press release," Cheryl said.

"Well, that's because the state police don't know yet. Only I do. This is my personal rabbit hole, Ms. Walker."

"Okay... " Cheryl said. "And what does this have to do with me?"

"I'd like you to follow me down that hole."

"Excuse me?"

"I want Checkmate to invite you into his network."

Cheryl blinked. "What?" RThen, regrouping, she asked something more sensible. "And how do you expect to arrange that?"

"We think we have a way."

"We?"

"Me."

"I'm a journalist," Cheryl said. "Not a spy."

"I don't believe 'spy' is the proper word. The goal would be for you to attract Checkmate's attention and encourage him to try to recruit you."

"Uh huh. How?"

"By making it publicly known that you intend to repeat your success with the Princetonian article with a second investigative piece about Checkmate," Bourbon said. "This one is to focus on the vigilante through the eyes of the people hunting him. It's why I came to Mr. Roman this morning. Your notoriety for the Hume article almost certainly caught Checkmate's attention. I'm hoping this second piece will pique his interest enough for him to make contact. "

Cheryl chewed on this. "Let me get this straight. You want me to help you... what? Trap Checkmate? Get him arrested?"

"No. No. Not at all. As I told you, all I want is for you to deliver a message."

"What message?"

Bourbon leaned forward and said, "He needs to know that his life is in danger. This isn't about the police anymore. He's being hunted by someone who doesn't want him arrested. They want him dead."

CHAPTER THREE

CHERYL'S ROOMMATE

WHITE KNIGHT TO QUEEN'S BISHOP THREE/
BLACK PAWN TO QUEEN FOUR

Saturday, July 5, 2048

TRENTON, THE CAPITAL OF NEW JERSEY, STOOD FOREVER BALANCED on a knife's edge between affluence and poverty. Despite a population of under 100,000, the small city suffered a high crime rate. This made travel outside of the riverfront area, where the State House and other government buildings resided, risky — especially at night.

Cheryl had learned this lesson the hard way when, just two weeks after moving here, she was mugged while walking home from work after dark.

Since then, she'd taken the bus the ten blocks to her apartment.

Unfortunately, while public transportation was safer, it was also crowded, stuffy, and claustrophobic, particularly for a "vertically challenged" young woman forced to stand for her entire commute. She spent the twenty-minute trip, twice a day, being squeezed and jostled by strangers, and clutching her purse under her arm like a football. One of the new, self-driving PeopleMovers would have been easier and much more comfortable, but Cheryl's pockets weren't deep enough to afford that on a daily basis.

So, the bus it was.

And tonight, by the time she let herself in through the street door, Cheryl was exhausted and anxious as hell.

Everything that Senator Bourbon had told her still rang in her ears.

Wearily, she turned left just inside the foyer, foregoing the steep staircase that led to the upper floors, and unlocked the door to Apartment 1A. As always, the hinges squeaked. This was an old house and, as her roommate liked to say, it talked to you.

The moment she was inside, a savory cooking aroma hit her nose and made her stomach growl. Grinning, her exhaustion momentarily forgotten, she followed it, uttering what had become the apartment's unofficial greeting: "Honey! I'm home!"

"Kitchen!" Sam yelled.

The apartment had a high ceiling in the manner of old houses, with a parlor, which Sam called the "front room," decorated in a weird mix of tastes. Two blue upholstered "womb" chairs flanked a worn leather sofa, with a glass-top coffee table connecting the three. An enormous, quartz-inlaid river stone hearth filled one wall. On the others hung examples of Sam's artwork, impressionist acrylics and oil-on-canvas still-lifes. Sam wasn't a particularly productive artist. Since moving in five weeks ago, Cheryl had seen exactly one new piece go up, only to be taken down again the next day because it wasn't "fully cooked."

The kitchen waited beyond a neat-as-a-pin dining room featuring an antique table, six matching chairs, and a china cabinet. This last was crammed with cherubic porcelain figures that Sam lovingly called "Hummels."

To Cheryl, they looked like something an old lady would collect.

However, while Sam Reshevsky was many things, an old lady wasn't one of them.

"Something smells good," Cheryl announced as she entered the kitchen. Though not a big space, it was Cheryl's favorite. Sam was a foodie, claimed to have once dated a Cordon Bleu, and cooked with the single-minded passion of a concert pianist.

"It better." Sam stood at the small gas stove, stirring something with slow, precise movements. "It's been simmering all day. How was work?"

Cheryl examined her roommate from behind. Not too many visual cues today: jeans, despite the heat, and a simple yellow t-shirt. Yellow usually meant "she," but not always. Cheryl checked the feet. Bare. No polish. Still inconclusive. No wig today, just the usual, close-cut dark hair. But that didn't necessarily mean anything either.

Still assessing Sam, she took a bottle of juice from the fridge and settled herself at the small butcher block table.

"What's for dinner?" Cheryl asked.

"You'll find out. You never answered my question. How was work?"

"Same old. Same old."

Sam laughed. Again, inconclusive, though Cheryl thought she sensed a "he" in the cadence. "Liar."

"Excuse me?"

Still stirring, and without looking at her, her roommate said, "You left early, skipping breakfast, on the morning after your favorite vigilante crashed the governor's party, and you're telling me the day was 'same old, same old'? I don't think so."

Cheryl screwed the cap off her juice bottle without replying.

"I read your article this afternoon," Sam said.

"We call them 'content pieces.'"

"Very mid-millennial of you. Congrats, by the way."

"On what?"

"Getting it published. I figured you wrote it on spec and offered it to Dag with your fingers firmly crossed."

"Is that what you figured?" Cheryl asked with a playful grin.

"What did he say when he read it?"

"He said, 'Good job writing that piece I assigned you.'"

Sam stiffened in surprise but still didn't turn around. "He assigned it to you?"

"Yep."

"Wow, kiddo! That's big!"

"You don't know the half of it."

"Well, get to it! You know I live vicariously through you."

"Turn around and I'll tell you everything."

"Gotta stir."

"Bullshit. You're playing with me. Now turn around."

"You have everything you need. Make your guess."

Exasperated, but only a little, Cheryl took another long look. That was when she spotted the thin gold chain fastened at the base of Sam's neck, partially hidden by the collar of the t-shirt. Her mother's locket, of course. And that only meant one thing.

"Turn around, Samantha," she said.

Smiling, Cheryl's roommate lowered the heat on the stove and faced her. The yellow t-shirt bore the words, "Lady of the Manor." Aside from that, though, today's cues were pretty thin. She wasn't even wearing much makeup.

"Good girl," Sam said, grinning. "We're having a Burgundy beef stew. Red potatoes and wild mushrooms."

"Sounds delish. When do we eat?"

"Right now. You can tell me about the other half of the 'half of it' while you set the table. Deep bowls, please, not plates."

"Yes, ma'am."

Cheryl had met Samantha Reshevsky, a.k.a. Samuel, back in late May when she answered an ad for a roommate. After four years in a crowded dorm at TCNJ and two more years sharing a two-bedroom walkup with three roommates in Princeton, she'd wanted to celebrate her entrance into adulthood with a living arrangement that was a bit more — well — adult.

But she'd discovered fast that rents were too high to allow her a place of her own. So instead, she'd focused on rooms-for-rent in the Trenton area.

A few disappointing leads had eventually brought her here, to a three-story brownstone off Prospect Street, less than a mile from the State House.

Samantha, it turned out, owned the entire building, which consisted of five apartments, all occupied. In fact, she'd grown up here, only converting it from a single home after her parents passed away suddenly. It wasn't something she liked to talk about.

Cheryl and Sam hit it off right away. What had started as a potential roommate interview turned into a home-cooked dinner followed by wine and conversation. Sam was twenty-eight and an orphan since nineteen. Her parents had left their only child with this valuable property and sufficient investments to keep her safely out of the working world. Sam was five-nine with a slim, athletic build, green eyes, and a thick mane of dark curly hair that, later on, Cheryl understood to be an expensive wig. Around her neck, she wore a locket with her parents' pictures in it — the same locket she had on now.

Samantha asked a lot of questions, which Cheryl dutifully answered. Her parents lived in Flemington, an affluent town well north of Trenton. Her father was a federal judge, her mother a retired teacher. She had a brother currently in law school and a sister recently divorced. For her own part, Cheryl liked to write and had her eye on a career in modern journalism.

That last part had delighted Sam, who dubbed Cheryl a "fellow artist" and proceeded to show off her own artwork. "I'm slow," she announced, proudly pointing out the pieces in the front room. "What you're looking at represents three years of painting. But I get there eventually."

"They're beautiful," Cheryl said. And they were.

By the end of the night, Samantha made a show of tearing Cheryl's application in half. "You're in, kiddo," she declared. "That is, if you think you can handle me!"

"Easy," Cheryl replied at once, both delighted and deeply relieved.

But Sam held up a lacquered finger. "I wouldn't be too quick to use that word where I'm concerned."

Cheryl grinned. "Oh, yeah? Why not?"

The next day, she found out why not.

When she arrived at her new apartment with all of her belongings in the back of a borrowed car, Cheryl met Samuel.

He opened the door wearing shorts, dockers, and a green Polo shirt that totally worked with his eyes. He had close-cropped dark hair, teased slightly in that way that looked natural but really took some doing.

Cheryl stared at him across the threshold, a suitcase full of clothes in one hand and a backpack full of sundries in the other.

"Right on time," he said with a smile.

"Samantha?" Cheryl heard herself ask.

"Not today. Come on in."

He had her drop her stuff in the bedroom that was now hers. In the meantime, he went out to the car, insisting on collecting the rest for her, the very soul of chivalry. While he was doing this, Cheryl tried to unpack, but the best she could manage involved standing in the middle of her new space feeling—confused.

A short time later, sharing coffee in the front room, Sam explained.

He was, and always had been, flexible when it came to his gender. "Some mornings Samantha wakes up. Other times, it's Samuel."

"But... yesterday, I could have sworn you were a woman."

"Kiddo, yesterday I *was* a woman. Try to keep up."

Cheryl, who'd always considered herself as "socially progressive" as anyone, was struggling to do just that. Almost without thinking, she asked, "But... which one..."

"Which one what?"

She struggled to find the words. "Which were you born?" The phrasing was seriously awkward, not a journalist's sentence at all.

"Are you asking me which toolbox I've got?"

Cheryl flushed. "No!"

"You sure? Because that's what it sounded like."

Cheryl tried to answer but couldn't. She felt like an idiot.

He laughed, the sound deep throated and entirely masculine. "Relax. Maybe one day I'll tell you my life story. But since we've just started living together, why don't you focus on the Sam who is, and not worry too much about the Sam who was? I'm not trans. I don't take any medication and I'm not considering any surgery. I'm what you'd call 'gender fluid.'"

Cheryl knew the term. Of course she did. It was 2048, for God's sake! Once, she'd met a girl who was—

She stopped herself. Had 'girl' even been the right term?

"Ask," Sam said.

"What?"

"You have questions. It's all over your face. Let's get it all out in the open right now. It'll make things easier." When she didn't respond right away, he said, "Look, I should have opened up to you last night. But the fact is I was enjoying your company, which doesn't happen too often, and I didn't want to see it go south. So instead, I told myself to wait until today and maybe... I don't know... shock you through it. That was a bad call, and if you want out of the lease, I totally understand. But for the record, I like you and I really hope you don't."

Cheryl licked her lips and asked, "Are you gay?"

"I'm pansexual, when I have a love life at all, which ain't often."

She absorbed this. "Okay. Sure. Um... what's your pronoun?"

He smiled broadly. "I don't go in for 'they' or any of the neopronouns like 'xer.' With me, I let who I am from day to day dictate what I want other folks to call me. The thing is, Cheryl, I don't bother too much with labels. For me, deciding my gender on a given morning is both as important and unimportant as picking out my clothes for the day. Oh, I've got some rules of thumb. It's usually Samantha who hits the bars on a Saturday. And it's usually Samuel who goes to the DMV. That said, sometimes I switch it up. I like to surprise myself. I can go a week or more as one, or swap daily for a month." He put his coffee mug to his lips. "It's a great way to live, honest to God!"

"Which will you be tomorrow?" Cheryl asked.

"Ask me tomorrow." Offering her one of the kindest and most patient smiles she'd ever seen, he added, "Just take it one day at a time. And don't pay me any rent. Not yet. Give yourself a week. If, after that, you find you can't handle it, we'll tear up the lease. But I hope you don't. As I said, I like you."

And, once the shock wore off, Cheryl found she liked Sam, too.

A lot.

Whether he or she, Sam was always Sam: funny, brilliant, and remarkably wise. Cheryl had never met anyone so comfortable in their own skin. This wasn't to say that life was a breeze for Sam Reshevsky. True, rental income and investments made working unnecessary. But even so, the world still managed to screw with Samuel/Samantha on a pretty regular basis.

Just last week, Samantha had visited Home Depot, only to return flustered and offended. "Some orange-vested creep decided the lady in the plumbing aisle couldn't possibly prefer a strap wrench over a pipe wrench. No matter how many times I insisted, he kept telling me the pipe wrench would be 'easier for me.' We must have argued for ten minutes. I swear, by the end I was ready to clock the jerk."

"Why not send Samuel?" Cheryl had asked at the time. "Wouldn't that have made things easier?"

"Sometimes, kiddo, it's not about 'easier.'"

In the here and now, while sharing a great stew dinner, Cheryl recounted her morning, the story assignment from Dag, and the subsequent surprise meeting with Senator Bourbon and Trooper Merryman.

"Wait a minute," Sam interrupted.

"What?"

"I get that Michael Bourbon wants you to write an in-depth investigative piece about Checkmate. But his underlying goal is to entice your favorite vigilante to... get in touch?"

"Something like that."

Sam chuckled. "Checkmate's ego must be almost as big as mine. And Bourbon thinks setting you up with big-wig interviews will get his attention?"

"So he says."

"And you figure that'll work?"

"Well, if it doesn't, then at least I'd get a great story out of it."

"Don't shrug this off. Are you telling me you wouldn't jump at the chance to meet your hero?"

"I never said Checkmate was my hero!"

"You wrote the article about him. And you talk about him, like, a lot."

"He's... interesting."

"Uh-huh."

"Stop making fun of me!"

"I'm not. I'm actually thrilled for you! Damn, girl! This could make your career!"

"Only if I don't screw it up. Blowing an opportunity like this by turning in some amateur sludge would hurt me more than not doing it at all."

"You'll knock it out of the park," Sam said matter-of-factly.

"You sound pretty sure."

"I am. I read last year's Princeton piece. It deserved that award, hands down."

"Thanks. I hope you feel the same way about this second story... if I write it."

"If? You mean you didn't say yes?"

"Not yet. I've got an appointment with Bourbon in his State House office Monday morning at nine to 'discuss it further.' He said he'll give me the interview schedule then, if I decide to accept the assignment."

"I'm surprised Dag's giving you a choice."

"So am I," Cheryl admitted. "It's not his style. He's more of a 'Do it, underling!' kind of editor. But this time he told me it's entirely my call. He's also waiving my word quota for the week so that I can focus on it."

"Damn!" Sam said again. "Who do you figure the interviewees are likely to be?"

"Law enforcement, probably. Rhona Johnson, the Superintendent of the State Police. Maybe Attorney General Portermann."

"And they're supposed to give you their impression of Checkmate?"

"Something like that."

"Do you think you'll be able to interview the governor?"

Cheryl laughed. "Not likely!"

"You should tell Bourbon you'll only do the story if you can interview the governor."

"Sam, that's crazy!"

"No, just bold. And, you know me, kiddo. I'm all about bold."

"You think I should write the story?"

Samantha laughed. "Oh, you're going to write the story! You can pretend all you want, but you made up your mind before you got home."

Cheryl didn't reply. Sam was always good at reading her.

"Fine. Play hard to get," her roommate said dismissively. "How exactly did you two leave it? You and Mr. Moneybags, I mean."

"I told him I was very interested... but that I had to sleep on it. He said okay and gave me his card. Said to call him if... and only if... I decided not to take the assignment. Otherwise, he wants me at the State House tomorrow morning at nine. To be honest, he looked... not annoyed, exactly, but maybe taken aback when I didn't accept his offer on the spot. Merryman seemed weirdly pissed off, though."

"Well, I don't know about the cop. But Bourbon's probably used to everybody just bowing to his whims."

"You don't like him."

"I don't know about liking him. But I sure didn't vote for him."

"Why not?"

"Because he's too goddamned rich, that's why not. I know we've got him to thank for these..." She held up her wrist, showing her Cuff. "And they're cool and all. But just how much can the guy represent 'the people' when he can pretty much buy and sell us like cattle?"

"Might be a little overstated," Cheryl said with a grin.

"Not overstated enough. But forget that. This is an amazing opportunity, and congratulations alone aren't going to cut it. There's that bottle of champagne we've been saving for a special occasion. This feels like it."

"That's sweet!"

"Go get changed," Sam said. "I'll clean up and find the bubbly."

"You cooked. At least let me help you clean."

"Nope. You're queen for today. Scoot!"

Laughing, Cheryl left the kitchen through a curtained doorway and entered the short hall beyond. On the left side was Sam's room, the door closed. On the right was her own. The two of them had few "roommate rules," but one was this: Your bedroom was your inner sanctum. Neither would enter the other's without explicit permission. In the weeks she'd lived here, Cheryl had barely glimpsed the interior of Sam's room, much less gone inside.

Cheryl ducked into hers, climbed out of her work clothes, and slipped into shorts and a comfortable t-shirt. She spent just a moment looking at herself in the mirror behind the door. She was a solidly medium woman, medium height at about five foot four, medium build with hips that always felt a little too wide and breasts that always seemed a little too small, medium length hair a kind of mousey, dirty blonde that she had to straighten almost daily to keep it from turning into a rat's nest. Her complexion was fair, her nose maybe just a skosh too big, and her grey-blue eyes always seemed a little too far apart.

All so friggin' medium.

This self-assessment was a common ritual for her.

She wondered if all women did it. She wondered if Samantha did it.

And that made her wonder if Samuel did it.

When Cheryl returned to the kitchen, she found Sam worrying the foil off the bottle of champagne that had been in the back of the fridge since Cheryl had moved in.

"There's one thing I don't get," Sam remarked as she expertly popped the cork. "Why was Merryman there?"

Cheryl replied, "I'm still not entirely sure. Bourbon told me that Trooper Merryman's been put on temporary leave pending an official inquiry into the Drumthwacket mess. Maybe the brass wants Merryman out of the spotlight while they investigate and, eventually, throw some blame around. I don't know, but the guy didn't seem very happy about the whole thing. I got the impression that the senator had hired him, at least in the short term, maybe as personal security."

Sam considered this. "Can't be a bad gig, bodyguarding the richest man in the state. Grab a pair of flutes out of the cupboard, will you? Oh, and show me his card!"

"Whose card?"

Sam chuckled. "Bourbon's! I haven't seen a real paper card in, I don't know, ten years. I can't believe the guy who invented Cuffs still uses them."

"That's a good point. I've got it right here." Cheryl opened her purse on the butcher's block table and started rummaging through it. "At least, I think I've got it. I hope I didn't accidentally —" She stiffened as a chill shot up her spine.

Alarmed, Sam asked, "What's wrong?"

Instead of answering, Cheryl reached into her purse and pulled out a chess piece.

A white pawn.

The two of them stared at it and then at each other. Slowly, as if by unspoken agreement, they both dropped back onto their respective chairs. Cheryl put the chess piece down between them before pushing her chair back as if it might be radioactive. For a while, they stared at the thing in silence. Finally, clearing her throat, Samantha remarked, "I guess I can assume that wasn't in your purse when you left this morning?"

"No."

"When was the last time you opened it?"

"After the meeting. I went back to my desk and put away Bourbon's card."

"And this chess piece wasn't in there then?"

"No way."

"You're sure?"

"It's not that big a purse. If this had been in there then, I'd have seen it."

"So, sometime between then and now," Sam said thoughtfully. "One of the other staffers, maybe? As a stupid prank or something?"

"I doubt it. I keep my purse with me most of the time. All of us do. We don't have cubes or desks to lock things up in. "

"Could it have happened on the bus?" Sam offered.

"It was under my arm the whole ride. I always do that."

Tentatively, Samantha picked up the chess piece and examined it. It was a standard wooden pawn, maybe two inches tall and painted an ivory white.

Then Sam turned it over in her hands and froze. "Oh!"

"What?"

She upended the piece so Cheryl could see. There, in the middle of the pawn's felt bottom, was a small black button, recessed so that just putting the piece down wouldn't trigger it.

"What's that?" Cheryl asked.

Sam raised her eyebrows, something she did whenever Cheryl was being needlessly oblivious.

So Cheryl asked instead, "Should we press it?"

"That's kind of the point of a button."

"What if it's... um... a bomb or something?"

"You think Checkmate's trying to blow you up?"

"It might not be Checkmate who put it in my purse."

"You think one of your rivals at NC22 is trying to blow you up?"

"It sounds stupid when you say it out loud."

Samantha laughed, but without humor. She put the piece back down on the table. "It's your call, kiddo."

Cheryl picked up the pawn and examined its button more closely. Small and definitely recessed, though her fingernail could press it easily enough. The piece didn't feel heavy at all. But did that guarantee it wasn't packed with explosives?

This is crazy! I'm being paranoid.

She looked up at Sam, who watched her intently. Finally, her roommate said, "Champagne's going flat. And the suspense is just about killing me."

Cheryl steadied herself.

Then, throwing caution to the winds, she pressed the button.

Nothing blew up.

Instead, a voice, decidedly computer-generated, said, *"Hello, Cheryl. Meet me at the State Street Pub at ten o'clock tonight. I'll have a table reserved for you in the back. I'll find you there. Do us both a favor and come alone."*

"Holy shit," Samantha whispered. She met Cheryl's eyes. "What are you going to do?"

Cheryl swallowed dryly. Steadying herself, she stood up and said, "I'm... going to get ready. Sorry about skipping the champagne, but it looks like I've got a date tonight."

With that, she headed into her bedroom, her heart pounding.

CHAPTER FOUR

HER BLIND DATE

WHITE PAWN TO KING'S KNIGHT THREE/
BLACK KNIGHT TO KING'S BISHOP THREE

Saturday, July 5, 2048

THE STATE STREET PUB, SITUATED ACROSS FROM THE STATE HOUSE, occupied the ground floor of a recently completed office building. The building and pub were both part of Trenton's latest effort at gentrification, a controversial and costly program that had been advancing, in fits and starts, for twenty years.

The neighborhood was a fairly good one, being so close to the seat of government, so Cheryl wasn't too worried about catching a late bus. Sam, however, felt differently—and said so.

"Are you sure about this?"

"It's my job, Sam."

"Since when does your job involve meeting strangers in bars in the middle of the night?"

"Ten o'clock isn't exactly the 'middle of the night.' Besides, it's Saturday and the place'll be crowded. So if Checkmate turns out to be a psycho, there'll be plenty of people."

"I still don't like it."

"Sam, you're sweet for worrying. But I'm going to be fine."

"This is crazy."

"It's my job," she repeated.

"You've already gotten mugged once since living under my roof!"

"I'll be fine."

Sam groaned with exasperation and commanded, "Stay put!" before hurrying back into her bedroom. Cheryl waited, her arms crossed, more bemused than angry. It was hard to get mad at Sam Reshevsky.

A minute later, her roommate returned carrying a small velvet pouch.

"What's that?" Cheryl asked.

"My self-defense gear." Samantha opened the bag, fished around, and pulled out the first item. "Rape whistle." This she blew hard enough to rattle the windows. Cheryl yelped and hugged her ears.

Sam next drew a black cylinder from the bag. "Pepper spray."

"I already carry pepper spray."

"Yeah, I've seen the pink thing on your keychain. It's adorable. But this is twice the legal concentration. Military issue. I got it from a soldier I used to date."

"Is that it?"

"Not quite." Samantha turned the bag over and dumped a set of brass knuckles into her palm.

"You've got to be kidding me!" Cheryl protested.

"Don't judge a book, kiddo." Samantha slid the knuckles over her fingers. "See this button here? Hold your thumb on it when you punch, and you deliver a hundred and fifty thousand volts. They're called shock knuckles, and they're the very latest in stun-gun tech."

"Seriously? Where'd you get this?"

"Don't ask."

"Is any of this stuff legal?"

"Just the whistle. So watch yourself out there. And keep at least one of them in a pocket. Purses can be hard to get into fast if you're in trouble."

"I got to tell you, Sam, this seems like a lot."

"Well, it isn't a lot, not if you're planning to meet notorious vigilantes at late-night pubs. Now, you're as smart as they come. We both know it. But without these things to keep you safe, you're just a light bulb on a shelf."

"A lightbulb on a shelf?"

"Waiting to be screwed."

At exactly 9:51 PM, Cheryl stepped into the State Street Pub. The joint was surprisingly small, just a long, narrow room with a row of round tables against the left wall, a polished bar and stools against the right, and a narrow aisle between them. A kind of old-fashioned ambiance filled the place, from the dim Tiffany lamps above the tables to the thirty-foot marbleized mirror behind the bar.

It was so crowded that Cheryl worried she wouldn't be able to find a table at all, let alone one in the back. But sure enough, after excusing herself past at least two dozen men and women to get there, she found the promised "Reserved" sign waiting. Looking around and seeing nothing and no one revealing, she dropped onto one of the two chairs, raised her wrist, and texted a message to Sam, reporting that she'd arrived safely.

Then she turned on her Cuff's voice recorder.

She was ready.

Her heart was beating very hard.

"Hey, honey!" someone said loudly, startling her.

A waitress loomed, a tired-looking redhead of maybe thirty wearing jeans and a skintight black t-shirt over an amble bosom. The cheap plastic name tag pinned at her collar read "Monika." Her long hair was tied in a ponytail and her lipstick-ed smile looked a little forced. A long Saturday shift, Cheryl supposed.

"Sorry," the waitress said. "Didn't mean to shout. It's so noisy in here."

"Yeah, it is," Cheryl replied.

"Anyway, I'm Monika. What can I get you?"

Cheryl considered a glass of wine. But this was supposed to be an interview, not a date. "Just coffee, if that's okay. Decaf."

"Sure, it's okay, honey. You want something off the menu?" She nodded to a single sheet of paper on the tabletop.

"Maybe later. I'm waiting for somebody."

"Gotcha. Be right back with the coffee."

Monika departed. Minutes passed. Ten o'clock came and went. Nobody so much as approached her. Fighting impatience, Cheryl scanned the nearby faces. Most were in couples or groups, but a few were youngish men drinking alone. One of them noticed her attention and offered a tentative, hopeful salute with his shot glass. Cheryl shook her head and looked away. She really didn't want to be hit on right now.

Her Cuff chirped. It was a text from Samantha, the words floating above her wrist. *"So what's he look like? A psycho?"*

Despite her anxiety, Cheryl smiled. She tapped back, "He hasn't shown up yet."

"Think you got stood up?"

"Maybe."

"Good. Why not call it a night and come home?"

Cheryl laughed. "You're relentless."

"I'm worried about you."

"I'm fine. And I'm staying put, at least for now."

"Okay. But promise me you'll be careful and think things through. There's more to life than a job."

"I promise."

Moments later, Monika returned from the bar balancing a coffee cup and wine glass atop a small round serving tray. "Here you go, honey," she said, her accent more Boston than Jersey.

She placed the coffee in front of Cheryl and set the wine down across from her.

"I'm sorry," Cheryl said, confused. "I didn't order that."

"Oh, that's for me," Monika replied as she took the opposite chair.

Cheryl gaped.

Monika sipped her wine and waited.

Cheryl whispered, "Checkmate?"

The woman smiled and offered the slightest of nods.

A weird sense of unreality gripped Cheryl, almost like a mind fog. "But you work here."

Monika tilted her head. "Do I? I don't recall saying that."

"You took my order."

"I asked what I could get you. That seemed only proper since I'm the one who invited you out."

"You have a nametag." She regretted the comment immediately. Last night, this person had posed as a state trooper, gained access to the governor's mansion, caused the arrest of the freaking speaker of the freaking state assembly, and then had escaped, all under the noses of twenty cops.

And I'm asking him how he got a plastic nametag?

Then she thought, *Him?*

"I thought you were a man," she said, steadying herself.

"I'm not."

"But your voice on the holo last night..."

"Voice changes are easy. It helps to have a good vocal range." She added in a deeper register, "Drop below two octaves, and most people subconsciously identify you as male."

The effect was jarring, almost as if Monika were lip-syncing a man behind her. "That's... impressive," Cheryl admitted. Her perceptions were still dancing the tango, but at least she was no longer mealy-mouthed.

"Thanks. But we're not here to talk tricks of the trade. I understand you have a message for me from Senator Michael Bourbon. Your coffee's getting cold."

"What?"

"Your coffee," Monika said. "I didn't know how you take it, so I got you sugar and creamer. I hope that's okay."

"Um... sure. Thanks," Cheryl replied, though right now how she took her coffee meant exactly zilch. "How did you know about Bourbon's message?"

Monika merely shrugged.

"How'd you get that pawn in my purse?"

Monika shrugged again.

"You must have pickpocketed it in there, but when?"

The woman took another sip of wine. "Pickpocketing's about theft, taking things. I'm more about giving things to folks without their knowledge."

"You think that makes it better?" Cheryl demanded.

Another shrug.

"Fine. Look, I don't much like being played with."

Monika regarded her. "Is that what you think I'm doing?"

"Aren't you?"

The waitress/not waitress—Cheryl couldn't quite think of her as "Checkmate" yet—clasped her hands on the tabletop. "This isn't a game, Ms. Walker. There's more going on, a lot more, than you're aware of. People have died. More people may die. That's what happens when you poke a nest of snakes. Don't bother with the senator's message. I already know it. I'm in danger. Well, that's true. It's been true for a very long time. But this is all much bigger than me."

"Then tell me," Cheryl said, her heart pounding again. "All of it."

"Then you'll be in danger, too."

Cheryl shivered, though she did her best to hide it. "I'm okay with that."

Monika smiled thinly. "Really? Ever been in danger, hon? I don't mean that little mugging last month. That kid was more scared than you were."

"How the hell do you know about that?"

Monika waved away the question. "This is a bigger kind of danger. This is killers with guns and zero moral compasses. This is seeing you, that roommate of yours, even your family, all in life-threatening jeopardy. If you drop this now, and I mean right now... if you call Senator Bourbon and tell him you're not interested in doing the second story, then all that can be avoided. But you have to decide right away, otherwise the choice will be taken away from you."

"By who?" Cheryl asked bitterly. "By you?"

"No."

"Then who?"

"Let it go."

"Tell me your name," Cheryl demanded.

"Tonight, it's Monika."

"Your real name."

Monika shook her head.

"Why not?"

"You're not naïve enough to need an explanation."

"Why are you doing this?"

"Doing what?"

"Bringing down corrupt politicians."

"Don't you think somebody should?"

"Why does it have to be you?"

"Because I can."

"The tech you used last night to jam police communications and hack into the holosystems at Drumthwacket... where'd you get it?"

"Here and there."

"That's not an answer."

"I didn't promise you answers. Frankly, you're getting more from me right now than anyone ever has. But that's just because I'm hoping you'll push past this dangerous curiosity and walk away when we're done."

"I'm not going anywhere," Cheryl insisted, though the words terrified her. What Checkmate had said—and, yes, now she was thinking of Monika as Checkmate—scared her. The thought of somebody going after Sam or her family because of her was the stuff of nightmares. But what kind of future would she have as an investigative journalist if she backed off at the first sign of trouble, especially on the say-so of a—

Criminal? Vigilante? Cocktail waitress?

"Look," Cheryl said. "How do I know you are who you say you are? You might be a plant, a practical joke served up by one of my so-called colleagues to punk me." She didn't believe this, but it bore suggesting, if only to see Checkmate's reaction.

Monika burst out laughing. "Okay, I admit that surprised me! Well, let's look at this logically. Do any of them know about the offer from Senator Bourbon? The second article?"

"I don't think so. But it's not impossible."

"Well, if you believe that, then get up and walk out of here. Forget the whole thing."

"Prove to me you're Checkmate."

"How?"

"Not my problem."

Monika sighed. "Believe it or not, I don't much like showboating." Without flourish, she placed something on the tabletop between them.

Cheryl stared at it.

It was her Cuff—Cheryl's own Cuff.

The most recent Cuff models were slim devices, designed to be unobtrusive, just a changeable band fitted to a thin, flat, unmarked panel, over which the user passed one fingertip to activate the heads-up display. Some bands had clasps. Others were elastic. Most were conveniently easy to remove since, once configured, no Cuff could be transferred to another user—ever. So there was little point in stealing them.

Yet, Cheryl's wrist was bare.

"But... you never touched me!"

Monika replied, "Didn't I? Are you aware that as many as thirty percent of what are called 'social contacts' go unnoticed? And the percentage is even higher for women." She picked up Cheryl's Cuff in her left hand, displaying her own. "These things are amazing. You're too young to remember life before them. People used to obsess about digital privacy. There used to be tech that would let you clone someone's phone just by putting it down nearby. The truth is, Cufflink hit the market with their 'next stage in the evolution of technological security' at exactly the right time. People had been trying to beat the privacy problem for decades, but he, Bourbon, was the first one to pull it off, and he's pretty much owned the market ever since."

"What's your point?"

"Do you ever worry about someone seeing what you tap into this thing, or what it shows you?"

"Of course not."

"Why not?"

"Can I have my Cuff back, please?"

"Sure."

Scowling, Cheryl took it and fitted its faux black leather band around her wrist where it nestled firmly against the skin, providing it easy access to her DNA signature.

"Feel better?" Checkmate asked.

"Thanks," Cheryl muttered. "But having nimble fingers, by itself, doesn't make you Checkmate."

"Hmm. What would?"

"I told you: not my problem."

"Then I guess we're stuck."

Cheryl fumed, still fingering her Cuff. Then she remembered something Merryman said at their meeting, a detail not in any of the press releases.

"Music," she said.

"Beg your pardon?"

"You piped music into the ears of every trooper at the governor's mansion last night."

"That I did."

"What was it?"

"Abbey Road by the Beatles. I've got a thing for classical."

Merryman had said as much that morning, citing a grandfather who'd been heavily into the mid-20th century band. For her part, Cheryl couldn't have named a Beatles song if pressed. But she'd armed herself with the album title before coming here.

"Okay," she said, maybe a little begrudgingly. "I accept that you are who you say you are."

"That's a relief. But you never answered my question."

"What question?"

"Why don't you ever worry about someone watching when you use your Cuff?"

"Is this some kind of quiz?"

"It's a question."

Cheryl sighed with exasperation. "Fine. I don't worry because the Cuff uses my DNA to encrypt everything on its heads-up display so that only I can read it."

"It projects what amounts to a kind of artificial prosopagnosia... face blindness... in the people around you. Real-time biometric encryption, both visual and auditory. Did you know the bulk of Bourbon's commercial sales come from the federal government? The CIA and NSA love these things. The president even wears one."

"Of course, I know. But—"

"The feds have even sued Cufflink, demanding the proprietary specs behind their encryption. But so far, they've lost in court every time. The free market keeps winning the day. The problem is that nobody else... anywhere... has ever been able to match the tech, at least not yet. And the Cuff's been on the market for twenty years. Most people walk around with them on their wrists, taking them for granted without a second thought about the miracle of technology they keep their shopping lists on. Impenetrable. Unhackable."

"You sound like you own stock," Cheryl said sourly.

"Who doesn't?"

But it was true. How many times had Cheryl's father pontificated about that very thing at family dinners? The Cuff had changed the world. With it, a hundred people could stand together on a train or bus, all with their wrists up and their life, photos, bank codes, and love letters flashing in the air in front of them—and know, beyond any doubt, that no other eyes but theirs could read them.

"What's the Cuff got to do with it?" she asked Monika.

"Something, I think. Otherwise, I doubt Michael Bourbon would be your point man on this story."

"So, what? Bourbon's more than the CEO of Cufflink. He's also head of the state senate."

"He's the president of the state senate. Not the same thing."

"You're splitting hairs. What do Bourbon and the Cuffs have to do with the danger you're talking about?"

"Uh uh," Checkmate replied, shaking her head. "I need a decision. Are you dropping this story or not?"

Cheryl studied the woman's face. The vigilante called Monika had high cheekbones and full, painted lips. Pretty, if not exactly beautiful. But definitely a woman.

Then again, this same person had disguised herself as a forty-something man well enough to pass muster in a brightly lit room.

How did somebody do that?

"What if I say no?" Cheryl asked. "I mean, what if I decide not to drop the piece?"

"Then I give Senator Bourbon what he wants. I invite you to join my crusade, immediately making you a target for the same forces that are currently after me. And I'm not talking about the state police."

Cheryl swallowed. She couldn't help it. Her coffee, cold and forgotten, still sat on the tabletop between them. "Is it really that dangerous?" she asked.

"Hon, it's very dangerous."

"How?"

"If I tell you that, it's already too late. I know this sounds funny coming from me, but I'm not being dramatic here. If you continue with this, I'll bring you in, but I can't guarantee your safety. I simply can't." Monika wore a hard look, all business, all straight talk.

And Cheryl believed her.

For a long moment, she couldn't manage a reply.

Checkmate took one of her hands. "It's okay. Just get up and walk out. I've got the check. Tomorrow... hell, tonight... text Bourbon and let him know you're out. Then go live your life. Please."

Cheryl met the woman's eyes and read what looked like a genuine plea there.

"No," she heard herself say. "No, I'm not quitting. I'm in."

Monika watched her for another few seconds. Almost reluctantly, she let go of Cheryl's hand, sat back in her chair, and sighed. "Well, then," she said, sounding regretful, but also something else—excited, maybe? "How would you feel about helping me bring down the chief justice of the New Jersey Supreme Court?"

CHAPTER FIVE

SALLY'S SINS

WHITE BISHOP TO KING'S KNIGHT TWO/
BLACK BISHOP TO QUEEN THREE

Saturday, July 5 – Sunday, July 6, 2048

AT FIFTY-SIX YEARS OF AGE, SALLY COOKER SHOULD HAVE BEEN AT the pinnacle of her legal career — a genuine American success story. Born to working-class parents in Asbury Park, she'd worked her way through first college and then Princeton Law, finally graduating third in her class. Then had come a successful career as a state prosecutor, followed by an appellate court judicial appointment, and culminating twelve years ago with her elevation to chief justice of the State of New Jersey.

Top of the world.

Right?

Sally sat behind the wheel of the high-end Cadillac she'd bought for herself just last year. It was a big car and she liked it, but right now a part of her wished for something a bit less conspicuous. It was with this thought firmly in mind that she'd parked the pretty behemoth in the darkest corner of the lot that she could find.

She did this every time she visited this place, which had been occurring with increasing frequency of late.

Her hands shook as she stepped out of the car, locked it with her Cuff, and headed slowly toward the warehouse's poorly lit frontage. As she did, another big car, this one a Mercedes, rumbled loudly into the lot. Its driver, evidently seeing her, pulled into a nearby space and killed the engine. Knowing who it was, Sally briefly considered ignoring the arrival and continuing toward the building's only lit door. But she knew the man too well.

Vladimir Antonov didn't suffer slights gladly.

The Mercedes' passenger door opened and the most notorious man in the state of New Jersey emerged. He cut an intimidating figure, Sally noted, not for the first time. Nearing sixty, the Russian-born gangster was a bear of a man—stockily built, with broad shoulders, a mostly bald head, and a more or less permanent scowl.

As the two of them eyed each other from a distance of perhaps ten feet, Antonov nodded and said in his deep, gravelly voice, "Delta."

"Beta," she replied. Steeling herself for the answer, she asked, "Do you have him?"

Antonov nodded. Then he opened the rear door and pulled a man from the backseat. He was trussed up with zip-ties and looked like he'd been crying. Just seeing him made Sally's insides tighten.

She knew him. Of course she did.

But calling on so many years of judiciary gravitas, she declared, "Good." And without another word, turned her back and walked on. It dismayed her, but didn't surprise her, to hear Antonov dragging his prisoner along as the three of them approached the only working door into the warehouse.

That was what they called it: "the warehouse."

Ironically, of all the businesses that had failed to make a go of this big building over the decades, not one had ever used it as a warehouse. Instead, it had always been a self-storage facility, one that had suffered many owners and many names, none for long.

These days, it stood derelict and forgotten—empty, except for the occasional Siblings meeting.

With Antonov and his prisoner crowding uncomfortably behind her, Sally knocked on the unmarked steel door. Seconds later, it was opened by someone wearing the usual long black robe and featureless white mask. For a moment, they all regarded one another.

"Welcome," the doorman said.

Sally, who'd suffered this ritual too many times, wordlessly crossed the threshold and squeezed past him. A moment later, Vladimir followed, dragging along his charge. "Got a gun?" he asked the man in the mask.

"No." The doorman suddenly sounded nervous. Vladimir Antonov had that effect on people.

But the big man merely nodded and shoved his prisoner into a nearby corner. "Face the wall. Don't move." Then, to the doorman: "Give me the outfit."

Wordlessly, the masked individual took two small bundles from a carboard box on the floor. These he handed out, first to Sally and then to Antonov.

Sally donned hers. As usual, the black cloak reached her feet. The familiar white mask hid her entire face and was as featureless as the doorman's, save for a blood-red symbol painted on the forehead. She knew what that symbol was, of course.

The Greek letter delta.

The mask was a cut above Halloween store fair — if not exactly comfortable, at least not uncomfortable. In the early days, they'd used hoods with eye slits, which had always made her feel stifled. These masks were a marginal improvement.

When she was done, she found Antonov similarly attired, except of course his mask bore a Greek beta. The tethered man, in the meantime, hadn't moved an inch, though by the way his shoulders shook, Sally guessed he was quietly crying.

She didn't blame him one bit.

"Good boy," Antonov said to the prisoner, taking hold of him again.

"Do you know where you're going?" the doorman asked them.

"Unit 23," both Sally and Antonov replied in unison, a moment of grim comedy that failed to bring a smile to either of their faces. The unit number, along with tonight's summons, had been transmitted to their respective Cuffs.

The doorman presented them each with a sheet of paper. "Here's a map."

Sally took it without thanking him.

But standing beside her now, Antonov asked the fellow, "Tell me something. Is it always you?"

"Always me?"

"Always you at the door?"

"Does it matter?"

"Don't play games with me," Vladimir growled.

"No. There are a few of us. We... get assigned."

"And do you know what everybody looks like?"

"What?"

"You know what I look like," Antonov said flatly. He nodded at Sally. "You know what she looks like. What about the others? What about *him*?"

"No!" the man said, almost yelped. "That is... I know some of the others, the ones who show up unmasked, like you. But not... I mean, never —"

"Relax," Vladimir said. "That's good enough."

The man visibly shuddered, and while Sally couldn't see the face behind the mask, she could imagine his expression of relief. This was one of the recruits. Not a Sibling and unlikely to ever be one, but useful and, with a few exceptions, loyal. The fact that he'd been given this responsibility and, through it, allowed to know the identities of at least some of tonight's attendees, was testament enough.

"Are we the last to arrive?" Sally asked, the first time she'd spoken since entering the building.

"Yes," the doorman replied at once, practically snapping to attention.

She nodded and, with a final look at Antonov, entered the labyrinthine warehouse. As before, Vladimir and his prisoner followed. Together, but without a word spoken, they navigated the seemingly endless, all-but-identical corridors, each one lined with big doors, all closed and locked. In these modern times, public storage places like this one offered biometric security and Cuff connectivity. But there was none of that here, nor were there cameras or microphones. The current patrons had no desire to be recorded.

Finding Unit 23 would have been all but impossible without the doorman's map. While each of the countless doors were numbered, those numbers frequently changed sequence from one corridor to the next. Sally had never understood why this was and had never cared enough to ask.

She finally spotted U23 by the fact that it, alone, stood open. Confirming this by checking the sign above the garage-style door, the three of them stepped into the windowless, dimly lit space.

The Siblings were already gathered.

"Welcome, Beta, Delta," Proprietor said. "Put our guest in the chair. Gamma, please shut the door."

Antonov did as instructed, dragging the groaning prisoner to a heavy steel, straight-backed chair that sat in the middle of the otherwise empty unit. He dropped the poor man onto it, securing his wrists and ankles with more zip-ties. At the same time, Gamma pulled down the unit's louvered door, pressing one leather-shoed foot on the pedal to lock it in place.

Unit 23 was now secure. No one could open it from the outside without a key, which Proprietor alone carried. Also, with the door closed, this concrete box was naturally soundproof. Even the most sophisticated eavesdropping tech couldn't penetrate so much masonry.

Nevertheless, no names would be used during this meeting. Proprietor was as practical as he was demanding, and he left nothing to chance.

Wordlessly, Sally regarded her fellow Siblings. They were all dressed as she was. Each mask bore a different, sequential Greek letter — though Zeta was conspicuously missing — except one. The forehead of Proprietor's false face remained blank. And unlike the rest, his mask and robe were both blood red.

Sally knew who most of the attendees were, of course. She had to. Secret societies were fine but, to get anything done, business had to take place among the members and, inevitably, faces and names had to be revealed.

In fact, the only identities she didn't know were Proprietor's and Alpha's. This was an ignorance she had long ago accepted, and one that she shared with the others. In fact, in no small way, that single mystery defined them as a group. They were the Siblings, and Proprietor led them, controlled them, and owned them, with Alpha as his only lieutenant. This servitude had been difficult for Sally to swallow at first. But ultimately, she'd come to rely upon it. After all, Proprietor was the reason she now occupied the state's highest bench.

Of course, that didn't mean she appreciated these ritualistic theatrics. But it did mean that she would never say so.

"Now then," Proprietor announced. "Let's discuss the matter of Zeta's arrest." The voice, as always, was disguised, electronically altered so that no one could tell the speaker's gender, much less their identity. Nevertheless, Sally had always assumed Proprietor to be a man, though she wasn't sure why. He wasn't especially tall, and the robe hid his body shape. Perhaps it was something in his bearing, or simply a long-buried social bias on her part.

"It's a disaster!" Epsilon exclaimed in his deep baritone.

"This kind of thing isn't supposed to happen!" Theta added. She was the newest member of the Siblings. "I was given assurances!"

"Calm down!" Alpha snapped. His voice was also electronically disguised, his identity as mysterious as Proprietor's. "The turn of events last Friday took everyone by surprise. But it will be dealt with."

This, of course, was the key topic on tonight's agenda. The man in the chair would come later. The Siblings had been jarred by Zeta's arrest at the governor's mansion. And some of them were scared.

"I've been in touch with him," Proprietor said, speaking reasonably. "He became careless and made mistakes that left him vulnerable. But he has no intention of saying anything and is denying all charges."

"He'll bring us all down," Gamma said. "He'll turn State's evidence."

"No," Proprietor replied. "He won't."

"How can you say that?" Eta demanded.

"Because he's one of us," Proprietor declared, not loudly but with conviction. "Tell me, Eta. Would you betray us simply to protect your personal interests?"

For several seconds, no one spoke.

Finally, in a small voice, Eta replied, "Of course not."

Proprietor nodded. "None of us would. Zeta will keep his peace. And in return, we'll make sure he receives the best possible defense and, most importantly, has not sacrificed himself in vain."

"Proprietor," Epsilon said in a more respectful tone. "The Checkmate situation's gone too far."

Sally, who'd watched this entire exchange without speaking, who in fact never spoke at these meetings if she could help it, now went cold at the mention of the vigilante. Checkmate had been nibbling at the edges of Proprietor's organization for years now. But the July Fourth Gala marked the first time they'd gone after — and gotten — a Sibling.

"He's taken down one of us!" Eta exclaimed, so loudly and abruptly that Sally started. "That wasn't supposed to be possible!"

"And it wouldn't have been," Alpha replied in a reasoned tone, "if not for this person here."

Antonov's prisoner, who'd been sweating and trembling throughout, now looked up with fresh alarm. Behind their masks, all eyes locked on him, as the Siblings came together in a loose circle around his shackled form.

Proprietor said, "Which brings us to our second order of business. Our guest tonight is Zeta's private secretary, Steven Woolsey. He's been responsible for Zeta's data security for... twelve years, is it?"

When the man stared mutely up at the red mask, Proprietor bent and removed his ball gag, doing so almost gently. For several seconds, the prisoner coughed and sputtered. Then he croaked, "Please. It wasn't my fault."

"First things first," Proprietor told him. "Answer my question."

"Oh... yeah. Twelve years. Listen, I'm sorry. This is all just a big misunderstanding."

"Given the circumstances, I can see why you'd say so. You see, Siblings, this man is the reason Zeta is awaiting arraignment tomorrow."

"How so?" Epsilon demanded. He took no step toward the prisoner, but the guy in the chair flinched anyway.

Proprietor replied, "By providing Checkmate with the lion's share of their evidence against Zeta."

"I didn't know it was Checkmate!" the man whined.

"How could you not know?" Theta demanded.

The prisoner whimpered piteously but offered no reply.

So Proprietor answered for him. "This man subscribed to one of the newer dating apps. He was contacted three months ago by someone calling themselves Monika, with a "k." The two of them struck up a friendship, and even engaged in physical relations... all online, of course."

"How do you have sex...?" Eta asked, then added, "Oh."

"He kept wanting to meet her, but Monika kept putting him off," continued Proprietor.

"Man got catfished," Gamma said.

"Our guest began to suspect the same thing," Proprietor replied. "The photos exchanged were no longer enough. So about two weeks ago, he insisted on an in-person meeting and Monika agreed. They met at a local bar, where he found her to be every bit as beguiling as her photos indicated. His crush turned into love... or, at least, obsession. Wouldn't you say so, Mr. Woolsey?"

Again, the prisoner didn't reply. His eyes were on the floor, and he seemed to be muttering to himself.

Again, Sally didn't blame him. She knew where this was going.

Proprietor remained unfazed by the prisoner's lack of response. "Monika started taking a keen interest in his work, which he was happy to talk about. Gradually, one might even say artfully, Monika asked for more and more. She wanted to see his office. She wanted to know Zeta's schedule, both personal and professional. And every time, our guest obliged. Apparently, the two hadn't yet engaged in any real physical contact. But he was hopeful. Isn't that so?"

This time Proprietor didn't give the prisoner a chance to not reply. "Then, just last week, Monika asked to visit Zeta's private office. She wanted to see where the 'coffee gets made," as she put it. And again, our guest agreed. But he insisted she come by the annex after Zeta was gone for the day, which she did. He then insisted that the visit be short, only a few minutes, followed by dinner and then, finally, back to his apartment for a nightcap. Monika agreed.

"But when they were in the office, Monika took something from her purse and sprayed it in his face. When he regained consciousness, he found Zeta's Cuff backups had been stolen and Monika was gone."

"Sevoflurane," Gamma remarked. "Just like at Drumthwacket last night."

Sally continued saying nothing. She didn't even wonder where Proprietor had come up with so many details about Woolsey's manipulation. The fact was she already knew the answer. They all did. Vladimir Antonov had spent the last several hours "talking" to the man, and had shared the results of that undoubtedly one-sided conversation with their collective leader.

"So it seems." Proprietor's mask shook sadly. "Our guest here was duped. That, by itself, could have been forgiven. This all happened four days before Friday's gala and the damage might have been mitigated had he come forward. But he didn't. Instead, he replaced the missing backup chips with fresh ones, locked the office, and never said a word. As a result, Checkmate exposed our Sibling."

"I'm sorry, okay?" the prisoner wailed. "I panicked! It was stupid!"

He was resoundingly ignored.

"So, Zeta was keeping backups?" Theta said. "I thought we weren't supposed to do that. Everything stays on our Cuffs."

"Obviously, Zeta didn't follow that particular protocol," Alpha remarked. "I certainly hope the rest of you do."

Every masked head nodded, including Sally's. She'd advised Victor—Zeta—more than once to avoid backups. Cuffs were secure, utterly so—and, once calibrated to their wearer's DNA, they became useless to any thief. But backups could be vulnerable. Regardless, the speaker had been distrustful of technology and had quietly insisted on protecting his financial records. It had been foolish of him, disastrously so, as things had turned out.

But God knew Sally had warned him.

"I don't understand," Eta remarked. "I thought Checkmate was a man."

"Did you?" Proprietor asked. "Why is that?"

"The hologram on Friday. Wasn't that voice male?"

Proprietor replied, "So was the homeless person that Checkmate paid a thousand dollars to create what, in hindsight, was a ridiculously obvious diversion. In both cases, I can't help wondering if prejudices were being triggered, pushing us toward an assumption that would remove half the population from suspicion."

Gamma said, "Or this Monika person could just be a member of Checkmate's network."

"Also possible," Proprietor admitted. "Either way, we're dealing with an adversary who rarely employs the same tactic twice. That makes him... or her... quite formidable."

"What was on the backups that proved so damning?" Epsilon asked.

Proprietor replied, "Without either Zeta's Cuff or the stolen backup chips, we can't be sure. But Zeta is insisting that all of our established communication protocols were followed in any emails or texts that he sent or received. Codenames only."

Sally, however, knew that had been a lie. Victor Cardellini had lied to Proprietor. And even worse, he'd placed her in the position of having to do the same thing.

"Still, it's bad." This came from Theta.

"There's no denying that," Alpha replied. "But it's manageable."

"First things first," Antonov growled, and that's what it was: a growl. He nodded toward the prisoner, who was looking frantically around like a mouse surrounded by cats. "What about him?"

Proprietor regarded the fellow as though having forgotten he was there. "Would you please take care of it, Beta?"

Without ceremony, and utterly without due process, Antonov drew a pistol from under his robe and shot Victor's assistant twice in the chest. Sally felt her throat catch. She'd expected this. They all had, as it had certainly happened before. Nevertheless, her stomach rolled over as Steven Woolsey—now dead—slumped in the chair, his eyes wide and spittle dripping from his slack mouth.

Antonov asked Proprietor, "Found or not found?"

"The latter. Given Zeta's arrest, it's probably to everyone's benefit if his private assistant just disappears. It might even give the defense team a possible scapegoat."

Practical, as always, Sally thought, more than a little bitterly. Proprietor had always subscribed to Machiavelli's favorite chestnut: "the end justifies the means." Sally didn't know what would happen to the poor

man's body, nor did she care to know. That was Antonov's responsibility, and he was welcome to it. Beta was a thug and Sally despised
him. But if she were honest with herself, she understood his value to
Argo.

"This unpleasant business attended to," Proprietor said, "all of you
should return to your lives and duties. The leak has been dealt with and
the situation with Zeta will be handled."

"How?" Gamma asked, sounding shaky.

"We'll know as things proceed. I've already taken steps to ensure
our brother is assigned a friendly judge. And that's just the beginning.
It'll be fine. Trust me."

"Of course, Proprietor," Eta said.

"What about Checkmate?" Epsilon asked. "Man or woman, they've
got to be stopped or another one of us is bound to be next."

It was Alpha who replied. "For the time being, avoid new hires.
Make sure your staff isn't backing up your Cuff. Checkmate can't
expose you if the evidence remains unreachable."

"Exactly so," Proprietor agreed.

"That's all well and good," Epsilon said, "but it's purely defensive."

"True," Proprietor replied. "Fortunately, a way to seize the offense
has been initiated."

Epsilon asked, "Are you talking about the journalist?"

"I am. Cheryl Walker of New Century 21 has been recruited,
unwittingly, to lead us to Checkmate. To do so, she will need access to
some of the people in this room. Interviews will be arranged over the
next few days, and it will be necessary for the Siblings involved to make
themselves available."

Sally, who was still thinking about Victor and his stolen emails,
heard herself ask, "Is that really wise, especially given what happened
to Zeta?"

Proprietor turned his attention to her, something she'd never cared
for. Even behind the mask, the man's presence intimidated her like no
one else had in her life, professional or personal. It was a feeling she
loathed.

"It's necessary, Delta. I'll be in touch to discuss what should and
should not be said to Ms. Walker." Addressing the whole of the
gathering, he added, "We're close, my friends, only days away from
changing everything. And the only remaining obstacle is Checkmate.

We need to find them, man or woman, unmask them, and then mitigate the threat they pose."

And to this, Vladimir Antonov added unnecessarily, "We gotta put him in the ground."

"Quite so," Proprietor agreed.

Chapter Six

SPIDER

WHITE PAWN TO QUEEN FOUR/
BLACK KNIGHT TO QUEEN'S BISHOP THREE

Saturday, July 5 – Sunday, July 6, 2048

CHERYL SAID, "ARE YOU TELLING ME SALLY COOKER, THE STATE'S top jurist, is corrupt?"

Monika smiled thinly. "Is it really so big a stretch? Look, Jersey's got a rep for being a shady place. Everybody knows it. The New York mob likes to dump its bodies in our Pine Barrens, and Jimmy Hoffa is supposedly buried under the endzone at Giants' Stadium. A former governor once shut down a bridge at rush hour because he was pissed off at the local mayor. Over the last century, there have been prostitution scandals, bribery scandals, embezzlement scandals... you name it."

"Same as everywhere," Cheryl remarked, maybe a little defensively. Like a lot of Jerseyites, she loved her state—even though, like a lot of Jerseyites, she rarely said so.

"You can make that argument, sure," said the enigma across from her. "But in the past fifteen years, things have amped up. And as far as I can tell, it started with Martin Sadler. Remember him?"

"Sorry. No."

"He was a state assemblyman out of East Orange. Started his political career on the local school board. Ran for freeholder and won. From there, he got his seat in the assembly here in Trenton. He was sharp and savvy, but he had this extremely unwise moral code. He started calling out his colleagues for minor corruption. Made enemies. Then he got himself appointed to the Oversight, Reform, and Federal Relations Committee and started investigating major corruption. Made more enemies.

"About a month later, he, his wife Alice, and their only child, Robin, were driving back from a weekend camping trip up at the Delaware Water Gap when they went off the road. Their car tumbled down a steep slope and into a rocky valley where it exploded, killing all three of them."

"Jesus..." Cheryl said.

Checkmate nodded gravely. "Witnesses reported Sadler drinking heavily at a local truck stop shortly beforehand. The official cause of death was ruled a drunk driving accident."

"And you're saying it wasn't?"

"Sadler didn't drink. A complete teetotaler. Pretty self-righteous about it, truth be told. No, hon. He was killed to protect the people he was going after."

Cheryl chewed on this. "Sounds a little paranoid."

"Does it? Well, Martin Sadler and his family died twelve years ago. Since then, eight more people have joined them in and around Trenton. And those are just the ones I know about. Most of the deaths were made to look like accidents, one a mugging gone wrong, one a suicide."

"How do you know they weren't accidents, a mugging, and a suicide?"

"Through good, old-fashioned detective work. It's there. Much of it's implied, but it's there. You just have to look."

"For so many murders to be orchestrated without any sort of police investigation... You're talking a large, organized conspiracy."

"Yes, I am."

"Fine," Cheryl said. "Let's say you're right. What are we looking at? Is this a single person or like a cabal or something?"

"I don't know. Yet."

"What do you know?"

"That whoever or whatever's behind this has their hands in everything that goes on in this state. They've turned the baseline corruption that's always been here into a cancer that reaches into every corner of the government. They've got resources, high-level contacts, and a ton of clout, enough to get away with what they've been doing for more than a decade."

Cheryl's bullshit meter was flashing red. If this had been anybody but Checkmate, she'd probably have been making them a foil hat.

But this *was* Checkmate.

"Do you have hard evidence to back this up?" Cheryl asked. "Anything at all?"

Monica smiled thinly. "If I did, it would already be over. But so far, whoever they are, they've been incredibly careful. All I've got are footprints in the sand. I know they're out there. But that's just about all I know."

"Do you believe Speaker Cardellini's involved? Is that why you targeted him?"

"Vic's the closest I've come so far. He's either one of the big wigs in this thing or thinks he is."

"And Sally Cooker?"

"I think so, yes."

"Why?"

"We'll get to that. For now, let's just say that I've been tugging at the edge strands of a very big web. I think Cardellini's arrest marks the first time I've really gotten the spider's attention."

"And you think the chief justice is the spider?" Cheryl asked.

"I don't know."

Cheryl sat back, ruminating. She'd always admired Sally Cooker. The idea of her being involved, or possibly even running, the kind of criminal confederacy that Checkmate described — well, "disillusioning" didn't quite say it.

"Might Vladimir Antonov be the spider?"

Monika shook her head. "No. I'm certain he's in it up to his neck and has been for a long time. But he's not running the show."

"How can you be sure?"

"I've studied Antonov. I know his M.O. When he was doing business as just Vlad the Importer, he was smart but had all the subtlety of a sledgehammer. Then, quite suddenly about fifteen years ago, his style shifted. He went from being an uncomplicated killer to a cunning assassin, planning 'accidents' rather than outright hits."

Cheryl considered. "And you're assuming that Antonov went into business with somebody who demanded he be more circumspect when he does his..." She couldn't quite convince herself to say "killing." So she went with an old spy novel term that, again in retrospect, sounded ridiculous. "Wet work."

She saw Checkmate suppress a smile and felt her own cheeks redden.

"So to speak. But it's more than that."

"More?" Cheryl asked.

"Prior to that fifteen-year-old trigger date, Antonov went after rivals and other corrupt importers, especially if they were Russian. Aside from occasional bribes, he had little or no interest in politics, state or local. But after that date, suddenly he's going into the infrastructure business. Roads, highways, bridges, you name it. He lands contract after contract. And anyone who starts poking around too much finds a way to get gone."

"Accidents or suicides," Cheryl said.

"Exactly. So if you buy into the theory about the ever-widening spider web, if you accept the conspiracy, it's an easy jump to connect it to Antonov. With me?"

"Yes." Then shaking her head, Cheryl added, "No. This is crazy!"

Checkmate said nothing.

Cheryl looked at her almost pleadingly. "None of this makes sense!"

"Really? Why not?"

"Because this isn't some third-world dictatorship! This is America, for God's sake! States aren't just taken over by faceless overlords! It's the stuff of bad action movies!"

"Honey, that right there, that denial, is what these people count on. It's why they're able to stay in the shadows. They rely on decent people shaking their heads and saying, 'it's impossible.'"

Cheryl sat back, annoyed at the way her hands shook when she rubbed her face. "I'll be honest. It's easier for me to believe that you're certifiable."

"So do that."

"What?"

"It's not too late. You could walk out the door, go home, and tell yourself whatever gets you to sleep. Then meet with Bourbon, do your interviews, write your second story about me, and go on with your life. Look, honey. By now it must have dawned on you exactly why you were recruited for this."

"What do you mean?"

"Think about it. Bourbon hopes the act of writing this article will attract my attention, all so he can deliver an obvious message? I don't think so."

"You think it's a trap."

"Of course, it's a trap. A variation on the old Honey Pot. He's hoping between that rather nice article you wrote about me at Princeton last year and this second one, done under his watchful eye, no doubt, he'll lure me out of the shadows. Then, finally, he'll get his first real crack at me."

"That assumes Michael Bourbon is involved in this conspiracy of yours."

"It does."

"Do you know it for a fact?"

Monika shook her head. "And I've looked. The guy's squeaky clean. But it doesn't matter. If you do what I said, just go on and write your story, then you're safe. Only make damned sure you never mention Martin Sadler or Antonov or conspiracies to anyone, ever."

"And what about the Honey Pot?"

"That only works if I get in touch. And if you walk out that door, I won't. By this time next week, Bourbon or whoever will decide I was too smart to be baited and chalk it up to a failed experiment."

"Are you sure?" It troubled Cheryl that her words sounded so desperately relieved.

"Sure as I can be."

And she almost did it. She almost got up and walked out of that bar without looking back. Hell, she wouldn't have to do the story at all. She could text Bourbon the minute she was out the door and decline, the late hour be damned. He'd be disappointed, of course. So would Dag. But it was definitely an option.

Doing so wouldn't be cowardly so much as rational, if even half of Checkmate's claims turned out to be true.

Then why am I still sitting here?

"I don't know what to believe," she said, more to herself than to Monika. "Or who to trust."

"Welcome to my world, honey. Seriously. Just go."

Cheryl locked eyes with her. "What happens if I don't?"

Monika looked back without flinching. "Then..." She seemed to hesitate. "Then like I said, I ask you if you're willing to help me investigate Chief Justice Cooker."

"How can I possibly help?"

"You can do something I can't. You can get in and talk to people, starting tomorrow with Bourbon. He's no doubt already set up interviews for you. Maybe Sally Cooker's even on the list. If she's not, ask for her. Hell, demand it. But then..." The woman's voice trailed off. Cheryl got the impression that Checkmate was debating with herself.

"What?" Cheryl asked.

Monika sighed. "But then you'll be in it, honey."

Cheryl just stared at the woman, the vigilante, the wanted criminal, unable to form a reply.

Monika said, "After tomorrow, if you agree to work with me, the things I ask you to do are *going* to get their attention. No way around it."

"Are you talking about Cooker, Bourbon, or Antonov?"

"Maybe all three. Once these people understand you and I are in cahoots, they'll use you to get to me. They're ruthless and they're scared, and that makes them dangerous, not just to me, but to you and everyone you care about. So if you're going to walk away, do it now." Monika tossed a lacquered thumb over her shoulder. "The door's that way."

"No," Cheryl said.

"You should, honey. You really should."

"Would you?"

Monika looked momentarily taken aback. Then she shook her head. "I committed to this a long time ago. There's no turning back now. Not for me. In a way, I kind of envy you."

Cheryl said, "I want to help."

She couldn't tell if Checkmate was relieved or horrified. "Are you sure?"

"Yes."

"I can't talk you out of it?"

"No, you can't. What's more, if you refuse to let me help, I'm going to my editor with everything you've told me."

"If you do that, the spider will find out."

"Yeah, that's the way I see it, too. So your best bet for keeping me safe is to bring me into your network."

"My network," Monika echoed. Then she laughed, though the sound had zero humor in it. With a sigh, she sat back again. "Okay, honey. I won't bother telling you that you don't know what you've just signed up for."

"Good," Cheryl said. "Because I'm not looking for a lecture. If anything of what you're saying is true, these people need to be stopped. What kind of person would I be if I just turned a blind eye to that much rot in my own state?"

"Smart?" Checkmate suggested wryly, though it struck Cheryl that the woman across from her looked regretful, perhaps even a little frightened.

Checkmate... Frightened.

That can't bode well.

"All right, then," she said, leaning close to her new — what? Collaborator? Partner? Cohort? "Tell me everything I'll need to know for tomorrow."

The woman across from her blew out a sigh before resignedly replying, "Fine. Let's start with a very specific question I want you to pose to our illustrious tech billionaire and senate president. I want you to ask him about something called... Argo."

CHAPTER SEVEN

IN THE STATE HOUSE

WHITE KNIGHT TO KING FIVE

Monday, July 7, 2048

NEW JERSEY'S STATE HOUSE, THE SECOND OLDEST BUILDING OF ITS kind in the U.S. — sort of, was built in 1792. It had been in continuous use ever since, through fires, wars, and additions — lots of additions. It boasted a hundred rooms, including the senate and general assembly chambers, state agency headquarters, and other offices. From overhead, the building loosely resembled a capital "H" — two big wings connected by a domed rotunda.

Cheryl had been here before on school field trips, though this was the first time she'd come on actual business.

But that wasn't why she was so nervous.

Samuel had spent most of Sunday trying to talk her out of it. After a restless night, Cheryl had shared with her roommate everything about her bizarre meeting with Monika, including Cheryl's decision to help with Checkmate's investigation.

"Kiddo," he'd said. "You know that's crazy, don't you?"

"I know it sounds crazy. But what if she's right? What if there is this cabal running the whole state?"

"Then call the frigging FBI! Don't go following some vigilante on a half-baked crusade!"

"Checkmate says that the FBI can't touch it without an indication that a federal law's been broken or some other clear threat to national security."

"I call bullshit! The FBI gets involved in state-level stuff all the time!"

"Not on the say-so of a vigilante."

"Are you hearing yourself? This is who you're cozying up to?"

"I know how it sounds. But I believe her."

"Why?"

That had flummoxed Cheryl. Why had she agreed to help Check-mate, despite the danger? Was she really that committed to "doing the right thing," or did the idea of breaking the biggest statewide story in fifty years tickle her ego?

Finally she'd answered, "Because if this cabal is real, then they need to be stopped!"

"Yeah? And why's that?"

Again she was flummoxed, but this time by disbelief. "Are you telling me you're okay with some faceless entity running your life, working above the law, and killing anybody who crosses them?"

Sam had the decency to look uncomfortable. "You know me. Apolitical. I don't even vote. But as far as I know, there's always been corruption. Isn't this just more of the same?"

What followed was a rare argument, one that ended with Cheryl storming off to her room. After that, the roommates largely avoided one another. Samuel went so far as to be out at dinnertime instead of preparing their now traditional Sunday meal. Meanwhile, Cheryl worked on her Cuff, researching the demise of Martin Sadler. She found considerable coverage of the tragedy, but nothing that questioned the ruling of accidental death. Sadler's alleged alcoholism was alluded to, but there wasn't so much as a whisper of conspiracy.

If Checkmate was right, then whoever this "spider" was, they were well concealed.

With Sam absent, Cheryl ended up ordering a pizza and eating alone at the kitchen table. Finally, around nine o'clock, the apartment door opened and she looked up to see Samuel standing in the dining room archway, dripping on the linoleum.

"Honey, I'm home," Sam said.

"You're wet," Cheryl remarked.

"It's raining."

"I'm sorry we fought."

"Shut up and hug me."

Gratefully, Cheryl did just that. Wet or not, Sam always gave good hugs.

"Be careful, kiddo," he whispered. "I really don't want to lose you."

"You won't."

"Promise?"

"Promise."

In the here and now, clinging to the memory of that hug like a warm blanket on a cold night, Cheryl entered the State House lobby. It was crowded, with at least two dozen people jostling through Security on their way to work or, like her, to other business in the state's seat of government. Three lines, managed by armed troopers, ushered everyone onto sensor plates that instantly detected and categorized any metal or liquid. Those items outside "safety parameters" were confiscated. There wasn't much of this; most folks knew better than to smuggle nail clippers into the State House, much less a weapon of any kind.

But there were a few outliers. One was a young man who screamed bloody murder when the troopers seized his energy drink after it tested positive for alcohol content. He raised such a fuss, in fact, that he ended up being ejected from the grounds, a result he accepted with all the grace of an enraged toddler. Several people laughed. Cheryl didn't.

Her turn came and went without incident. She'd had the good sense to leave Sam's shock knuckles and mace safely at home, and her house keys and rape whistle crossed the sensors without a blip.

A minute later she was standing at one of the receptionist stations.

"I've got an appointment with Senator Bourbon," she told the fellow, who confirmed this on his Cuff and perfunctorily initiated a Cuff-to-Cuff transfer that provided Cheryl with directions to the senator's offices.

These led her through what was once the original building and into the rotunda. This was a pretty space, though far smaller than its D.C. counterpart. It had a polished, diamond-patterned, marble floor, walls painted a vivid burnt orange, and three floors extending upward that culminated in a 145-foot dome covered in gold leaf and copper. In the floor's center stood a pedestal and a bronze sculpture of Abraham Lincoln, a two-foot-tall replica of the one at the Lincoln Memorial in Washington.

Paintings of local statesmen adorned the walls, along with a Latin phrase that Cheryl had to ask her Cuff to translate. "Fiat Justitia Ruat Coelum."

Let justice be done though the heavens fall.

With her wrist up and her path within the building clearly indicated, she turned a corner and found an elevator — one with an OUT OF ORDER sign slapped onto it. Groaning, she looked left and right for a staircase but found nothing obvious. So feeling foolish and not sure why, she wandered down the corridor until she came upon a door labeled FIRE EXIT.

"That not it, miss," said a woman in janitor's garb, who was dusting baseboards with a dry mop. She looked about fifty, tall but with the thick frame of someone "who works for a living," as Cheryl's father sometimes phrased it. Her salt-and-pepper hair was pulled back into a tight ponytail, and she wore very thick glasses.

"I'm sorry?" Cheryl asked.

"That door alarmed," the woman said. She had an accent. Baltic maybe? "You bump it wrong and police come running. If you want out, go back the way you come."

"Oh. No. I have a meeting with one of the senators."

"Ah! Most of them gone for summer."

"Not this one," Cheryl said. "Senator Michael Bourbon?"

The janitor laughed. "Oh! Is always here! He has big-shot office on second floor. Take stairs. Elevator broke."

"I know."

"Stairs, there. You find easy." She pointed.

"Thank you."

"Is no worry. When you reach second floor, turn right. Office behind two doors back of senate gallery. You find easy."

"Thanks again."

The janitor nodded sagely. "When lost, always ask cleaning lady. No one knows place like us." She offered Cheryl a wink and went back to her work.

Once on the second floor, her Cuff directions made sense again, and Cheryl found Senator Bourbon without any further trouble.

His offices were busy, despite the state senate being out of session. Apparently, a senate president's work was never done.

He had a staff of eight, all young people. They filled a large outer room, most of them working on their Cuffs. A few looked up when Cheryl entered, but only one, a smartly dressed woman close to her own age, greeted her.

"Ms. Walker?"

"Um, yes."

The woman offered her hand. "I'm Tammy, Senator Bourbon's chief of staff. The senator's been waiting for you." She motioned to an unlabeled door on the room's far side. "Just knock first."

Steeling herself, Cheryl did as instructed. Bourbon's door was one of those polished, solid oak, quarter-panel numbers.

A big shot's door.

"Come in."

She stepped inside the large office expecting an inner sanctum much like her father's, full of shelves of leatherbound law books, all unopened, since each one was available on his Cuff. Bourbon, however, wasn't a lawyer. He was a tech magnate, a computer engineer who'd invented the Cuff twenty years ago while fiddling with AI encryption algorithms in his attic workroom. Now the company he'd started, Cufflink Incorporated, was one of the largest employers in the state, its flagship product having secured both Bourbon's wealth and his legacy.

Beyond that, however, the man was a surprising enigma. Married for thirty-six years and with two grown sons, he made his home in wealthy Berkeley Heights up in Union County and, for most of his life, had shown no interest whatsoever in politics. Then, about fourteen years ago, he'd launched an unexpectedly successful run for the District 21 state senate seat. Everyone had been astonished. There'd been vague accusations that he'd somehow bought the election, but the rumor gained no traction.

And Senator Michael Bourbon had been getting re-elected, easily, ever since.

Interestingly, Bourbon still maintained control over Cufflink, something that was, at best, frowned upon in government. In fact, the opposition had launched no less than four investigations into possible conflicts of interest. These efforts had not only failed, but they'd also ultimately revealed that Bourbon personally financed numerous public works projects. This revelation had sent his approval ratings through the roof and his opponents slinking away, disgruntled but impotent.

He now occupied the state president's office in easy triumph. And on his shelves were not law books but pictures of his family — and, on a number of custom-made stands, every iteration of the Cuff since its introduction two decades before.

The man himself was seated behind a glass-top desk that, on closer inspection, proved instead to be a genuine Cufflink "Cuffdesk." These sold for around forty thousand dollars retail, which surely meant Bourbon had bought it on his own dime. Cheryl had heard of them but had never seen one before. The Cuff's biometric encryption didn't extend to too many other devices, but this desk was a rare exception. With it, Bourbon could summon a heads-up display and desktop virtual keyboard that would be completely incomprehensible to anybody who wasn't, well, him.

"Wow," she said. She'd never been all that much of a gadget nerd. But that desk would impress even the most dedicated Luddite, much the same way a Lamborghini "wowed" anyone who'd ever driven a car.

Michael Bourbon grinned and came partway out of his chair. It wasn't quite a "gentleman's stand," but more than Dag's usual grunt and curt nod. "Good morning, Cheryl."

"Good morning, Mike," she replied.

It was flippant and she knew it. Her mother would be cringing and her father fuming if they'd heard. But she couldn't help it.

To his credit, Bourbon took it in stride. "Please, take a seat."

She did. Unlike Dag's office, the senator's guest chairs were made of leather-upholstered hardwood.

Bourbon sat back down and regarded her. "So since you're here, should I assume you've decided to accept my assignment?"

In her ear, a voice said, *"An interesting choice of words."*

Despite herself, she flinched a little. It was the first time Checkmate had spoken through the small flesh-colored earpiece she'd given her the night before. "It's standard police issue," Monika had explained at the time. "All but impossible to spot, and it won't set off the building's security."

And of course she'd been right.

Out loud, Cheryl said, "I called my editor this morning and told him I'd write an in-depth, follow-up article on Checkmate. Frankly, it's a great opportunity. But we need to be clear on this, Mike... it's not your assignment."

"Watch his eyes. This isn't a guy used to defiance. And keep calling him 'Mike.' It's got to be rankling him."

Except it wasn't, not as far as she could tell. Instead, he simply smiled and declared, "My God, you're a journalist down to your toes, aren't you, young lady?"

Cheryl didn't reply.

"There you go. Defiance met with condescension. This guy always thinks he's the smartest person in the room. Let him. It's useful."

Bourbon asked, "May I at least assume that the underlying goal remains the same?"

"He means trapping me."

"You mean 'sending a message' to Checkmate?" Cheryl didn't add the air quotes. She didn't have to.

"Exactly. I can't tell you how important this is."

"Well, if you're hoping for me to get his attention..." She almost said "her," but caught herself. "I'll need to interview the right people."

"Already arranged." He tapped something in the air in front of him and the Cuffdesk's heads-up display illuminated, filling the space between them with pictures and words. Except, of course, the pictures were all blurred out and the words were gibberish—Cufflink's unbreakable encryption at work. As Cheryl watched, Bourbon swiped through a number of screens, found what he was looking for, and tapped something on his Cuff.

The heads-up display suddenly clarified into perfect readability.

Cheryl was astonished. Cuff encryption couldn't be bypassed, not even by the owner. This was part of its cutting-edge security protocols. No one could be coerced, threatened, or otherwise forced to display unencrypted data. Doing so just wasn't an option. You could send something to another Cuff and receive in return. But you couldn't share.

Apparently, Michael Bourbon's Cuffdesk could.

"The interviewees are all high-profile law enforcement and judiciary. If my theory about Checkmate's network is accurate, by week's end his informants should pass him word about this new story being written and, most especially, who's writing it. My chief of staff, Tammy, will transmit to you a copy of this schedule, of course."

Reading the list, Cheryl remarked, "I see I'm meeting with the attorney general tomorrow and Rhona Johnson on Friday, but I'm not going to see Chief Justice Cooker until next week. Any chance we could get that moved up?"

"There are limits even to my influence, Cheryl," the senator replied. "To be honest, you're lucky to be seeing these people at such short notice as it is. In addition to Colonel Johnson, you'll be interviewing two of the troopers that Checkmate assaulted last week. With luck, that alone will earn us a tug on the line. If not, we'll continue with the schedule. If necessary, I can probably arrange an interview with the acting assembly speaker, once one is selected."

"Nice," Checkmate noted.

"That's all well and good," Cheryl said, "but I still think I need to talk to Cooker sooner than next Tuesday."

"May I ask why?"

"Give him nothing. Let him wonder."

Cheryl met Bourbon's eyes with as neutral an expression as she could manage. "I'm not at liberty to say."

"I see." Bourbon's caterpillar-eyebrows dipped as he considered. "Cheryl, these interviews and the story you'll be writing are a means to an end. You do realize that."

"Say nothing."

Cheryl said nothing.

"Fine. I'll try," the senator finally told her, sounding less than happy about it. "I'll reach out to Sally Cooker personally and see if she can spare you some time in the next day or two. Is that good enough?"

"Thank you, Mike." Then Cheryl said, "I'd also like to talk to Victor Cardellini."

Bourbon's frown deepened. "That's... difficult. He's being arraigned this morning. Given the circumstances and his personal wealth, he may be deemed a flight risk and not get bail. Poor Vic isn't expected back in the office for the foreseeable future."

"'Poor Vic.' Interesting."

Cheryl silently agreed. "Then maybe I can visit him at the jail?"

"Maybe. I'll see what I can do." But he looked dubious.

"Thanks." Then, screwing up her courage, she said, "And depending on how things work out with the chief justice, I'm wondering what day would work for interviewing the governor."

"Oh, snap! And I get accused of having too much chutzpah! Honey, you are full of surprises!"

"Excuse me?" Bourbon said.

"I'd like an opportunity to probe Governor Lapidus's views on Checkmate. After all, on Friday night she didn't simply order an investigation of Speaker Cardellini. Immediately after Checkmate exposed him, she had him arrested, right there on the spot. I find that interesting, don't you?"

"Well, yes," the senator stammered. "I see your point."

"She's been surprisingly quiet about the vigilante in the media. Some might say 'loudly' quiet."

"Be that as it may, she *is* the governor. I'm not at all sure—"

"If you really want Checkmate's attention," Cheryl pressed, holding the man's eyes. "then putting me with Susan Lapidus is the way to do it."

Michael Bourbon drummed his fingers atop the Cuffdesk. Finally, begrudgingly, he said, "You make a good case. As it happens, the governor owes me a favor. I'll let you know if I can make something happen."

"Thank you."

"Well, Cheryl," the senator said. "If there's nothing else…"

"Do it now."

"Actually, there's one thing," Cheryl said. Suddenly, her heart was in her throat. She looked at Bourbon, who looked back at her expectantly. Steadying herself as best she could, she asked, "What can you tell me about Argo?"

"Watch his eyes."

For a second, Michael Bourbon's gaze seemed to lose focus. It was there and gone in an instant, so quick that Cheryl would have missed it—if she hadn't been instructed not to.

During last night's prep, Checkmate had explained that, contrary to popular wisdom, most people didn't glance "up and left" when they lied. In fact, they rarely broke eye contact at all, making a semi-conscious decision that holding someone's gaze conveyed sincerity. The truth was that honest folks often looked askance while thinking. Instead, Cheryl should watch for a momentary glazing over of the eyes—a "tell"—a loss of focus indicating that the imagination has been triggered. Apparently, it only worked when the subject was taken off-guard, forced to improvise. But in such cases, it was pretty close to infallible.

"Spotting it takes practice," the vigilante had schooled her. "But once you get in the habit of looking for it, you see it everywhere."

"That's a very cynical way of approaching the world," Cheryl had pointed out.

"Perfect cynicism is perfect awareness," Checkmate had quipped without a trace of irony.

And now, here it was.

Sitting across from her, one of the most powerful men in Trenton feigned confusion. "Argo? I'm afraid I have no idea what you're talking about."

In her ear, Monika asked, *"Did you see the tell?"*

Cheryl cleared her throat. It wasn't hard as it already felt arid. This was the signal she and Checkmate had pre-arranged.

And in her ear, sounding almost jubilant, the vigilante declared, *"Bingo!"*

Bourbon leaned forward. "May I ask where you heard that word?"

Cheryl shrugged. "I came across it in my research. But I won't take up any more of your time." At this, she stood — or tried to. For a moment, her knees didn't seem to want to support her.

"Are you all right?" the senator asked, looking genuinely concerned.

Cheryl wouldn't meet his eye. "I'm fine. Leg's asleep, that's all."

"Time to go, honey," Checkmate said. When Cheryl didn't respond, the woman added, *"Listen to me: I've got your back. Whatever happens now, I'm with you."*

Cheryl didn't know why those words helped, but they did. With a sigh, she pulled herself to her feet and mustered up a smile. "Thanks for your time, senator." She held out her hand.

Michael Bourbon shook it. "Thanks for sticking your neck out on this," he said, and the poignancy of that statement almost made her knees buckle all over again. "We'll touch base later in the week, and I'll have someone on my staff let you know about any changes in the schedule."

As she nodded and went to the door, Checkmate whispered in her ear, *"Welcome to the game, Cheryl Walker."*

CHAPTER EIGHT

HIS SIDEKICK

BLACK KNIGHT TO KING TWO

Monday, July 7, 2048

CHECKMATE STAYED QUIET IN HER EAR AS CHERYL BACKTRACKED her way down to the first floor. The janitor from earlier was nowhere in sight, but then Cheryl spotted the woman in the rotunda, dusting the portrait frames and the Lincoln statue on its pedestal.

"Ah, miss," the janitor said, grinning. "Did you get the job?"

"It wasn't an interview," Cheryl replied with a smile. "At least not that kind of interview."

The janitor nodded and went back to her cleaning.

"Can I ask you something?"

The woman shrugged, which seemed to be a yes.

"How long have you been here?"

"Me, miss? Only some months. Why?"

"Well, I'm a journalist and I'm doing a story that'll bring me back here in a few days."

"More big shots?"

Cheryl laughed. "Yes. But they're only part of it. Do you know about Checkmate?"

"Da. I play chess."

"I mean the vigilante."

"Oh, him! We no talk about him too much around here."

"Why not?"

"The big shots no like."

"Would you let me interview you about it? It would make an interesting counterpoint. I mean, big shots are fine, but sometimes the opinions of..." She considered how to put it. "...hard working folks like yourself count even more."

"Hmm," the woman replied, looking wary. "I need ask permission."

"I don't want to get you in trouble. This can be quick, just five minutes. If you'd prefer, I won't even name you in the article. Um... I'm sorry. My name's Cheryl. Cheryl Walker. What's yours?" She held out her hand.

The woman looked at the hand. She quickly wiped her palm on her overalls and shook it. "I am Val, Miss Walker. Nice to meet you."

"Call me Cheryl, okay?"

Val nodded.

"Well, then, can I call your Cuff later? To set things up, I mean."

Val seemed to chew on this for a moment. Then she held out her left wrist. Her Cuff was an older version, bulkier and less advanced than current models—maybe halfway along Bourbon's shelf of prototypes. But a Cuff was a Cuff, so when both women tapped their heads-up displays the right way, their contact information jumped into each other's device.

"There," Val said, looking somewhat uncomfortable. "No sure, though. I no want to lose job."

"That won't happen. I'll ask Senator Bourbon to clear it with your supervisor."

Val wrung her hands. "Then is okay."

"Do you know the senator?"

"He say hello sometimes. Most don't."

"Well, I promise you won't get in trouble. And during the interview, we'll skip any questions that make you uncomfortable. Sound good?"

"Guess so."

After exiting the State House, Cheryl made straight for the World War II Memorial. Located across the street in Veterans Park, the memorial consisted of a small domed gazebo above a statue of Lady Victory, holding a sword in one hand and a wreath of peace in the other. Often a popular meeting place, today's drizzle had mostly emptied it. So Cheryl settled herself under the relative shelter of the gazebo and waited.

A few people wandered by, some pausing to examine the six service markers that surrounded the statue, each representing a different branch of the military. Cheryl scrutinized every face, but nobody glanced her way, and none of them looked anything like Monika.

Finally, a man in a plastic poncho and wearing a New York Jets baseball cap walked right up to her. "I'm sorry," he said with a Brooklyn accent. "Got the time? My Cuff's gone dark."

Cheryl, who often forgot to charge hers, could sympathize. So she raised her wrist and replied, "About ten-fifteen."

"Thanks." Then in Monika's voice he said, "You did great in there."

Cheryl blinked.

He grinned.

She asked in a stunned whisper, "Monika?"

"Actually, it's Peter today," he said, once again in the Brooklyn accent.

"Peter?"

"Peter Leko. I'm in Trenton for the day, sightseeing. Never been a huge fan of Jersey. The Big Apple's my town, you know?"

Cheryl felt her head start to spin. "But you can't be..."

"Be what?"

"You look... different."

"Than who?"

"Than Monika."

With a sly smile, Peter Leko's voice changed registers again, replacing the Brooklyn accent with a Boston twang. "Honey, none of us are just one thing. We all have different people inside us. I've just gotten better at zeroing in on them."

Cheryl almost laughed, but instead covered her mouth, afraid of how it might sound. After a few seconds, she swallowed and said, "This is completely crazy."

"Since when is life sane?"

"Are you ever going to tell me your real name?"

Suddenly, Peter was back. "Now, Cheryl. We've only had one date." He grinned. It was a remarkable grin, crooked and thoroughly male. Looking at him, it was a herculean task to accept that this—person—was the same woman from the bar.

"Why won't you level with me?" she asked.

"You're not that naïve."

"Is it naïve to expect trust from someone you're partnering with?"

"That's a loaded question. We only met last night. How much do *you* trust *me*?"

"Enough that, by your own admission, I just put a target on my back for you."

"Interesting. You did that for me?"

"You know what I mean," Cheryl told him crossly.

"Well, you're not wrong. Right now, the good senator is probably Cuff-calling someone, maybe more than one someones, informing them that their trap is baited."

"Are you that sure Bourbon's involved?"

"Not as sure as I am about Sally Cooker, but sure enough. That Argo question pretty much cinched it."

"But you said you don't even know what this 'Argo' is."

"I don't. But it's mentioned in emails sent from Cardellini to Cooker in a context that implies it's both a big deal and something they're not supposed to be talking about. Add to that the good senator's tell, and, well, let's just say I'm now confident he's as involved as anyone. That said, I'm glad he seemed open about moving up the Cooker interview. He also seemed receptive to having you talk to Cardellini and even Governor Lapidus. I'm assuming he Cuffed you the complete interview schedule?"

"Actually, not yet," Cheryl replied. "He just showed it to me on his Cuffdesk."

That took Peter by surprise. "On a Cuffdesk?"

"Sure. His company did invent them, after all."

"Natch," he said again. "But he shared it with you directly? He actually dropped the encryption?"

"Yes. I didn't know they did that."

"They don't. The thing that makes Cuffs so impossible to hack is that, when they're calibrated to an owner, the entire operating system is rewritten and encrypted using biometric markers. Once established, that encryption can't be changed or bypassed. It's why Cuffs can't be resold and you can't ever buy a refurbished one. Security. Security. Security."

"But he bypassed it," Cheryl said.

"Obviously, his Cuffdesk is different, special. There may be an opportunity there. I'll have to think on it."

"I'm now wondering if he's going to renege on some of those scheduling requests, now that I dropped the Argo bomb on him. Maybe he'll even cancel the whole story."

"He won't," Checkmate said, shaking his head.

"You sound sure."

"I am. Think it through. He knows about Argo, which is evidently something secret and scary. Now he finds out you know about it too, which has to be setting off alarm bells in his head. Where did you get that knowledge? You told him it was research, but he knows better. Right now, he's got to be assuming that you learned it from just one source."

"You," Cheryl said.

"Yep. So he has to assume that you and I have talked."

"We have."

"And will talk again."

"Like we are now."

Peter Leko grinned. "Exactly! Believe me, right now he's surer than ever that you're the way to get to me. So he'll keep you closer than ever. The story won't be cancelled and the scheduling changes will get made. You'll see."

"Fine," Cheryl said. "I'll take your word for it. Now, how can I help?"

"Right now, you can't. Go straight home. They're watching you as it is."

"What?"

"Don't look around. They've been here since before I showed up. A man and a woman. She's at the bus stop about fifty yards away, just standing there, not-not-watching us, despite the three buses that have come and gone. The man's over by the Naval Marker, taking pictures. Damn it! Don't look!"

"Who are they? Do they work for Bourbon?"

"State senators don't keep spies on their payroll. Besides, they're both dressed in gray suits, almost the same shade. No, not spooks. Muscle. And I know only one guy who insists his people wear gray suits like uniforms."

"Who?"

"Vlad the Importer."

"Are you kidding me?"

Peter shook his head. "It's something Antonov got into early in his career. Just his security staff, of course. Not his dock or warehouse workers. Nobody knows why he does it or, if they do, they're afraid to say. I think he digs feeling like the president surrounded by his Secret Service detail. I tend to think of them as the 'People in Gray.' Anyway, if we needed any more evidence that Bourbon's involved in all this, there it is. He must have signaled Antonov to have his people begin surveillance."

"That fast?" Cheryl protested. Fear had settled in her belly like a cold, hard stone. "I just walked out of there!"

"He probably had people nearby. Or maybe, and this worries me more, they've been watching you since you got the assignment."

"Including Saturday night when I went out to meet with you?"

"Probably not. I'd have noticed them."

"Why would somebody like Vladimir Antonov care about me?"

"I'm sure he doesn't. But he cares about me and you're the Honey Pot, remember?"

"Jesus. Do you think they're listening to us?"

"No, that's harder. Given the distance, they'd need a directional mic, and even the smallest of those is hard to conceal."

"But they must know we've been talking for longer than it takes me to tell you the time."

"Yeah."

"Aren't you worried?"

Peter shrugged. "When we split up, it'll be in opposite directions. Chances are the man will follow me and the woman you. In any event, don't make eye contact and don't let them know you're onto them. Just go home. If you get nervous, call 911 and report a stalker. These folks don't want attention. But chances are you're safe enough. This is only surveillance."

"Are you sure?"

"No," Peter admitted. "So be careful."

"What about you? Won't they suspect who you are?"

"They probably do already. But I'll lose them."

"How."

"Tricks of the trade."

"How will you get in touch?"

"Keep wearing your earpiece."

"Oh," she said. "I'm... scared."

"I know," he replied. "But I meant what I said. I've got your back. Go home."

With that, Peter Leko turned and strolled away, his hands in his pockets. As Cheryl watched, her heart pounding, he headed down the block and right past the bus stop. There, a fit-looking woman in a professional gray pants suit studiously didn't look at him as he went by.

A moment later, he was swallowed up by the city.

Cheryl remained rooted for another minute. Then, trying to appear casual and failing miserably, she glanced at the Naval Marker. Nobody was there.

Shit.

And with that, she started walking.

Chapter Nine

SALLY'S HUSBAND

White Bishop to King Three/
Black Pawn to Queen's Bishop Three

Monday, July 7, 2048

"Welcome home, Justice Cooker. He ate well for both breakfast and lunch. He's currently in the study watching television and drinking his electrolyte formula. He's been in good spirits most of the day."

"Thank you, Mindy," Sally said. "I'll check on him. But after, I'll be working in my office for the remainder of the afternoon."

"Of course. Are you hungry? I have some strawberry salad left over and I could make you a sandwich."

"No, thank you. One of my clerks fetched me something from the cafeteria. I'm fine."

She left the caretaker and slipped quietly down the hall to the study. During their first years in this house, nestled amongst others of its ilk in the affluent Glen Afton section of Trenton, Harrison's study door had always been closed. Back then, he'd been a private and reflective man who favored solitude while working.

These days, of course, it was nailed open for safety reasons.

As she slipped into the smallish but tastefully decorated room, she caught a glimpse of herself in the mirror that she'd hung on the wall nearly twenty years before. The woman who looked back at her was a stranger, the lean face lined from years of long hours and little rest, the hair a stark gray. She always told people, those few who ever asked, that she'd come by her gray hair "honestly," through the passage of years.

But that was a lie.

The color of her hair, like the nails in the study door, had their direct cause in a single night more than a decade ago, when New

Jersey's powerful Superior Court Judge Sandra "Sally" Cooker had found out what real power was.

Harrison sat in the high leather wing chair. It used to stand in the corner, more a show piece than anything else. But it had long ago been repositioned six feet from an old-fashioned flat-screen television.

A cartoon she didn't recognize played on the TV, the sound low. Harrison didn't like loud noises.

"Hello, darling," Sally said, coming around the big chair to gaze down at her husband of thirty-eight years.

Harrison James Bartleby, historian and author of fourteen books on the American Revolution, kept his eyes glued on the colorful images that romped about on the screen. He flinched but didn't otherwise react when Sally bent and kissed his sunken cheek.

"I talk to Harry today," Sally said. "The new baby's doing well. They expect to come back east for a visit sometime next month. You're a grandfather, darling. Isn't that wonderful?"

Harrison didn't reply, but Sally hadn't expected him to. There'd been a time when she'd sit with him for hours, just talking and hoping—praying, even—for some kind of response. But none ever came. Some years ago, she wasn't sure when, she'd stopped trying. She told herself this was acceptance, blessed acceptance, of a terrible but irrefutable new reality. But occasionally, while she lay sleepless and alone in the king-size bed the two of them had bought together just months before Harrison would no longer need it, Sally knew better.

Harrison was dead.

This was just 160 pounds of meat, run by a brain that generated barely enough power to keep its heart beating.

With a sigh so familiar she didn't notice uttering it, she left the thing that had been the love of her life and went down the hall to her office. This space, nestled at the front north corner of the house, was even smaller than Harrison's study. But its many windows and abundant natural light suited her, and the antique desk that held court here had belonged to her father.

Sally would, as had become her habit, lose herself in the briefs, opinions, and precedents of her profession. And by the time Mindy came in to report that Harrison had received his dinner and been put to bed, she would have been able to forget he existed, if only for a time.

Twenty minutes later, her Cuff chimed.

The caller was Michael Bourbon. She and the senator had little to do with each other professionally, aside from occasional mandatory public appearances, like last Friday night's gala. So if he was calling her directly rather than going through one of her law clerks, he was doing so in a capacity other than that of president of the state senate.

A knot, cold and hard, formed in Sally's stomach as she opened the call.

"Gamma," she said.

Proprietor's protocols were clear. Cuffs were secure; no one doubted that. But protocols reinforced learned skills and prevented slip-ups at times when they could matter. And Sally's master—there was simply no other word for it—did not abide slip-ups. That much had been evidenced on Saturday night.

"*Delta,*" Bourbon said.

"What do you want?" Sally asked. She knew her tone with him was short. But she hadn't slept in days.

He was quiet for a moment. To be honest, Sally had nothing against the senator, per se. Like herself, he was beholden to the man in the red mask. But whenever a Sibling meeting was called, which had been happening with increasing frequency, the time and place invariably came from Michael Bourbon's private number. Furthermore, at the gatherings themselves, Bourbon was always the gopher, doing this or that at Proprietor's whim.

It was hard to respect such a person.

"*I've just met with Cheryl Walker,*" he said.

This, of course, had been expected. Sally waited.

"*She wants to interview you, first.*"

A simple statement, but one that turned her icy with fear. She stared down at her Cuff, which only displayed Bourbon's number. Siblings never shared face-to-face calls. That was another of Proprietor's many protocols.

"Why?" she heard herself ask.

"*I'm not certain. But she was adamant. Honestly, she was adamant about a few things. She wants a meeting with the governor and, more worriedly, Zeta.*"

Victor.

The mention of the disgraced speaker's name made Sally's hands shake. She thought of Harrison, already a lost cause. Then she thought of their sons, Harry and Trevor, who weren't.

"Do you think she knows something?" Sally asked, astonished at how calm she sounded.

"Maybe. She mentioned Argo to me."

"She did *what?*" Her fear blossomed into terror. "How? I mean, how did she even happen across the name?"

"I don't know and didn't ask. I simply told her I'd never heard of it."

Sensible. But Michael Bourbon had always been a sensible fellow. "So she doesn't know what it is?"

"I didn't get that impression. If she had, I think she would have pursued it more than she did."

"Could Checkmate already be involved? Did she get the name from him?"

"I don't know."

"Has Beta been watching her?"

"Of course. His people have been shadowing her from the moment she left the State House."

"Good. All right, let me check my calendar." She did so, but only perfunctorily. Sally made it a point to know her schedule. *"I can see her this evening. At my home."* Sally glanced at her guest chair, a simple, modern straight-back with no arms. Harrison had never approved of her more contemporary tastes, saying it didn't befit a superior court judge.

If only you could see me now, darling.

"I'll pass that along. But, Delta, be careful. We're walking through a minefield here."

When aren't we?

"I can handle some mid-millennial with a master's in journalism," Sally replied, her condescension deliberate and almost automatic. She'd used that haughty tone a thousand times from the bench. It intimidated. It controlled. It elevated her above others.

Proprietor would approve.

But Bourbon didn't seem to notice. *"I'll pass your willingness for an evening interview along to Ms. Walker. Is eight o'clock workable?"*

Harrison would have been put to bed by then. "That's fine. Goodbye, Gamma."

She broke the link without waiting for his reply.

For several long minutes, she sat at her desk, trembling. Everything around her, her entire life both professional and personal, felt as though it had been built on sand. Until a few days ago, she'd been secure in her success and power, despite the fealty she owed to Proprietor. But that had been before Victor Cardellini had been publicly arrested, and before Checkmate had stolen his Cuff backups.

Cuff backups that almost certainly included certain email conversations with her.

If the vigilante knows, he'll bring me down. If Proprietor finds out, he'll punish me. Or, worse, he'll punish one of my boys.

She wanted to cry but didn't. Sally Cooker never cried. Tears changed nothing. She would deal with this situation the same way she dealt with every new threat. She would address it head-on and without emotion.

Very well, Cheryl Walker. You and I will talk this evening. Ask your questions. If you simply want to pick my brain about Checkmate, so be it. I'll tow the party line, just as Proprietor wants.

But if you know something you shouldn't, something that could put my children in danger — I will kill you.

OMAR AND STUFF

WHITE PAWN TO QUEEN'S ROOK THREE/
BLACK PAWN TO KING'S ROOK THREE

Monday, July 7, 2048

DESPITE CHECKMATE'S SUGGESTION, SHE DIDN'T GO HOME. IT WAS, after all, only ten-thirty in the morning.

NC22's offices were nearby. Nevertheless, with every step along the way, her nerve endings sizzled. It was hard not to actively look for the "People in Gray" who were presumably following her, sent by Jersey's scariest mobster. By the end of the short walk, Cheryl's face glistened with sweat, and it took all her courage to keep putting one foot in front of the other.

There was a comforting normalcy to the typical Monday morning activity she found waiting for her when she arrived at the collective. Dag was holding court in his office, and staffers were scattered about, working on their individual content. Nobody so much as looked up when she entered.

Feeling somewhat better, Cheryl settled down on one of the couches and worked on her Cuff. She started by entering her thoughts on the day. Doing this always relaxed her, kind of like cleaning a kitchen after a particularly messy meal — order from chaos.

Just when she'd finished with her notes on the Bourbon interview and was about to move on to the encounter with Peter Leko, a familiar voice asked, "You okay?"

Omar stood over her. He was dressed in khakis and a blue plaid long-sleeve shirt, with the tail out and the sleeves rolled up halfway to the elbow. "Young Journalist on the Go," Sam had dubbed the look when Cheryl had described it. "Do they all dress like that?"

"The guys do, but they take their cues from Omar."

Samuel had laughed. "Alpha male. The biggest lion on the Serengeti."

And it was true. Omar ruled the roost at NC22, at least among the politicos. Maybe it was his writing creds, which were admittedly solid. Or maybe it was something a bit less cerebral. Omar was good looking — very good looking, which had to help him with managing the other lions in the pride.

"I'm fine," she replied with a smile. "Why?"

Omar hesitated. Finally, turning away, he said, "It's nothing. Never mind."

"No," Cheryl pressed. "Come on. Tell me."

"Well... " He looked uncertain. It was a rare expression for him, and she found she rather liked it. "It's just that you're always so put together. But today you seem, I don't know. Nervous, I suppose."

Is it that obvious? The thought made that now-familiar cold rock in her belly even colder and rockier. "A tough couple of days, I guess."

"Been there," he noted with a wry smile. To his credit, he didn't ask her if she wanted to talk about it. They didn't have anywhere near that kind of relationship. Instead, he said, "That was a great piece you did on the gala at Drumthwacket."

"Thanks," she replied, wondering if he was being straight with her. He seemed so, but she had no idea how far she could trust that.

Then he remarked, "Dag told me he's got you on some kind of long-term assignment."

Did he? That didn't sound like Dag; the editor was a vault.

"I can't talk about it."

"I get it. Hey, look. I know some of the others have been riding you pretty hard since you got here."

"Have they?" Cheryl asked sweetly. "I hadn't noticed."

"Cute." He smiled. It was a great smile, a thousand lumens at least. "But seriously, maybe I have, too. If so, I'm sorry. It's kind of a rite of passage for newbies. And, let's face it, there's an element of jealousy in it."

"Jealousy?"

His smile turned rueful. "You don't get it, do you? Mark and Edwina think this humility of yours is an act, something to ingratiate you with Dag. But you honestly don't see it."

"See what?"

"You're the youngest person to ever win a Hume. I read your Checkmate article in the *Daily Princetonian*. It was better than good. You're a prodigy. You have to know that!"

Cheryl felt her face redden. "I got lucky."

"That's bullshit. Why do you think Dag picks you for so many choice assignments?"

Cheryl uttered an uncomfortable, "Oh."

"Anyway, I just figured it was time for somebody, one of your peers, to drop the envy and hazing and properly welcome you to NC22. So... Welcome."

It seemed sincere, so much so that Cheryl muscled through her discomfort and met his eyes. "Thank you, Omar. That means a lot."

He offered up another great smile. "Okay. I'll leave you to it." And, with that, he turned and headed off, only to stop and look back. "Um..."

Cheryl looked up again. Somewhere along the way, her cold rock had turned into fluttering butterflies.

Omar regarded her with an expression she'd seen before, plenty of times, but not on him. Never ever on him.

After a long, fidgety pause, he asked, "You want to get a drink after work?"

At first, Cheryl was thunderstruck. She stared at him, her mouth kind of falling open. Had Omar Polat, ace reporter for NC22 and six years her senior, just asked her out?

He seemed to take her stunned silence as rejection. "Hey, sorry. That was inappropriate. Forget it."

"No, it's okay. I—" Cheryl stopped, just stopped and considered. Omar was good-looking. And smart. And talented. But he'd also been ignoring her or riding her, on and off, since she'd started here. She recalled vividly his first words to her, uttered as Dag was introducing her around. He'd treated her to a cursory glance and muttered, "fresh meat," which had made his entourage laugh.

And this was that guy?

"Okay," she said, her interest piqued. "Drinks. About six?"

"Works for me!" he exclaimed, sounding almost schoolboy relieved. "Now get to work," he added with a touch of his usual condescension— though, this time, Cheryl thought it might be affected. "You've got a deadline."

"How do you know?" she asked, wary again.

He treated her to another grin. *God, what a grin!* "This is New Century 22. We've all got deadlines!"

This time, when he headed off, he didn't look back.

It was turning out to be an interesting day, a real star on her Cuff calendar.

Cheryl went back to her notes.

At lunchtime, Omar stopped by again. He was ordering out and asked if she wanted anything. From his eager expression, Cheryl sensed that, if she took him up on it, he'd buy her that lunch and eat it with her—or maybe the two of them would go out. There were a few pretty decent places within walking distance.

But while the notetaking had helped with her anxiety, she didn't feel ready for that. So, she told him no, she was fine.

"Still on for drinks though? After work?"

"Still on. Now beat it. I'm trying to be a journalist."

He laughed, but he obediently beat it.

She used her Cuff to peruse the net, continuing her background research. She'd gone over the Sadler case yesterday. But Checkmate, as Monika, had given her other names.

One was the wife of a state senator named Tim McAvoy. Caitlin McAvoy had been walking home from the market through a comparatively safe neighborhood when she'd been mugged, knifed, and left dead in an alley, her purse and wedding rings taken. She'd left behind six children. A tragedy, and still unsolved.

A week later, after burying his wife, McAvoy had done a complete one-eighty on the senate floor, voting for a controversial highway bill after arguing vigorously against it. He called the reversal a "change of conscience."

But Checkmate thought differently. "Whoever they are, they didn't want to kill McAvoy. They needed his vote. So they killed his wife as a message: play along or the kids are next."

That was crazy, completely off-the-rails nuts.

Except...

McAvoy resigned after the vote and moved out of state. These days, he had a law practice in Michigan. A grieving husband starting over, right?

Maybe.

Cheryl's Cuff chirped. She checked the ID. She groaned, sighed, and answered it. A face shimmered into view in front of her, projected an inch or two above her wrist. To anyone else, it would be an amorphous blob and the voice it generated gobbledygook. All any eavesdropper would be able to hear was Cheryl's end of the conversation.

"Hi, Mom," she said.

"*Hello, sweetheart! How's it going? We haven't heard from you in a while.*"

"Just busy. Long hours."

"*Sounds awful.*"

"I'm getting used to it."

"*Are you staying safe?*"

"Sure," she lied.

"*Do you have enough money?*"

"Plenty. Thanks, though."

"*Of course, sweetheart. Now, I'm calling to remind you about your father's birthday.*"

"I didn't forget," Cheryl replied, though she kind of had. With everything going on, her family had all but vanished from her thoughts.

"*I'm sure you haven't. We're planning a simple dinner for him. Your sister and brother will be there.*"

Cheryl ran through a mental list of excuses; she didn't feel like spending another evening defending her life choices. But then she realized that this would mark the first time she'd been home since coming up to Trenton—what had it been? Five weeks now?

And it is Dad's birthday...

"That would be nice," she said.

Barbara Walker sounded almost relieved. "*Wonderful! It's tomorrow night.*"

"Tomorrow!" Cheryl exclaimed. "You're having a party on a Tuesday?"

"*No party. As I said, all your father wants is a small family dinner. He's hearing an important appeal starting on Wednesday and thinks the hours may be long. So he wants to get his birthday 'out of the way' before then.*"

That sounded like him.

Cheryl stammered, "It's just that, with the hours I work, I'm not sure if—"

"*Cheryl Walker, this is your father we're talking about!*"

There was more to that lecture, she knew—oodles of guilt-spreading, conscience-tugging momspeak. But Cheryl had heard it so many times that evidently her mother didn't feel the need to repeat it. Just the first line was enough to make her point.

"What time?" Cheryl asked, grinding her teeth.

"*Seven o'clock.*"

"Okay."

"Are you going to take the train? I can have E.J. pick you up."

"Probably. I need to look at the rail schedules and get back to you."

"Let me know by tonight please, sweetheart. Your brother has his own plans to make."

"I will. Gotta go, Mom. "

"My worker bee. All right. Oh! One more thing. Your father and I want you to bring your roommate. What's her name? Samantha?"

Cheryl felt a rather shameful stab of pure panic. For a second, the cold rock returned with a vengeance. "Y…yeah," she stammered. "Samantha."

"Well, we'd love to meet her."

"I'm not sure she'll be available."

"Oh, she is, sweetheart! I've already called her."

"You... what now?"

"I called Samantha. She's lovely. At least she sounds lovely."

"You called my roommate?"

"That's what I'm telling you."

"How'd... you get her number?"

Her mother laughed. *"From you, silly! You gave it to me. You know, for emergencies."*

"Yeah, emergencies!" Cheryl snapped. "Not so you could call whenever you felt like it!"

"Why are you so upset? I told you. She's lovely. I invited her to dinner tomorrow night, and she said she'd be happy to come."

Cheryl's mouth went dry. "She did?"

"Yes. So, it's settled. Just let me know what time E.J. can pick you both up at the train station, all right?"

Cheryl went functionally mute. Too many scenarios, too many possibilities, swirled around in her head. And the biggest one, perhaps the most unfair one, was this: They're Methodists! They're all freaking Methodists!

"Sweetheart? You still there?"

"Yeah."

"We're all set for tomorrow night, yes?"

"Um, sure. Mom, I've got to get back to work."

"All right. We'll see you tomorrow night."

"Okay."

Then she broke the connection and thought, *Shit*.

Cheryl tried to clear her mind; she really did. And in that spirit, she dove into another of Checkmate's touted "victims."

Joseph Manning had been a Department of Corrections guard working at New Jersey State Prison, right here in Trenton. Three years ago, an inmate had stabbed him. Subsequent charges had been filed against Adrian Genrich, who'd been serving fifteen years for manslaughter. Later, when Genrich had been up for parole, Manning was scheduled to appear at the hearing. Everyone in the prison figured it was a slam dunk. Once Manning testified about the stabbing, which had happened without witnesses, Genrich wouldn't see the light of day again for another decade.

Except Manning recanted. He told the board there'd been no stabbing. He'd confiscated the weapon from another prisoner and had been carrying it on his person. Later, while escorting Genrich, he'd slipped and fallen on the blade, stabbing himself. He even insisted that Genrich had aided him, staunching the bleeding and calling for help.

As a result, Genrich got paroled.

Then, two days later, Manning and his wife were both killed when a fire destroyed their home. The cause turned out to be a gas leak. Arson was not suspected.

Adrian Genrich had since disappeared, though he was known to have ties to Vladimir Antonov.

The whole thing was circumstantial, just like with McAvoy, but it did seem to indicate, as Checkmate had said, a pattern. Cheryl knew she should keep digging and familiarize herself with the other names on Checkmate's list. But she kept thinking about the birthday party, and the idea that, tomorrow night, she'd be introducing her family to Sam.

I can't believe Mom called her!

I can't believe she accepted!

Her Cuff chirped a second time. Irritated, she looked down at it. The ID was for Senator Bourbon's office. Feeling a flush of excitement that pushed away, at least for now, her worries about tomorrow's party, she opened the line. A moment later, Tammy, the senator's aide, shimmered into existence above her wrist.

"*Ms. Walker? It's Tammy from —* "

"Hello, Tammy." Cheryl piped in, only to kick herself for seeming over eager.

The woman grinned. "*I'm calling to see if you would be available to interview Chief Justice Cooker at her home this evening.*"

The question was so ludicrous that Cheryl almost laughed out loud. "I think I can manage that," she replied, keeping her tone as carefully neutral as possible. "What time?"

"8:00? I'll send you the chief justice's home address."

"Perfect. I'll be there." Then, if only to make herself feel better about her professionalism, she added, "Any word on the interview requests for the governor or the speaker?"

Tammy didn't miss a beat. *"The senator's still working on that. If something develops, I'll let you know."*

"If," not "when."

"Thank you, Tammy."

They said their good-byes and Cheryl broke the connection before sitting back and marveled. Last Friday she'd been the newbie around here. This morning, she'd interviewed the president of the New Jersey Senate. And tonight, she would be doing the same with the state's highest-ranking member of the judiciary.

What a difference a few days make.

What a difference Checkmate makes.

She'd have to reach out to the vigilante and let them know about the Cooker interview. Monika, or Peter, or whoever, would no doubt want to strategize. After all, Cooker was their next target, the next strand in the spiderweb—always assuming that the web and its spider truly existed. And despite everything she'd read today, Cheryl still wasn't convinced of that.

"Well, I've had enough," said a voice.

She opened her eyes to see Omar wearing a bemused expression.

"Enough?" she asked.

"Work for the day. It's past five. Are you ready for that drink?"

Cheryl blinked. "Oh! Crap. I'm sorry, Omar. Something's come up. Raincheck?"

He looked so crestfallen that she wasn't sure if she should feel flattered or guilty. "I hope it's a good something and not a bad something."

For a moment, she considered telling him, but she rejected the idea.

Then she did it anyway. "I just found out I'm interviewing Sally Cooker at her home this evening."

To her surprise, Omar grinned broadly. "Seriously? That's big! How'd you land that? Never mind, you shouldn't tell me. But I hope once you blow us all away with whatever piece you're writing, you'll let me buy you that drink while you crow about it!"

Again, he seemed sincere, so much so that Cheryl felt an urge to say more. This time, however, she fought the urge and won. "That's a nice offer," she replied instead. "I might just take you up on it."

He nodded and started to turn away. Then he paused and asked, "How are you getting there?"

"Excuse me?"

"Well, I happen to know that Justice Cooker lives in Glen Afton. That's a long and pretty iffy walk, especially at that hour."

"Oh," Cheryl replied. "I guess I'll call a PeopleMover."

"You could," he said. "Or you could save yourself the expense and let me drive you."

"That's really great of you," she said automatically, "but I'm serious about completing this assignment alone."

"I'm not saying I'd go into the house with you. I'll stay in the car. Then I can drive you home and... Who knows? We might get that drink on the way back."

"You'll sit out in your car while I go spend an hour or more inside?"

He laughed a little. "It won't be an hour. This is the chief justice. You'll be lucky if she gives you fifteen minutes. Listen, if it makes you uncomfortable, forget I offered."

"Why *are* you offering?" she asked, treating him to a pointed look.

But he met her gaze evenly and replied, "Is that really so hard to figure out?"

Despite herself, Cheryl felt her cheeks redden. Turning away for a moment, she said, "Fine. Sure. I'll take the ride."

"And the drink? Afterward, I mean."

This time it was her turn to utter a brief laugh. "And the drink. Maybe."

"Good enough for me. We'll leave around 7:30, if that works for you."

It did. It even left her time to finish her Checkmate research and contact the vigilante about the unexpected turn of events.

"7:30," she agreed. Then, for no other reason than that she figured he'd like it, she added, "It's a date."

And to her quiet gratification, he *did* seem to like it.

CHAPTER ELEVEN

BAD INTERVIEW

WHITE KNIGHT TO QUEEN TWO

Monday, July 7, 2048

"ARE YOU ALL RIGHT?" PETER LEKO ASKED INTO CHERYL'S EAR.

She stood on the brick-inlaid front drive of a large, elegant colonial on a quiet tree-lined street in Glen Afton, right on the Delaware River. The houses here would never stand up against New York's Upper West Side, nor even West Princeton. But while the pretty mid-20th century homes might not scream wealth, they certainly whispered it.

"You got this," Omar said from behind her.

She looked back and gave him a smile. He sat behind the wheel of a black Ford Mustang, brand new or close to it. He'd tried to make small talk with her during the trip up from downtown, letting the car do its own driving through the Trenton streets, but Cheryl had simply been too preoccupied to hold up her end of the social contract. Her thoughts had been on Sally Cooker and on Checkmate's advice, given to her while she'd excused herself to the restroom just before she and Omar had set out.

"Thought I told you to go home," Peter Leko had said into her earpiece.

Cheryl, her back instantly up, replied, "I've already got a mom, thanks."

"Okay, I might have deserved that. But you don't want to play it fast and loose with Antonov's people."

"Are you even sure those two at the memorial were Antonov's people?"

"Sure enough. Go home, please."

"Sorry, can't. I'm interviewing the chief justice at her residence in about forty-five minutes."

"Are you? That was quick!"

"I guess Senator Bourbon pulled some strings, just like he said he would. Maybe he's not as involved as you think he is."

"Or maybe he's the one pulling the strings. For now, though, let's focus on the chief justice."

"Fair enough. How do you want me to handle it?"

"Depends on how much you're willing to take on. Risk-wise, I mean."

"Don't do that. I already said I'm in. That means I'm all in."

After that there'd been a long pause, so long that Cheryl started wondering if their link had been broken. But Checkmate said, still in Leko's voice, *"All right. Start the interview the way you normally would. But then I want you to ask a few more pointed and aggressive questions. Finally, just as it's about to wrap up, hit her with Argo. But don't lead with that. If you do, you might not get any further. How does all that sound?"*

"Okay, I think."

"Good. And don't forget to watch her eyes. This woman is going to lie to you, Cheryl. Be ready to spot it when it happens."

Now, with a July twilight settling around her, distant highway traffic noise in her ears, and handsome Omar at her back, Cheryl stiffened her spine and marched up three steps to a whitewashed porch, crossed it to a set of highly polished oak doors, and rang the ornate bell.

Her heart pounded the whole time.

The person who answered wasn't the chief justice but a younger woman in blue scrubs. Her straight brown hair had been pulled back into a ponytail and her nametag read "Mindy." She peered out at Cheryl, and then beyond her at the Mustang sitting in the driveway. "You're the reporter?"

"That's me," Cheryl said.

"Come on in." Mindy stepped aside, allowing Cheryl into a high-ceilinged foyer. "Sorry," the woman said, almost sheepishly. "I don't usually answer the door. But we just had a little crisis. Justice Cooker's in the study, down the hall on the left. I'd show you the way, but I have to get Mr. Cooker upstairs to bed."

Cheryl glanced past her at the base of a long staircase. Standing there, one hand on the banister knob, was a frail-looking man in his sixties. His hair was white and disheveled, and he wore an expression that Cheryl could only describe as empty.

"Hello, Mr. Cooker," she said, automatically.

"He can't answer you," Mindy replied. She turned, went to the old man, and began helping him into a stair-chair, following dutifully along as the mobility tool buzzed its way to the second floor. Cheryl stood watching them for a moment. Then she walked down the short hall and into a small, decidedly masculine study.

The chief justice of the New Jersey Supreme Court knelt in front of an upholstered wing chair, busily wiping at something on the area rug beneath it. When Cheryl entered, she looked up, her expression weary — "haggard" might not have been too strong a word.

"Ms. Walker," she said.

"Yes. I'm sorry, Chief Justice. Is this a bad time?"

The woman blew out a sigh and stood. "No. That is, it wasn't until five minutes ago. My husband had some soup that apparently didn't agree with him. My apologies. Family concerns. My office is just up the hall. You passed it on your way here. Why don't you wait for me there. I'm going to wash my hands."

"Are you sure? We can reschedule." Though that was the last thing Cheryl wanted.

"That won't be necessary," Cooker replied. "Just give me a minute."

So Cheryl left and found the justice's office without difficulty. This proved to be a smaller space but more modernly appointed than the study had been.

"Ask her about her husband," Checkmate said into her ear.

"Why?" Cheryl whispered.

"A hunch."

A chessboard stood under a nearby window, two straight-back chairs on either side of it. Beside it, at least two dozen chess books filled a narrow bookshelf. Cheryl, who very much liked the game but lately had little opportunity to play, wandered over to it. The board looked hand-made, as did the stylized pieces.

"Arthurian knights," Sally Cooker said from behind her.

"I'm sorry?" Cheryl asked, turning.

"The chess pieces. My husband and I purchased them in Wales some years ago. Personally, I prefer the more standard Staunton look, but he cherished them. I've always liked the game, but he was a true aficionado. We used to play all the time." As if remembering herself, the woman held out her hand. "Welcome, Ms. Walker."

Cheryl shook the proffered hand. It was just slightly damp from its recent washing. "Thank you for seeing me on such short notice, Justice Cooker."

"Why don't we sit?"

They did, Cooker behind a big wooden desk and Cheryl in one of its guest chairs. "Now then," the chief justice began. "I'm afraid I don't have too much time. How can I help you?"

Cheryl hesitated, wondering how to broach the subject of this woman's obviously ailing husband. Finally, she decided on the direct method, "I met Mr. Cooper in the foyer just now."

"You met Mindy, his caregiver. My husband may have been there, but I'm afraid he's no longer able to interact with anyone."

"A frank enough answer. Pursue it."

Cheryl felt a stab of reluctance. This line of inquiry was, of course, unrelated to her Checkmate story. But more than that, it felt wrong to pry—though admittedly that wasn't a very journalistic viewpoint.

Finally, she said, "May I ask about his situation?"

Cooker regarded her steadily. "Is this for your story?"

"No," Cheryl replied. "It's just... My grandmother died of Alzheimer's. She used to wear the same look that I saw on your husband's face just now."

"I see. My condolences. But my husband's condition is different. Ten years ago, he was assaulted, mugged, while coming home from his office. I'm afraid he took a rather severe beating."

"Oh my God," Cheryl said. "I'm so sorry!"

Cooker nodded gravely.

Chery asked, "Did they catch—"

"No," the justice replied, cutting her off. "I'm afraid poor Harrison is just another Trenton statistic. Now, if you don't mind, it's not a pleasant topic for me. Can we get to the matter at hand?"

"That's something I didn't know," Checkmate said into Cheryl's ear. *"She's kept it very private."*

Cheryl thought that "tragic" would probably be a better word. "Of course," she said. "As I'm sure you know, I'm writing an in-depth analysis on Checkmate."

"At the behest of Mike Bourbon, I believe."

"In agreement with my editor," Cheryl replied.

"All right, then," the chief justice said, leaning forward with hands clasped and forearms resting on her desk. "Ask your questions."

"Who, in your mind, is Checkmate?"

"His identity is unknown," Cooker replied.

"No, I'm sorry. I wasn't clear. Some have labeled Checkmate a watchdog, others a vigilante. I want to know where you land."

"Checkmate is a person of interest in a number of on-going investigations. It would be inappropriate for me to comment."

"Well, that wasn't very helpful, was it?"

So Cheryl tried a different tack. "Checkmate is said to use guile and deception to secure evidence of his targets' corruption—"

"Alleged," Cooker interjected.

Annoyed, but trying not to show it, Cheryl conceded. "In some cases, yes. So far, his evidence has held up in court, despite having been obtained without warrant or other due process. As the state's top jurist, how do you explain that?"

Cooker nodded. "It's a better question than your first. As a rule, I don't like speculating. But in this case, it's a matter of law. Checkmate, whoever he is, isn't a member of law enforcement. Nor is he an officer of the court, at least not as far as we know, so evidentiary protocols don't apply to him. Investigating officers and prosecutors can act on the evidence he provides as they would with any civilian informant. They corroborate it, of course, but as I understand it, that's relatively easy to do. Finding something hidden is always easier when one knows where to look."

Cheryl said, "So, without Checkmate's involvement, the people he's exposed would have remained undiscovered."

"That's not something we'll ever know." Cooker replied.

"Always nice to meet a fan."

Cheryl had to fight a smile. "Yet, for all the state government's talk about arresting him, to date, no indictments have been made against Checkmate."

"You can't indict an alias, Ms. Walker. First the vigilante must be found and unmasked. Then indictments can take place."

Cheryl felt her face flush. She should have known that.

But Checkmate said, *"Now that's interesting! Now, are you ready to fire the first volley?"*

As previously arranged, Cheryl cleared her throat. A signal of ascent.

"Okay. Go ahead. But tread lightly. There's a lot of power in that woman."

"Do you have more questions for me, Ms. Walker?" Cooker asked, not sounding impatient exactly, simply a bit dismissive.

"How well do you know Victor Cardellini?"

"Watch her eyes."

Cheryl did.

Sally Cooker's expression never changed.

"Anything?" Checkmate asked.

She didn't respond, the signal for "no."

The chief justice replied, "Our paths have crossed at various official functions, especially since he took the speakership, but we've had no direct professional or legal dealings." After a pause, she tacked on, again dismissively, "Why do you ask?"

In her ear, Checkmate audibly sighed. *"She probably saw that coming. Let's turn up the heat."*

"Do you think he did what he's been accused of?"

"Accused by Checkmate, you mean," Cooker replied, her tone flat.

"He was arrested by Governor Lapidus on the spot and arraigned this morning. The case is with the state prosecutor now."

"Very true."

Cheryl pressed. "So my question stands. Do you think he's guilty?"

"It wouldn't be appropriate for me to comment." Another flat answer.

"Did you find Checkmate's evidence in previous cases to be compelling?"

"I did. But each case is different. It's entirely possible that the so-called "proof" in Speaker Cardellini's case won't hold up to scrutiny."

"She sounds hopeful, like maybe she has a stake in the outcome. Ready to hit her with the Argo question?"

Cheryl cleared her throat again, both a signal and a nervous tick. Convenient, that.

"Do it," Checkmate said.

So Cheryl did it. "What can you tell me about Argo?"

This time, the loss of focus was there. It only lasted half-a-second, but Cheryl didn't miss it. "I'm afraid I don't know what that is," the chief justice replied.

Cheryl cleared her throat a third time.

"Bingo. Keep pushing."

Cheryl took a long, steadying breath. "Really? Then how can I have three emails sent from his Cuff to yours that state otherwise?"

This time there was no loss of focus, absolutely zero. Instead, the face of the woman across from her, the highest-ranking jurist in the state, went from pale to beet red. For a moment, her eyes grew wide, perhaps with shock, only to narrow to slits as she slowly stood up behind her desk.

"How. Dare. You?" Cooker demanded, dragging out the three words in a single hiss that would have made a snake proud.

Cheryl felt her insides turn to ice, even as, in her ear, Checkmate celebrated, *"You just hit a nerve!"*

Cooker pointed an index finger at her. "Did you just call me a liar, young lady?"

Cheryl swallowed. She simply couldn't help it. But she stiffened her spine and said, "I asked a question, Chief Justice. Isn't that what you invited me here to do?"

Behind the other woman's glare, Cheryl could see wheels turning. Sally Cooker was anything but a fool, and that sterling legal intellect got her from Point A to Point B very quickly indeed. "Who is Checkmate?" she asked, growled really.

"I have no idea," Cheryl said, which was of course true.

"You got that information from somewhere."

"I'm not at liberty to discuss my sources."

"Ms. Walker, I believe you to be in league with the most wanted fugitive in the state. As soon as you leave my home, which will be in the next ten seconds, I intend to contact the attorney general and recommend that you be arrested for criminal conspiracy."

"No, she won't," Checkmate said calmly. *"She can't. She's all but admitted to knowing about Argo. That's not something she's going to want exposed in a courtroom."*

Maybe so. Maybe no. But Cheryl still felt like a cornered mouse. With visible effort, she stood and faced the older woman, who continued to regard her as one might regard a particularly abhorrent insect. "What is Argo, Chief Justice?"

"Get out!"

Cheryl didn't move. "It's a question I'm just going to keep asking."

"I said get out of my home!" To emphasize the demand, Cooker pointed a trembling finger at the foyer door, which still stood open.

"Go," Checkmate said. *"We've got what we need."*

Did they, though? By Cheryl's reckoning, they had a verbal denial followed by authoritative anger, certainly nothing that could be used in a news story.

But Checkmate wasn't a journalist; the vigilante had their own agenda.

"Justice Cooker," she said, as levelly as she could, "you can rail at me all you want. But I have the emails. I'm giving you an opportunity to comment on them. But regardless of what you say, they're going to be made public."

Sally Cooker looked close to exploding. With her eyes fixed like daggers on Cheryl, she raised her Cuff and said, "Call 911."

Cheryl left.

CHAPTER TWELVE

SALLY'S MARKER

BLACK KNIGHT TO QUEEN TWO

Monday, July 7, 2048

SALLY COOKER WATCHED THE WOMAN — A GIRL, REALLY, YOUNGER than either of her sons — walk out the front door without another word.

Her entire body felt like it was aflame, though she couldn't have named exactly what she was feeling. Anger, yes. Outrage at Cheryl Walker's impertinence, yes. But also fear. In her mind's eye, she kept picturing that man in the chair in the storage unit, ball-gagged and terrified. He'd made a mistake, let Checkmate get the better of him, and Proprietor had killed him for it.

But he needs me.

He won't kill me.

No, he'll do worse than that.

She went to her desk and sat down, thinking furiously. Throughout most of her life, the law had been both a passion and a refuge, a way to force order onto a disorderly world. She'd made it her mission to not just know the law but to understand it, to use it, to wield it like a holy sword if need be.

But all that had ended ten years ago with a single Cuff call.

These days, the law was no longer her ally. Nor, of course, was it an enemy. Instead, it had become impotent, as meaningless as the illusion Sally now knew it to have always been. The law depended on accountability. Without that, it had no teeth.

And Proprietor was above accountability.

Still trembling, Sally raised her Cuff and opened her contacts, running through the list of names that danced in the air above her wrist.

She'd filed the particular listing she wanted under "Miscellaneous," the only identifier a single word: "Cable." For a moment, her finger hovered over the link, poised to make the call.

If she did this, she'd be crossing a line, another line. The last line. But if she didn't do this—

She initiated the call. Moments later, the face of a woman approaching forty, her features lean and her mouth turned downward, shimmered into existence and spoke, *"This isn't a good time."*

"I'm calling in the debt I'm owed, Ms. Cable," Sally said.

The face didn't reply, not immediately. Instead, the woman's mouth worked as if she'd bitten into something sour. *"I'm listening,"* she finally said.

"Do you know who Cheryl Walker is?"

"Sure. We're tailing her now."

"I…" Sally began, only to find that her mouth had gone dry. *The last line,* she thought bitterly. "I need her to die," she said. It sounded so callous as to be almost comical, but dancing around the issue seemed worse than pointless.

Cable, however, took the request in stride. *"I don't know if I can do that. The boss made it very clear that Walker's to be untouched, at least for now."*

Sally had to fight to keep her expression neutral. "So you're saying the timing is an issue? Interesting. I seem to recall you coming to me one night five years ago because of a timing mistake. You were scared and desperate and you begged me to help you, which I did. I even set you up with your current employment, did I not?"

"Yeah, you did, Judge. But what you're asking could put me in the ground."

"Then you'll have to do it correctly, won't you?" Sally said impatiently, at the same time hating the words that were coming out of her mouth. "She disappears. Her body's never found."

There came a long pregnant pause. *"He won't buy it."*

Sally, of course, knew exactly which "he" they were discussing. And if she were honest, the woman's concerns were justified. Certain persons would look at this act not merely as murder, which could be countenanced, but betrayal, which couldn't. "Can you do it or not?"

"Of course I can do it."

"*Will* you do it?"

Another long, unhappy pause. *"I owe you. So, yes. But it's going to cost."*

"How much?"

When the woman told her, Sally closed her eyes, refusing to shed a tear as she considered. There was, of course, the money in the Caymans. Every Sibling kept such an account. She didn't think Antonov or even Proprietor had the means of watchdogging those funds—but she wasn't sure. Nobody ever knew what Proprietor did or didn't know. It was one of the ways he maintained control.

"Agreed," she said into her Cuff.

"I'll try to keep it low-key. Me and a partner. We'll look for an opportunity. But if that first volley doesn't pan out, I may need to hire a team and put something more elaborate together. Don't worry. I'll keep your name out of it. But a simple disappearance isn't going to cut it here. The boss doesn't like coincidences. So for both our sakes, I'm going to have to stage an accident. Something tragic but unavoidable. Just one of those things."

"One of those things," Sally heard herself echo. She could almost feel what little remained of her self-respect withering like a rose in winter. For the thousandth time, she asked herself how she'd come to this point.

But the answer remained, as ever, glaringly obvious.

"Let me know when it's done," she said.

"This will square us," the woman replied, almost a warning.

"Yes."

She broke the link, sat back in her chair, and, for the first time since Harrison had been crippled simply to teach her a lesson, cried. As she did, two words rolled to and fro inside her head—simple words, and yet so exquisitely painful.

I'm sorry.

CHAPTER THIRTEEN

FIRST VOLLEY

WHITE PAWN TO QUEEN'S BISHOP FOUR

Monday, July 7, 2048

CHERYL SAID LITTLE ON THE DRIVE BACK INTO DOWNTOWN Trenton, and Omar, bless him, didn't press. In fact, he asked no questions at all as Cheryl marched out of the chief justice's house and climbed wordlessly into the passenger seat of his Ford Mustang. For several minutes, the two of them sat in silence as the self-driving electric sports car buzzed through the deepening twilight.

As it did, Cheryl's mind churned and, unheard by Omar, Checkmate talked into her ear using Peter Leko's voice. *"She knows exactly what Argo is. What's more, she's scared of it. Very scared of it."*

That had been Cheryl's assessment as well, which she confirmed by clearing her throat.

"You okay?" Omar asked, mistaking the noise as an invitation to talk.

"I'm fine," Cheryl replied, a little curtly. Again, bless him, he took the hint.

"I'm kind of wishing you hadn't pushed her so hard there at the end, though. Fear can often turn into desperation, and desperate people are dangerous."

This time, Cheryl didn't clear her throat or, in fact, offer any other flavor of response. What she'd said to Cooker at the end of their aborted interview she'd said as a journalist, not a vigilante's sidekick.

"Fine. I get it. I need to think about what comes next. You're interviewing the attorney general tomorrow, aren't you?"

Cheryl cleared her throat again. Omar glanced at her but said nothing.

"Good. I'll be in touch. But right now, and I mean it this time, you need to go straight home."

Cheryl sighed. With the state house's golden dome in view, she finally addressed Omar. "I'm sorry. I'm being terrible company. But do you mind if we take a raincheck on that drink?"

"Of course," he replied. "Cheryl, if there's something you want to talk about, I'm here for you. I get that you're working this story, possibly the biggest story in town, and we both know full well how easily a coveted story can get poached. But I've never stolen a story from a colleague in my life, and I won't start now."

He looked at her when he said this, his expression earnest. And his eyes, as far as Cheryl could tell, never lost focus.

Maybe he's telling the truth.

And maybe he's just had enough time to prepare the lie.

"Let me think about it, okay?" she asked. "But right now, I just want to go home. It's been a really long day."

"Then I'll take you home."

In her ear, Checkmate said nothing.

Ten minutes later, Omar's Mustang hummed to a stop on Cheryl's street, with the front door of Sam's brownstone just a few doors up the block. For a minute or so, Cheryl just sat there. She felt tired, perhaps less physically than emotionally.

Omar said, his manner tentative, "Any chance I could buy you dinner one night this week?"

She regarded him. He was very good-looking; there could be no denying that. He also seemed kind and had displayed more sincerity than she'd ever credited him with before now. However, between the whole Checkmate thing and her father's birthday tomorrow night, Cheryl wasn't at all sure she had the extra bandwidth for dating. "I'm... kind of taking it a day at time right now."

He nodded. "I get that. Well, it's Monday. How about tomorrow night? That's just one day, right?"

He smiled. He had a disarming smile, one that managed to penetrate her anxiety and exhaustion. Despite herself, she laughed.

"I'm headed to Flemington tomorrow night. It's my dad's birthday."

"Oh." He looked crestfallen.

Almost without thinking, she asked, "How about Wednesday?"

Omar brightened. "Works for me."

At that moment, Cheryl glanced past him and just up the street. Samantha stood at the open front door, wearing a knowing smile. "There's my roommate," Cheryl said. "I'd better go."

She started to let herself out of Omar's car but paused. For a second, their eyes met. Then she leaned over and kissed him, just a peck on the lips, so cobra quick that it didn't have time to be awkward, or so she hoped. She half expected him to be too surprised to kiss back, but he returned it fine. More than fine.

"Wednesday," he said.

"Yep." Feeling her face flush, she stepped out into the night.

A moment later, the Mustang hummed away, leaving her there on the sidewalk, looking up the stoop at her roommate. Samantha wore a flowered summer dress, with Birkenstocks on her perfectly pedicured feet. Atop her head was one of her better wigs, a strawberry-blonde number that looked absolutely natural. Cheryl had never met anyone who could pull off a wig like Samantha Reshevsky.

"Busy day?" Sam asked, grinning.

"Shut up."

"Who's the eye candy?"

"That's Omar," Cheryl replied, her face positively burning now.

"*Omar* Omar? Asshole Omar?"

"I may have been wrong about him."

"Get in here. I'll pour the wine and you can spill the beans."

Cheryl laughed. "Okay."

"Ms. Walker?"

The new voice startled her so badly that she jumped. Gasping, she whirled around to find two people standing on the sidewalk within arm's reach of her, a man and a woman. Behind them, idling at the curb, was a nondescript black sedan. Its rear driver's side door stood open.

"W — what?"

"Are you Cheryl Walker?" the woman asked. She wore a gray pants suit. Her tone was clipped, authoritative.

"Um, yes."

"We're federal agents, Ms. Walker," the man said. His voice was deeper, and he was a head taller than his companion. But he was dressed in an outfit as gray as hers, making them look like bookends. "Would you please come with us?"

People in Gray.

"What?" she asked again.

"Please don't make a scene," the woman said. "We have some questions to ask you, that's all."

As her shock wore off, Cheryl said more firmly, "I'm sorry. Who are you again?"

"Federal agents," the woman replied, now with an impatient edge. "We need you to come in for questioning."

"Let me see some ID."

"Don't make this difficult."

Like a switch getting flipped, Cheryl recognized the woman with an almost electric shock of fear. "You were at Veterans Park this morning! You were watching me from the bus stop!"

"Enough," the man said. His hand came up as if he meant to take her arm.

"I'm not going anywhere until I see some identification!" Cheryl exclaimed, recoiling.

The woman shook her head. "You're only making this—"

"Excuse me!" Samantha called, almost chirped. Cheryl's roommate still stood on the stoop, but now she held her Cuff arm up at an angle that anyone would recognize. Cuffs sported cameras, which could be activated in any number of ways. The most common was to lift one's arm, wrist facing the subject, and just click. Still pics or video.

When the People in Gray looked toward her, reacting to the interruption, Sam grinned and said, "There we go! A couple of nice full-face shots! I wonder what would happen if I posted these to social media with the words, 'Do you know this scary couple?'"

The man's face darkened. To Cheryl's horror, he reached for something inside his jacket, something she'd have bet wasn't ID. But his partner restrained him with a touch. To Samantha, she said, "This isn't your business, miss."

Sam grinned. "No? Well, it's a free country, so I think I'll vid it anyhow." To Cheryl she added, "Kiddo, why don't you come inside? I figure we're about done with these two, don't you?"

Cheryl's entire body trembled. It was an effort to think, much less move. But stiffening her spine, she took a step back from the two "federal agents." As she did so, she half-expected the man to make a grab for her then and there. But the couple didn't move.

Cheryl risked another step. Then another.

The woman said, her voice low and dangerous. "We'll connect with you another time, Ms. Walker."

"Come on, kiddo," Sam pressed, and something in her tone made Cheryl move faster. She backed awkwardly up the stoop to her roommate's side, while the two on the sidewalk watched them in stony silence. "By the way," Sam said. "I got the license plate, too."

The man uttered something close to a growl, but the woman steadied him. "You have a good night, ladies."

The two of them climbed into their non-descript sedan and pulled away.

Cheryl felt an arm close protectively around her shoulder. Suddenly, there were tears in her eyes. "Jesus," she muttered. Then, with a frightened and utterly humorless laugh, she added, "Honey, I'm home."

"Yeah, you are," Sam replied. "Let's go in. All of a sudden, wine seems like an even better idea than before."

The two women went inside. As soon as they did, Samantha double-locked the apartment door and lowered Cheryl onto the sofa. "Easy," she said, handing her a glass of wine and settling down beside her with one of her own, a merlot they both liked. "It's over now."

As Cheryl drank more greedily than was probably wise, she walked Samantha through her day, from the interview with Senator Bourbon to the meeting with Checkmate in Veterans Park to her brief and contentious interview with the chief justice. The only thing she didn't mention was Argo. Checkmate had warned her repeatedly that doing so could put whoever she talked to about it at risk.

Sam listened patiently, silently refilling Cheryl's empty wine glass. "And you're sure Pants Suit just now was the same woman from the park?"

"I'm sure. Checkmate said that Antonov's people always wear gray suits."

"Weird. I wonder why?"

"No idea. But Checkmate called them the 'People in Gray.'"

"That's cute."

"Jesus, Sam. I don't believe this! What did those two want with me?"

"Nothing good. Maybe they figure you know who Checkmate is, or at least how to find her."

"She wasn't a 'her' today. She was a 'he.'"

Sam chuckled. "I like them already." Then, more seriously, she added, "Look, didn't that Monika person warn you this investigation was going to be dangerous?"

"Yeah. But—"

"But it wasn't real then," Sam finished. "Not like it is now."

"Pretty much. Should I go to the cops?"

"And tell them what?"

"That two people accosted me on the street claiming to be federal agents. You got them on video! You got their license plate!"

"And we can give them all of that and, I don't know, swear out a complaint or something. But think about it. How likely is it that Antonov, if that's who sent the Grim Twins out there, used a traceable car? Besides, if this conspiracy Checkmate's describing really is a thing, how do you know the police won't be in on it?"

"So then, what? Should I call Checkmate and tell him... or her... what happened?"

"Can you? This person doesn't strike me as someone to just throw their number around."

Cheryl took out the earpiece. It was less than an inch long and shaped like a little pink plug. "Monika gave me this. I can use it to reach out if I want."

"Okay, but *do* you want?"

"I'm not sure. I'm scared."

"Sensible."

"I feel like I'm in over my head."

Sam nodded. "Go with that. Just remember when you're in deep water you've got three choices."

"Three?"

Sam raised a lacquered index finger. "You can drown."

"Not a fan."

Sam raised a second finger. "You can swim."

"Maybe. What's the third?"

"You can get the hell out of the pool."

Cheryl considered that. "How?"

Sam made a face, as if unhappy with what she was about to say. "You can go home. I mean your Flemington home."

"What about my job?"

"You quit. You leave Trenton and state politics behind and just lay low. And then... "

"And then what?"

"And then you find something else to do with your life. Something safer."

The cold rock resettled itself in Cheryl's belly. For a long time, neither of them spoke. Instead, they just sat together in companionable silence. This was something she really loved about her roommate. Sam knew when not to talk.

Finally Cheryl whispered, "Do you think that would work?"

"I don't know."

Cheryl wiped her eyes. "I don't want to leave."

"And I don't want you to leave. But if it'll keep you safe..."

Cheryl took another long drink of wine. Her head was starting to feel light, but she held her empty wine glass out to Sam anyhow. Her roommate dutifully filled it, though only about a quarter of the way.

Cheryl said, "I need to think about it."

"Sure you do. You also need to work remotely tomorrow. You're not going anywhere."

She'd already told Omar as much. Besides, she had her father's dinner party to prepare for, not to mention a Cuffcall with the attorney general.

Still, sheltering at home felt like a cop-out, like—well—cowardice.

"I don't want to live in fear," Cheryl whispered.

"Who does? But, kiddo, are you afraid now?"

She wiped her eyes again. "Yeah."

"I mean right now?"

"Well, no. Not at this second, I guess."

"That's good to hear. But why not?"

It seemed an odd turn in the conversation. "Because you're with me," Cheryl said. "Obviously."

"Obviously," Samantha muttered. She took another sip of wine.

"Sam? You okay?"

When her roommate grinned, Cheryl sensed a lot behind it. "I'm always okay."

"Did something happen to you today?"

"To me?"

"Yes. I'm sitting here all freaked out and focused on myself. But I've got this vibe that maybe you had a hard day too, and my drama's been overshadowing it."

"I'm right as rain," Sam replied without meeting her eyes. "Sam Reshevsky is right as rain."

"Okay, Sam. Tell me or don't tell me. I'm still glad you're here."

Her wrist chirped, announcing a text message. Reading it drew from her another of those small, humorless laughs.

"What is it?" Sam asked. "A love note from Omar?"

"It's Tammy from Bourbon's office. Seems I'll be interviewing the governor at Drumthwacket on Thursday morning."

"Wow! Seriously?"

Cheryl nodded.

"Was that Bourbon's idea, or yours?"

"Yours, really. I just took your advice."

"Damn straight! Cheryl Walker, I am and will always be the secret of your success."

This time, Cheryl's laugh was genuine. Then she remembered her mother's call, and said, "Well, 'Secret of My Success,' governors and gray people aside, we've got something else to discuss."

"Do we?"

"My mom called me today."

"Always a treat."

"She invited me to dinner tomorrow night. It's my dad's birthday."

"Lovely," Sam said off-handedly. "It'll be good for you to get out of this cesspool of a city, at least for an evening. Besides, I understand an hour northeast of Trenton is beautiful this time of year."

"Smart ass. But then she mentioned that you're invited, too."

"How nice!"

"And that she'd already talked to you, and you'd accepted."

"I seem to recall that, yes."

"Sam!"

"What? I'd love to meet your folks!"

Cheryl gave her a sour look. "Stop playing games. You know exactly what I'm talking about."

Sam's look traded sour for pointed. "Do I? What have you told them about me?"

Cheryl felt her face redden. "Not everything."

"I figured that when your mom called me Samantha. I take it she doesn't know about Samuel?"

"No. Sorry."

"Then maybe I'm not the one playing games."

When Sam looked away and took a bigger than usual swallow, Cheryl felt a stab of guilt. But to be fair, she'd been living with this person for barely five weeks. She'd waited longer before bringing actual boyfriends home, much less a roommate who would (what was the right word?) challenge her parents' perspective as much as Sam would.

"They're a little..." she began.

"A little what?" Sam prompted. "Conservative? Strait-laced? Kind of set in their ways?"

"All of the above. My grandfather was a Methodist minister."

"Methodists aren't so bad. I've run into a few. They're actually pretty open-minded."

"Maybe not so much my folks."

"You think they'd kick me out of their house?"

"No!" Cheryl exclaimed, perhaps a bit more vehemently than she'd intended. "And my mom would probably be okay with it, with you, at least once the... uh..."

"Shock wore off?" Sam suggested, and Cheryl was relieved to see a hint of a smile back on her lips.

"Yeah. But my dad's another matter."

"Tough guy?"

"Let's just say that his moral compass points in exactly one direction. Ever since I was a girl, there were things you did and things you didn't do. No wiggle room. No compromise. No extenuating circumstances."

"Probably a good philosophy for a federal judge."

"I suppose so."

For about a minute, neither of them said anything, the only sound the *tick tick tick* of the mantle clock. Finally, and in a whisper, Cheryl said, "You're the only friend I have here, Sam."

"Same."

"But... you grew up in Trenton, didn't you?"

"Sure. The thing is: after my parents died, the idea of 'home' kind of died with them. Now, in the same house where I grew up, I'm pretty much just the landlord."

Cheryl took her friend's hand, her small fingers closing around Samantha's longer ones. "Not to me."

"Don't make me cry, okay? I don't like crying."

"I'm sorry."

"You didn't do anything wrong."

"I betrayed you," Cheryl whispered.

"What? To who?"

"To my parents, when I didn't... explain."

"You didn't betray me. Okay, maybe you denied me, at least by omission. But that's forgivable." With a sigh, Samantha added, "I'm sorry, too. I shouldn't have accepted your mom's invite, not once it was clear she didn't know about my... stuff. It was a pride thing, and not fair to either of you."

"Still want to come?" Cheryl asked.

Sam blinked. "Do you want me to?"

"I'm not embarrassed by you. In fact, it's more like the opposite. You're the most amazing person I've ever known, and I've met Checkmate twice!"

To her surprise, Samantha burst out laughing. After a moment, though she wasn't exactly sure why, Cheryl joined her and, still holding hands, the two of them laughed together. It felt great, better than crying, and way better than panicking over mysterious People in Gray.

As the moment finally passed, Samantha asked, "So, who's going tomorrow?"

"To dinner? It's not big. Just my mom and dad and my brother E.J. and sister Megan."

"Good to know. But I mean, who's going: Samantha or Samuel?"

"Oh. That's up to you."

"Listen, I love that you've got my back on this. But I've got yours, too. Your mom clearly thinks you're living with a woman. So if you want, a woman is what she'll get."

"Just do you, Sam. They'll deal."

"You sure?"

Cheryl nodded. "Whoever wakes up tomorrow, that's who goes to dinner."

Samantha offered up her glass. Cheryl clinked it. "Fair enough, then. Either way, it should be an interesting evening!"

CHAPTER FOURTEEN

ANOTHER BAD INTERVIEW

BLACK PAWN TO QUEEN'S KNIGHT THREE

Tuesday, July 7, 2048

CHERYL SLEPT FITFULLY, PLAGUED BY DREAMS THAT, COME MORNING, she couldn't quite remember. She awoke in a haze of anxiety, due partly to Checkmate and her next interview, and partly because of the People in Gray. But, perhaps only a bit surprisingly, most of her nerves jangled at the thought of tonight's dinner. It was an angst that only worsened when Samuel emerged from his bedroom, all smiles, and promptly made them a hot breakfast.

Cheryl watched him from the kitchen table, nursing a coffee and letting her morning mind-fog slowly lift.

With his back to her, he said, "It's not too late."

"What?"

"It's not too late," he repeated, looking over one shoulder. "You could say something like, 'My mom's expecting Samantha tonight, so maybe Samuel isn't the way to go.' I'd understand."

And for just a second, Cheryl considered it, only to reply, "You do you."

He seemed to find the statement vaguely amusing. "Okay, kiddo." He turned back to the stove.

Cheryl spent the morning trying to work, digging deeper into Checkmate's list of conspiracy victims. Dag called at one point, just to touch base. So did Omar, which was — interesting. She told neither of them about the confrontation on the sidewalk last night; it seemed pointless. Dag would want to pull her from the story and Omar might — well, she wasn't sure what Omar would do. He didn't strike her as the "I'll protect you, fair maiden!" type and, despite his assurances, she didn't entirely trust him not to run to Dag and insist, if only for her sake, that Cheryl be reassigned.

Around eleven, she finally remembered to call her mother and say that she wouldn't need the train station pick-up, that Sam would be driving them. She spent the next ten minutes apologizing for having forgotten to let her know last night.

It was exhausting, and it didn't bode well.

At lunch, Sam asked her if she was nervous about the coming teleconference with Edgar Portermann.

"What? Oh. No, not really. I'm way more nervous about tonight." Just as he was about to say something, she pointed a finger. "Don't you dare! You do you, like I said. My nerves are my problem."

"If you say so. But look at you!"

"Look at me?"

"You just got back from interviewing the chief justice and you're about to get it on with the attorney general, and you're acting like it's nothing!"

"'Get it on'? How old are you?"

"It's a big deal! Or has being pals with the senate president left you immune to the pull of power?"

Cheryl laughed. "I don't think he likes it when I call him Mike."

"Good! Keep doing it."

"As far as the interview goes, it's not going to be anything to Cuffcall home about. I'll ask questions. He'll answer them. Frankly, it's easier to do over Cuff than in person."

"If you say so," Samuel said, digging into the kale and spinach salad he'd made for lunch. "But I'd be beside myself. Between you and me, I find Eddie Portermann sexy as hell."

This time, when she laughed, Cheryl almost choked on her food.

By 3:30, she'd returned to her bedroom. While Sam puttered in the backyard garden, Cheryl worked on her Cuff, reviewing her list of interview questions.

That was when her earbud chirped and Checkmate asked in Peter Leko's voice, *"You ready for Portermann?"*

"Ready as I can be."

"The guy's a bully. Keep that in mind. He's going to come at you from multiple fronts and then gauge your reactions, looking for signs of weakness."

"That's a very military take on things."

"This is war, Cheryl. Don't kid yourself into thinking it's anything else."

"Only if Portermann's involved in this nameless conspiracy of yours."

"Of mine? Still doubting me after the way Sally Cooker reacted?"

"No," Cheryl admitted. "There's something here. But neither one of us understands how big it is. Or isn't."

"Fair enough. We'll know more after you ask Portermann about Argo."

Cheryl blew out a sigh, flashing back on the chief justice's reaction. Whatever Argo was, the mention of its name had been enough to elicit anger.

No. Not anger. Fear. Sally Cooker had been scared.

How would the A.G. react?

"I hope so," Cheryl said. "Anyway, I'm ready."

"I'll stay in your ear."

"Not this time. This time, I'm going it alone. I'll let you know what happens."

"Really? Edgar Portermann prides himself on being very intimidating."

"You've never met my father."

"Okay. If you're sure."

"I'm sure." After a moment's debate, she added, "I think Antonov's People in Gray came after me last night."

"I know they did."

"You do? How?"

"Tricks of the trade. Let's just say I keep tabs on some of Vlad the Importer's more relevant employees."

"Should I be scared yet?"

"Maybe. But you handled it beautifully."

"My roommate came to my rescue."

"I'm glad you have somebody looking out for you. You probably shouldn't go anywhere alone for a while."

"Great. Okay, I'll talk to you later," she said with a familiarity usually reserved for friends and family. Was that what she and Checkmate were now? Friends?

Not hardly.

She removed the earbud and placed it on her nightstand. Then she set herself to waiting.

At 4:00 sharp, her Cuff buzzed. Tammy in Bourbon's office had told her not to call but to wait for an invite, and here it was. Sitting alone in her room, Cheryl steeled herself and answered it. Instantly a glowering visage shimmered into view above her wrist. The man looked to be in his sixties, smooth-faced with heavy jowls and thinning gray hair.

"*Ms. Walker,*" Attorney General Edgar Portermann said. He had a very deep voice; it reminded her of her father's.

"Hello, Mr. Portermann. Thank you for taking the time to talk to me." A rote, professional way to establish rapport.

Portermann's reaction, however, made clear that rapport would not be forthcoming. "*Let me start by saying that I disapprove of both the story you're writing and the fact that you were chosen to write it. I read your Hume piece. It came off as a bit too pro-criminal for me.*"

"Pro-criminal?" Cheryl echoed.

"*Pro-Checkmate. I came away with the impression that you admire him.*"

Cheryl swallowed back a knee-jerk reaction to defend her work. "I'm not the subject of this interview, Mr. Portermann. Maybe it would be best if—"

He cut her off and cut her off hard. "*Who is Checkmate, Ms. Walker?*"

"W—hat?"

"*His name. I think you know it.*"

"Do you?" Cheryl replied carefully. "And why is that?"

Portermann ignored the question. "*If you have any information about Checkmate, his identity, whereabouts, or intentions, you are legally bound to share it with the authorities. To do otherwise puts you at risk of criminal charges.*"

"What charges would that be?"

"*Aiding and abetting.*"

Cheryl fumed, trying to think. While Cuff video wasn't known for its display resolution, there could be no mistaking the predatory look in Portermann's eyes. It was as if he were a prosecutor and she simply another defendant on the stand.

Time to change that dynamic.

"*Attorney General Portermann,*" she said with deliberate formality, "*what do you know about Argo?*"

If the Cuff's display had allowed for it, Cheryl felt sure Edgar Portermann's face would have turned red. As she watched, his expression darkened like gathering storm clouds.

"*Young lady,*" he said in a voice like a knife's edge, "*I've known your father for years. Now, I have no idea what game you think you're playing, but I'm quite certain if he knew he would have something to say about it. I think I'm going to call him and tell him what you've been up to and who you've been associating with.*"

There was a lot to unpack there.

"First of all," Cheryl replied, "don't refer to me as 'young lady.' I'm an adult and a journalist. Second of all, my father despises you and has said so on many occasions. He finds you overbearing and a bit of a bully and, frankly, sir, so do I. That said, if you want to contact him, that's certainly your right. It's a free country, or so they say. But I'd be surprised if he even took your call, and more surprised if he lent the slightest credence to anything you might tell him. Now, if the condescension and intimidation tactics are out of the way, would you care to answer my question, or should I put you down as a 'no comment'?"

Good words. Strong words. Too bad that, despite them, Cheryl's insides had turned to jelly. The very idea of this powerful man calling her father and — what? Snitching? Reporting? Tattling? — well, it scared her on a level she didn't want to closely examine.

She could only hope that bit of bravado she'd conjured up out of thin air would serve as a bluff.

And to her astonishment, it did.

The attorney general looked like a volcano about to erupt. His eyes flashed. His mouth worked. Finally, he replied darkly, *"You're playing with fire."*

"I'm doing my job. One more time. What do you know about Argo?"

"I have never heard that name."

Like hell, you haven't, she thought.

Aloud, Cheryl said, "Noted. Next question."

"This interview is over," Portermann declared. His face blinked out.

For several minutes, Cheryl sat on her bed, feeling a thousand things at once. A lot of it was fear: fear of the People in Gray, fear of whoever or whatever was behind all this, and — yes — some fear of Checkmate as well. Since finding that chess piece in her purse, her life had ramped up onto the Highway to Weird, and there didn't seem to be an exit in sight.

Jesus, what if Portermann actually did call her father?

As if she didn't have enough angst about tonight's dinner.

At five o'clock, Sam rapped on her door and, as per house rules, he waited for her to open it.

When she did, she half-expected to find Samantha looking back at her, that Sam had decided to make the change after all. But no, he was still Samuel, dressed smartly in dark slacks, a salmon button-down shirt, and a grey sport coat. He'd even gone so far as to include a blue pocket square, a trendy addition.

"You clean up nice, Reshevsky," Cheryl told him.

He stuck his nose in the air. "You insult me merely by pointing it out."

She laughed.

He said, "It's five o'clock. We want to leave by 5:45, yes?"

"Yeah. Okay. I'll get dressed. Thanks."

"Kiddo?"

"Yeah?'

"It's going to be fine."

"I know," she said, though she knew nothing of the kind. The cold rock was back in her stomach, only this time it had brought some friends.

Alone in her room once more, Cheryl pulled out a summer dress, one that her dad especially liked. As tokens of confidence went, it wasn't much. But the way Cheryl saw it, the more tokens that she could pile on her side of the scale, the better.

She brushed her hair and applied just a touch of makeup. Afterward, regarding herself in the full-length mirror, she decided to declare victory. With a sigh, she stepped out into the hall, through the kitchen, and into the front room.

Samuel was seated in one of the womb chairs, looking at something on his Cuff. When she appeared, he stood like a proper gentleman and gave her a smile. "You clean up nice, Walker."

"You insult me just by pointing it out."

"Ready?"

"Nope."

Sam's smile vanished. "I can stay home. You can borrow my car."

"No. No, you're coming, if you still want to."

"I wouldn't miss it. But if it's screwing with your head this badly..."

"But that's on me, not you or even them. Besides, if I'm honest, I think I'm worrying about the dinner mostly to distract myself from some of the other... stuff... that's been happening."

"Very self-aware of you," Sam noted without a trace of irony.

"Thanks," Cheryl replied dryly. Then she blew out a sigh and added, "Now. Let's go."

So they did.

CHAPTER FIFTEEN

GUESS WHO'S COMING TO DINNER

WHITE PAWN TO QUEEN'S KNIGHT FOUR

Tuesday, July 8, 2048

SAM'S OLDER PRIUS—ONE OF THE LAST MODELS MADE WITHOUT AI-Drive—arrived at Cheryl's family home promptly at 7:00. This would be a plus since the judge had a thing about punctuality. The big house occupied a spacious, hilly lot with a backyard that overlooked a golf course. The borough of Flemington, situated forty-five minutes north of Trenton and about twice that from New York, was the seat of Hunterdon County. Its roughly five thousand residents were mostly upper middle class, a far cry from the poverty that hung over Trenton like a shroud. Lots of Jaguars and BMWs. Lots of McMansions. Lots of country club memberships.

And the Walker family was no exception.

"Being a judge pays well," Samuel remarked, looking up at the three-story, faux-stucco palazzo where Cheryl had spent her youth.

"Some of it's my mom's."

"What's she do?"

"Retired English teacher. These days she's mostly about charity work. She inherited a lot of money from my grandparents."

"Always the easiest way to get rich. Come on, kiddo. There's somebody peeking at us from behind the drapes. Let's head inside before they think we're doing something we shouldn't be."

Cheryl felt her face flush. "No jokes tonight, Sam."

"Doesn't your mom have a sense of humor?"

"Barely. My dad, none at all."

"Tough crowd."

"Still glad you came?"

"Gladder than ever."

The front door opened as they approached. Backlit by the foyer chandelier, Cheryl saw her mother's smile shift from welcoming to confused. Approaching sixty, Barbara Walker was a handsome woman who took great pride in never having "required" the attention of the top-notch plastic surgeon who lived next door. She wore a pink blouse and white pleated skirt, her small feet tucked into expensive high heels. Diamonds sparkled at her ears, her throat, and her fingers.

"Cheryl!" she declared, stepping out and spreading her arms.

Knowing what was expected, Cheryl met her in a quick, almost chaste embrace. Steeling herself, she stepped aside and said, "Mom, this is Sam Reshevsky, my roommate. Sam, this is my mother, Barbara Walker."

Samuel put his hand out. Barbara shook it, her lipstick-ed smile wavering. "I'm at a bit at a loss here. Where's Samantha?"

Sam looked pointedly at Cheryl, who said, "This is Samantha, Mom." When her mother's face clouded over, she added, "Let's go see Dad. In fairness to Sam, I'd like to explain this just once."

"I see," Barbara replied. "Why don't you both come in? Your father's in his den."

The inside of the big house was beautiful but oddly sterile. As a child, Cheryl had learned to navigate the first floor carefully, touching as little as possible, as though she lived in a museum. The upstairs, with its bedrooms and play areas, had been much more comforting. Down here — well, her mother believed wholeheartedly in presenting a genteel and sophisticated face to the world.

Her father's den lay just off the family room, a dimly lit space of dark woods and shelves of law books. There was an ornate desk, but Cheryl had seldom seen him sit behind it. He preferred instead a large leather wingchair by the window. In fact, he was seated there now, dressed in his usual suit and tie, with a large tome in his big hands and a glass of scotch within easy reach.

"Happy birthday, Dad," Cheryl said as they all stepped into the small, oddly intimate space.

The Honorable Elliot J. Walker lowered his book and rose. At sixty-three, his hair had gone gray and there were wrinkles around his eyes. But if anything, this made him seem even more intimidating than when Cheryl had been a little girl, desperate for his approval and almost pathologically afraid of his wrath.

"Thank you, sweetheart," he said with something like a smile. "I'm glad you were able to come."

"Of course."

"And who's your companion? Your mother told me your roommate... Samantha, I believe... would be joining us."

"Well—" Cheryl began.

But Sam beat her to it. Stepping smartly forward, he thrust out his hand. "Judge Walker, I'm Samuel Reshevsky, Cheryl's roommate. I'm also gender fluid. I was Samantha yesterday when your wife called and graciously invited me to your home."

Elliot Walker regarded first the hand and then the man it belonged to. Finally, with a nod, he shook it. "I understand. Nice to meet you, Mr. Reshevsky. Is that title acceptable?"

"Why don't you call me Sam," Samuel replied with an easy smile. "That always works." Turning, he presented Cheryl's mother with the bottle of wine he'd insisted on bringing, a decent if not particularly high-end cabernet sauvignon.

"Oh!" Barbara Walker cooed as if guests hadn't been bringing her bottles of wine for thirty years. "What a lovely surprise! Thank you!" Her smile faltering a little, she said, "But I'm afraid I don't quite understand Sam's... situation."

"Sam's gender fluid, Mom," Cheryl replied, willing her eyes not to roll. Questions like this were to be expected. "Some days he identifies as male, other days female."

"Oh. I see." Barbara looked to her husband, who nodded. "Well, then, why don't we all repair to the dining room? Your brother and sister are already there. Coming, dear?"

"In a moment," the judge replied. "Cheryl, might I have a quick word?"

"I don't want to leave Samuel alone to—"

"I'm sure he can take care of himself for two minutes, can't you, Sam?"

"Yes, sir," Sam replied. Then he turned to the judge's wife, who still looked a bit flustered. "After you, Ms. Walker."

"Please, call me Barbara," she replied—more by habit, Cheryl thought, than inclination.

Alone in the den, Cheryl faced her father. He stood at ease but still seemed as cold and imposing as any Greek statue.

"How are things going in Trenton?" he asked.

"Fine," Cheryl replied. Suddenly, two sharp memories jabbed at her. The first was of the People in Gray, presumably Vladimir Antonov's well-dressed thugs, trying to coerce her into their car. The second was of Edgar Portermann threatening to "snitch on her."

Dear God, what if he did?

For a moment, she considered telling her father the whole thing: Checkmate, Antonov, all of it. But the words wouldn't come. She insisted to herself that she didn't want to worry him. But that was at least partially a lie.

She didn't want him to shut her down. And he would. If he thought this story put her in anything even resembling risk, he'd never let her leave Flemington. He'd make a Cuffcall and have her fired from NC22, then likely send her to her room.

Am I really so sure I don't want that? she suddenly wondered.

And maybe for the first time since last night's sidewalk confrontation, she realized that she *was* sure.

Then her father said, "I'm concerned about this roommate of yours."

That snapped her back to the here and now. She felt her eyebrows knit. "Sam? Why?"

He took a slow, deliberate breath. "Are you romantically involved with this person?"

"The person has a name, Dad."

"Samuel one day and Samantha the next? That's not a name. It's an affectation. But you didn't answer my question."

"That's because I'm not sure it's any of your business."

And just that easily, the old ire was back. As a child, she would never have dreamed of challenging her father. But that changed after high school. These days they frequently bumped heads, and often about matters far less consequential than Sam. It was one of the reasons she rarely came home. She steeled herself, preparing to be scolded for her disrespect, but he surprised her.

"Perhaps not. You're a grown woman. But I'm still your father, which means I have something of a stake."

Cheryl wasn't sure if she agreed with that sentiment. Nevertheless, she replied, "No, we aren't 'romantically involved.' Sam's my roommate and my friend. That's it."

"I'm relieved."

"Why? I'd be lucky to have him."

"Or her."

She didn't reply.

The judge said, "I realize I'm old school about such things. Your mother, too."

"Dad, LGBTQ recognition is nationwide. Same-sex marriage has been legal for decades."

"True. But we're not dealing with something as straightforward as homosexuality here. That, at least, is as old as civilization. This is altogether different. Do you know if Sam considers himself queer or straight?"

These were old terms, very 2010. Just hearing them set Cheryl's teeth on edge. "Sam's sexuality is nobody's business but his."

"Should I infer that you don't know, or know but won't tell?"

"Take your pick. But I'll tell you this much: Sam and I don't keep secrets."

The judge shook his head in that pitying way that always drove her crazy. He thought she was being naïve. Maybe that was part of their problem; he always thought she was being naïve.

"Look, sweetheart. He... or she... is obviously intelligent and well-mannered. But I can't help thinking that such a lifestyle speaks to underlying issues."

"Excuse me?"

"Get off your high horse. This is between you and me. Sam's charming, and I can see why you've become fond of him. I just want you to be careful."

"Careful? What are you talking about?"

"Nobody lives the way he does without some degree of, well, damage. Tell me, over the course of your... what is it?... month-long 'no secrets' relationship, has he talked about his childhood?"

"Of course."

"Do you think you know it all?"

"I know enough."

"Do you?"

"Dad, what are you afraid of?"

"I don't want you to get hurt. It's really that simple."

Cheryl thought, yet again, of the People in Gray. "If I get hurt, it won't be Sam who does it."

"You're sure of that?"

"Totally."

"Very well, then. I've said my piece. Let's go join the others. I'm sorry if I upset you."

Cheryl reminded herself that her father meant well. But there were times when his prejudices peeked out like mildew in the shower. And perhaps worse, they usually did so accompanied by just enough logic to make their sickness sound reasonable.

But she loved him.

So what was she to do with that?

The dining room was as elegantly sterile as the rest of the first floor, with a long, polished oak table surrounded by eight chairs. One whole wall was windowed, with the late-afternoon sun filtering through tinted glass and lending everything a warm, if somewhat surreal, glow.

Mom was elsewhere, probably in the adjacent kitchen. Sam was speaking with Megan, Cheryl's older sister and the Walkers' middle child. The eldest, Elliot "E.J." Walker, Jr., was popping tiny, toothpicked meatballs into his mouth as if they were the last he'd ever see. It was their father's favorite appetizer. E.J.'s too, apparently. Cheryl's brother had a thick neck and a stomach that, at only twenty-seven, drooped over the belt of his suit trousers. His dark hair was already thinning, making Cheryl suspect he'd be bald by thirty-five. Their grandfather had been so, and she'd heard such things often skipped a generation. E.J. was in law school at Rutgers University and kept an apartment in New Brunswick.

In contrast, Megan was thin and barely five feet tall, with long auburn hair and skin as flawless as fine porcelain. She wore a simple blue dress with a string of real pearls around her neck to lend the outfit just the right touch of class. Megan taught second grade in Flemington. She and her husband had lived in a much smaller house nearby, but after the divorce, Megan had moved back into her old bedroom upstairs.

As Cheryl and her father entered, Sam said something that made Megan laugh. She had a sweet laugh that Cheryl envied. In comparison, her own always sounded like a horse's whinny.

Standing nearby, however, E.J. scowled.

"Save some for your old man!" their father called just as his namesake popped another meatball.

"These are good," the future lawyer said.

"I know. It's why I like them. I see you've both met Cheryl's roommate."

Megan grinned and, as was her way, ran over to deliver a warm hug. "I love him!" she whispered in Cheryl's ear. "If you don't want him, I do!"

Cheryl laughed. Megan, at twenty-five, was an order of magnitude more flirtatious than Cheryl had ever been. She secretly wondered if that coquettishness had contributed to the collapse of her marriage.

"Yeah," E.J. said. "We've met. Hi, sis."

"Hey, bro," Cheryl said, untangling herself from Megan. Her eyes touched Samuel's. He offered her a tiny shrug. Something had evidently gone down while she and her father had been posturing in the den.

As the judge approached the table and helped himself to a meatball of his own, E.J. threw a thumb in Sam's direction and asked Cheryl, "Is this guy legit?"

"Legit?" Sam echoed. He looked amused.

"Not sure what you mean," Cheryl said, her hands on her hips.

"I mean, is he really a woman half the time?"

"I wouldn't necessarily say 'half,'" Sam remarked thoughtfully. "To be honest, I don't track it that way." He turned to Cheryl and asked with a sly wink, "Do you, by chance?"

"I don't," Cheryl said. "Since I've known you, though, it's probably pretty close to fifty-fifty."

"Ugh!" Sam groaned. "I hate being predictable."

Megan chimed in, "I don't see it. I really don't." She appraised Samuel as if he were a racehorse at auction. "You're so masculine."

"Thanks," Sam replied.

"I just can't see you as a woman."

"Well, if after tonight I ever get invited back, maybe you can meet Samantha."

"Is that how you think of her?" their father asked. "As a separate person."

"Figure of speech," Samuel replied.

"Crazy," E.J. muttered.

"E.J.!" Cheryl snapped.

"Well, it is! Look, Sam, I gotta know. What do your folks think of this lifestyle of yours?"

Cheryl started to protest, but Samuel simply said, "My parents passed away when I was a teenager."

"Figures," E.J. muttered.

"Son, you're being rude," their father said, his tone admonishing, though not yet impatient. Still, impatience approached; Cheryl could feel it in the air. E.J. locked horns with the judge more often than even Cheryl did.

"It's okay," Sam said. "My mother and father knew I was gender fluid. We all found out together when I was about eight years old."

"Eight years old?" Megan asked, agog.

Sam nodded. "It was a pretty big adjustment. I really flipped their sixes."

"I'm sorry," the judge said. "What was that?"

Sam laughed. "Apologies. It was a family joke. You know those old sitcoms where somebody's house or apartment number is six, but then a nail pops out or something and the number flips over and becomes a nine? It's a trope that was used more than a few times and always led to all kinds of merry mix-ups. So many TV shows used it that when I was a kid, my father gave it a name: 'flipping the six.' It came to mean anything unexpected that throws you for a loop or challenges your perspective."

"I like it!" Megan remarked.

"So do I," their father said. He turned to E.J. "Sounds like that's what Sam's doing to you, son. Flipping your six."

"Forget it," Cheryl's brother groused, turning away and downing yet another meatball. "When's dinner?"

"I'm surprised you have room," the judge remarked in his judgiest way.

E.J. ignored him, opting instead to march into the kitchen, presumably to direct his question to their mother.

Cheryl said to Sam, "Sorry about that."

He shrugged. "Not my first rodeo."

"I imagine not," the judge remarked. "Can I get you something? Wine? Beer? Something stronger?"

"I'm sure whatever you're having would be fine."

"I like dark beer. It's an acquired taste."

Sam asked, affecting a grave tone, "Schwarzbier, porter, brown ale, or stout?"

At that, Cheryl's father offered a rare laugh. "All of the above. But tonight, I'm thinking something Belgian."

"Then I'd be happy to join you."

The judge nodded, looking begrudgingly impressed. "Cheryl?"

"Wine for me."

"Megan?"

"Mom's serving prime rib, isn't she?" Cheryl's sister asked.

"She is."

Megan raised a glass of red wine. "Then I'm good to go."

After that, the evening settled into a fairly undramatic groove, for a while. They all sat and ate, with Cheryl beside Sam on one side of the table, Megan and E.J. on the other, and her parents, as usual, at either end. In addition to the prime rib, the menu consisted of roasted red potatoes, fresh summer corn, and baby peas. Frankly, the meal couldn't have been more American if it were waving a flag. Barbara Walker took pride in her cooking. The meat was broiled to perfection and the potatoes seasoned with rosemary and sea salt. Even Sam, who could be a bit snobby when it came to food, was visibly impressed.

"Wonderful, Barbara! Michelin would run out of stars."

Cheryl's mother beamed at the praise.

"So you cook, huh?" E.J. asked. He hadn't said much since dinner started. But then, he rarely did when he ate.

"I dabble."

"He's being modest," Cheryl said. "Sam's a great cook."

"More a stovetop chef," her roommate elaborated. "Stir fries, crepes, pasta. Our oven is too small for anything like this." He touched his fork to what was left of the prime rib on his plate. "I've tried."

"The right appliances do make a world of difference," Barbara agreed.

"Equipment is key in most endeavors," the judge added sagely, making it sound like an edict from the bench. Cheryl smiled to herself. Her father was putting on airs, something he only did when he wanted to make a good impression on someone.

Sam, you're winning the night!

But her brother said, "Speaking of equipment, Sam. What kind do you have?"

"I'm sorry?" Sam asked.

"I know I'm being indelicate. But I've been looking at you all evening."

"I'm flattered."

E.J. reddened. Cheryl took a swallow of wine to drown a laugh. "Not like that," her brother said quickly. "Just curiosity. Cheryl tells me you dress up like a woman some days."

"Nope."

"Nope?"

"Big nope."

"You don't dress up like a woman?"

"Some days I am a woman. And so I dress appropriately."

"But which are you really?"

"E.J.," Cheryl's father said, a bit of warning in his voice. "I don't think—"

But her brother barreled on. "I just want to know if this 'person' can pee standing up."

"Enough!" Cheryl's mother exclaimed, so loudly that E.J. actually flinched. "Sam is a guest in this house!"

But Samuel said, "It's all right, Barbara."

"No, it's not," the judge declared. "Elliot, you are embarrassing yourself and our family!"

But E.J. was anything but cowed. "I'm just looking out for my little sister! She's living with this guy, or gal, or whatever. Don't you want to understand who, or what, he is?"

Cheryl's stomach turned queasy, her appetite gone. She couldn't come up with a word to describe what she was feeling. But then, quite suddenly, she did.

Mortified. She was mortified.

"Elliot," Judge Walker said, rising to his feet in a slow, authoritative way that Cheryl had witnessed a thousand times. "May I please see you in my den."

"Forget it," E.J. backpedaled, looking sullen. "Let's forget it."

"This is your father's birthday, E.J.!" their mother admonished.

"Sorry."

But from the look on her husband's face, "sorry" wasn't going to cut it. And Cheryl thought: *this went south faster than usual.*

Sam said, "Hold on a second, please." He announced this loudly, and with a vocal quality that Cheryl had never heard before. The words themselves were casual, but the tone had a touch of command to it. It was rather like the way a skilled teacher can quiet a roomful of rowdy kids with a single phrase.

Both E.J. and Cheryl's father looked momentarily taken aback, as if Sam had cursed at them. Megan blinked in surprise. But Cheryl's mother, who'd been witnessing the rising altercation with dismay, looked at their guest with something like hope.

Into the silence, Sam said evenly, "My 'equipment' isn't the point. My 'equipment' isn't me."

"The hell it isn't!" E.J. replied sharply.

But Sam raised a hand. "Hear me out." Again, everyone quieted, even E.J., though he glowered plenty. "Your sister Megan is a lovely woman."

"Um, thanks," Megan replied blushing.

Sam smiled. "But what was your original hair color?"

Her blush drained away. "Excuse me?"

"It's a perfect chestnut right now. But were you born that way? Or are you 'really' a brunette? Flaxen-haired? A redhead?"

Cheryl expected someone to jump to her sister's defense, but no one did.

"Um... " Megan said again, looking uncomfortably around the table. "That's not... " Her words faded, washed away in a tide of social awkwardness.

"My business?" Sam finished for her. "Not important? Of course it isn't. The hair color you're born with doesn't define you. Why should it?"

"It's different!" E.J. snapped.

"How so?" Sam asked passively.

"Because... Well, damn it! Because there's a goddamned difference between hair color and whether or not you've got a dick!"

"E.J.!" Barbara protested.

Judge Walker slammed his hand on the table hard enough to rattle the dishes. Everyone jumped, except Sam, who locked eyes with Cheryl's red-faced brother.

"That's the mistake you're making," Samuel said. "Biological sex is just a physical attribute, isn't it? Like height. Or weight. Or the color of one's eyes. The first can be changed with lifts, the second with diet and exercise, and the third with contacts. And like them, biological sex can also be reimagined, or even outright ignored. Your sister has dared to decide, 'I want to change this about myself. I don't want it to say who I am.'"

"Mid-millennial nonsense-speak!" E.J. scoffed. "Anybody with half a brain knows there's a difference."

"The only difference is in your head. Right now, I'm every bit as male as you are, Elliot Walker, Jr. Tomorrow, I might be every bit as female as Megan here. Who I was when I was born doesn't enter into my day-to-day life. I am exactly who I choose to be. The only question is: what's that to you?"

"You're with my sister!"

Cheryl hadn't said much during all this. She wasn't sure why. Part of it was like watching a slow-motion car wreck. Here were the nightmares she'd had last night coming to pass before her very eyes. But now the outrage boiled up inside her like magma and, almost before she knew she was going to, she stood up, walked around the table, and slapped the back of her brother's head.

"Cheryl!" Barbara exclaimed, further scandalized.

Her father said nothing.

E.J. yelped in surprise. Before he could protest further, she leaned over between him and Megan, the latter of whom slid her chair back as if her siblings had suddenly become radioactive.

"He's my friend, you asshole!" Cheryl yelled in his face. "And even if I were sleeping with Samuel, Samantha, or both, you know what? It's none of your goddamned business!"

"Cheryl!" her mother exclaimed again, this time at the curse. Cursing was a big no-no in the Walker household, right up there with being rude to guests.

But hadn't someone once said rules were like a house of cards?

E.J. jumped to his feet and stormed from the room. For a second, Cheryl thought he might be headed to the den, as the judge had wanted. But no, he marched straight through the foyer and out the front door, slamming it as he left.

For a long time, everyone stayed where they were in a kind of stunned silence.

Then Megan, either from a breathtaking case of denial or a very inappropriate sense of humor, stood up and announced, "Well. I think it's time to bring out the cake!"

CHAPTER SIXTEEN

LOSING FOCUS

BLACK PAWN TO KING'S BISHOP THREE

Tuesday, July 8, 2048

THERE WASN'T GOING TO BE ANY CAKE.

Cheryl's father followed E.J. out the door, their muffled argument vibrating the dining room windows. With this going on, Sam cleared his throat and said, "I'm sorry, Ms. Walker. I didn't mean to stir up so much trouble."

"You didn't do anything wrong, dear," Barbara replied, though the fact that she failed to admonish Sam for not using her given name made Cheryl wonder if she meant it. "E.J. has been—" She picked through her words. "Dealing with some things."

"What things?" Cheryl asked.

"That girl he was seeing broke up with him," Megan said.

"Oh. I liked her."

"We all did. E.J. messed it up, as usual. She wanted a ring and he wouldn't give her one."

"Megan," their mother said, "let's not bore our guest with family drama."

"That ship has sailed, Mom," Cheryl remarked.

With a sigh, Sam said, "I think I should go." Turning to Cheryl, he added, "You might want to stay."

"What? What for?" When she looked at him, Samuel wore a pointed, plaintive expression that, at first, Cheryl couldn't decipher.

"Yes!" Megan chimed in. "Spend the night! Come on, sis. It's been forever!"

"You're welcome to stay, dear," her mother added.

"I can't," she said, speaking to Sam. "And you know it."

"You could reschedule," he suggested.

"You don't reschedule the kind of interview that I've got on Thursday. And tomorrow I need to be home to prep."

"The governor will understand," Sam said.

Cheryl could have kicked him.

Everyone's attention perked right up. Megan gasped and her mother looked wide-eyed. "Cheryl? You're interviewing Governor Lapidus?"

"Yes."

"This Thursday?"

Cheryl nodded.

"Why didn't you tell us?" Megan demanded.

"I was kind of saving it for Dad. Call it a birthday surprise."

Her mother shook her head ruefully. "That bit of news might have made things go more smoothly tonight."

Cheryl bristled, but Megan beat her to it. "Don't put that on her, Mom. That was all E.J."

"I know. I just..."

Cheryl faced Sam and declared, "Let's go."

"You sure?" he asked.

She gave him a hard look.

"You're sure," he said.

"Cheryl, wait!" Megan begged. "Give Dad a minute more with E.J. Even if you leave, you'll have to walk right past them to do it."

As if on cue, an engine hummed to life—E.J.'s big Escalade; Cheryl would have bet on it.

"He's gone," she said. "Let's go."

The front door opened, and the judge came in wearing the mother of all scowls. Returning to the dining room, he and his wife locked eyes for a long, unhappy moment. Then he turned to his daughters and their guest and said, "I'm sorry about that."

But Sam shook his head. "The apologies are on my side."

"No," Cheryl insisted. "All you did was defend yourself. I was the one who smacked him."

"He had it coming," Megan remarked.

"Be that as it may," their father said, sounding tired, "I'm not really in the mood for cake just now. I think we should make it an early night. Sam, I apologize. We invited you into our home and treated you very disrespectfully."

Samuel said nothing. He looked—regretful. It was an expression Cheryl didn't think she'd ever seen him wear before. She didn't like it.

"Dad!" Megan declared with forced exuberance. "Cheryl's interviewing the governor!"

The judge's eyes lit up—a little. "Is that true, sweetheart?"

Cheryl nodded.

That actually earned her a smile. "Exciting! This is for NC22, I assume."

"Of course."

"What sort of article are you writing? A personality piece? Something topical?"

"Checkmate," Sam remarked before Cheryl could.

"I don't understand," Barbara said.

Cheryl stammered, looking between them. "It's kind of a follow-up article to that one I wrote last year, only this time from the perspective of high-level law enforcement. Yesterday I met with Senator Michael Bourbon and Chief Justice Cooker. And this afternoon I had a Cuffcall with Attorney General Portermann."

At the mention of Portermann's name, her father scowled again. Cheryl hadn't been lying when she'd told the attorney general that her father despised him.

"And Thursday's the governor?" her mother asked.

"I have to be at Drumthwacket by nine a.m."

"It's a silly name," Megan noted.

Ignoring the comment, the judge said to Cheryl, "What's the point of this article?"

"The point?"

"What is it you hope to convey to your readers?"

Cheryl chose her words carefully. "A better understanding of Checkmate's motivations and how those motivations are viewed by people in power."

"His motivations? He's trying to undermine our judicial system."

Cheryl knew she should simply agree and get Sam and herself out of there.

But she couldn't.

"Is he? By exposing corruption in Trenton?"

"Vigilantism doesn't solve anything. It may seem noble, even romantic, but it's a crime. And, while this particular criminal has a certain flair, what he's doing is undermining the public trust."

"Maybe the public trust *needs* a little undermining."

Cheryl froze, because these words hadn't come from her lips.

They'd come from Sam's.

The judge's manner shifted from patronizing to condescending. "Society needs order to function, Sam. Idealistic individualism is all well and good, but without order, everything unravels, crime skyrockets, and people get hurt."

Nobody in the room, which now had as much birthday party vibe as a Catholic wake, missed the inference.

Idealistic individualism, huh? Cheryl thought.

"Who fixes a broken system, judge?" Sam asked.

"There are mechanisms to fix it from within."

"Are there really?" Sam was standing ramrod straight, his eyes almost blazing. "You can't put out a fire from inside the house."

"Don't quote Jefferson to me, young man."

"I didn't. Jefferson wrote, 'If our house be on fire, without inquiring whether it was fired from within or without, we must try to extinguish it.' That's true, but I'm taking it further. If your house is on fire, the first thing you do is get out, get safe. Then you call someone to put it out, or try to, from the street, from the outside. You can't fight it yourself."

"So you're proposing that this vigilante is a metaphorical fire-fighter."

"Something like that."

"Then I would counter that it's more accurate to say he's the fire."

The words were out before Cheryl could stop them. "Corruption is the fire, Dad. And Trenton, the whole state, is lousy with it. An organized and pervasive conspiracy. The more I work with Checkmate, the more I realize just how deep the cancer goes."

She realized her mistake a half-second too late. All of them stared at her, except Sam, who blew out a sigh that sounded almost painful.

"'Work with Checkmate,'" the judge echoed, his eyes as hard as granite. "Is that what you said?"

"They're a source," Cheryl heard herself reply. She glanced at her mother and sister, only to find them staring at her as if she were a stranger. That shook her badly, more so than her father's intimidating but familiar glare.

"Young lady," her father said. And the echo of Edgar Portermann was anything but lost on her. "If you know who this person is, you need to tell me right now."

"I don't know, Dad," Cheryl replied.

"But you've spoken with him?"

Cheryl hesitated before deciding that the good old Rubicon had just been well and truly crossed. "Yes, I have. What's more, I believe them. I've spoken to two high ranking state politicos today, and both of them are hiding something, something very big."

The silence that fell was heavy as lead and so profound that Cheryl thought she could hear her own heartbeat. Finally the judge said, "You're going to drop this story."

"No," Cheryl replied.

But her father just kept talking. "You're just out of graduate school, for God's sake. I don't know what Dag Roman was thinking, giving it to you."

"I'm not dropping the story." She pointed a finger at him, a disrespectful gesture she knew he hated. "And don't you even think of calling Dag and trying to get me pulled from it. This is my life and my career, and I decide what I can or can't handle."

"Cheryl, this is dangerous." The hard glare was gone now, and his words almost sounded like a plea. He'd never spoken to her like that before. It startled her, shook her badly.

Nevertheless, she declared, "Victor Cardellini was just the beginning. Michael Bourbon's in it, too. And Chief Justice Cooker. They're connected to something. A cabal that's been running this state from behind the scenes for years. It has to be exposed. I know you don't believe me."

But then Judge Walker did something that shook her far worse than his plea, something that turned her insides to ice.

His eyes lost focus, just for a moment. No one else would have noticed it. But Cheryl did.

Then he said, "There's no such cabal." But the words, the edict, had an edge to them. They whispered, or at least so it seemed to Cheryl, of something held back, something unspoken.

She gaped at him.

"Drop the story," he repeated, this time with even more entreaty.

Cheryl didn't—couldn't—answer.

Finally, averting his eyes, he turned from them all, went into his den and shut the door.

"Oh, dear," Barbara said.

"Sorry, Mom," Cheryl muttered.

"Are you really in danger, sweetheart?"

"No," Cheryl replied, wondering how much of a lie she'd just told.

"Do you promise?"

"I promise," she said, tasting something bitter.

Her mother sighed. "I'll talk to him," she said. "I'm so sorry this evening went so poorly."

"'Poorly?'" Megan remarked. "It positively exploded! Party guts are hanging off the walls!"

CHAPTER SEVENTEEN

THE DETOUR

WHITE KNIGHT TAKES PAWN AT QUEEN'S BISHOP SIX

Tuesday, July 8, 2048

CHERYL AND SAMUEL LEFT A FEW MINUTES LATER AND WITH VERY little fanfare.

They were twenty minutes into the return drive to Trenton before either of them said much of anything. All at once, Cheryl felt her eyes fill up.

"I'm really sorry, Sam."

"Don't be. It was my fault as much as anybody's. I should have come as Samantha."

"But you weren't Samantha when you woke up this morning."

"I'm not a slave to my nature, kiddo. I could have done it. I *should* have done it, for you. Nobody would have known a thing."

"That's sweet, but my family's issues aren't your problem."

He didn't reply.

They drove on, the daylight fading to their right as they followed State Route 202. Traffic was heavy, the kind of heavy that always intimidated Cheryl. But Sam handled it with ease, even when a light rain began to fall.

After another long silence, Samuel asked, "When are you going to tell me what else happened?"

Cheryl felt her stomach clench. "What?"

"Something your father said or did hit you, really knocked you for a loop."

It took her a moment to muster an answer. "It did," she finally said, annoyed at how her voice cracked. "But I don't know what it means."

"Then spill, and we'll figure it out together."

Cheryl said, "I think he knows there's a conspiracy."

"He does? What makes you say that?"

"Checkmate told me that someone's eyes lose focus, just for a second, if they're trying to conjure up a lie. Well, my dad's lost focus just before he insisted that the cabal doesn't exist. I think he was lying. I think… I think maybe he's a part of it somehow."

"Seriously?"

"He's a federal appeals court judge, Sam. In his way, he's as powerful as Senator Bourbon, or close to it."

"Jesus," Sam said. "Maybe we should go back. You should talk to him about this."

"I can't."

"Cheryl, this is a big deal! This matters!"

"It does, but you don't know him like I do. He's not going to talk to me. He's not going to talk to anyone. If he really is involved in whatever's going on, he's going to keep everyone in our family as far away from it as he can. If I push him, at least before I know a lot more than I do now, he might actually call Dag and get me pulled from the story."

"So you're just going to let this go?"

"Yes. No. No, of course not. But I have to figure out the best way to approach it. I've got that interview with the governor on Thursday. Checkmate's got this specific question he wants me to ask her, kind of a lie detector. Maybe, if she passes the test, I can, I don't know, talk to Lapidus about all of this."

She expected Sam to ask what this "lie detector" question was, but he didn't. Instead, he glanced sideways at her and pointedly said, "You're going to talk to the Governor of New Jersey, someone you've never met, about your father's possible involvement with a statewide criminal plot. That's your plan?"

"Sounds stupid when you put it like that."

"Hmm."

"Okay, what do you think I should do?"

"Me?" He laughed, a dry humorless thing. "I'm an artist, not a politician. Maybe you want to talk to Dag."

"Dag?"

"He assigned you the story. Besides, you trust him, don't you?"

It wasn't something she'd ever considered. Trust Dag? She respected him, sure. Sometimes, she even liked him. But that wasn't the same as trust, was it?

"I don't know," she finally told Sam.

"Then put it down. Sleep on it. We can talk more tomorrow."

"Yeah. Okay."

The onboard GPS abruptly announced, "Road work ahead. Detour advised." Then it flashed a route on the windshield's heads-up display indicating an approaching jug-handle that would take them off 202 and onto the far less traveled Dutch Lane.

Secondary roads that were closer to New York and Philadelphia had a reputation for congestion and flatlands. But deeper in the state and the more north one went, the more hills one found. Not mountains exactly. Jersey would never be Colorado, or even Pennsylvania. But away from the cities, rural routes were often narrow with steep grades. Dutch Lane was one of these.

Frowning, Cheryl said, "Roads are bad tonight."

"No biggie," Sam replied, signaling his way into the exit lane.

They left the highway in favor of the two-lane country road. Here the streetlights became fewer and the houses fewer still. There remained some traffic, mostly motorists who, like them, had taken the detour, their headlights shimmering in the increasing rain.

"Can I ask you something?" Sam said.

"Sure."

Following the posted detour signs, Sam turned them onto Westerville Road, where pastures flanked them, looking oddly forbidding in the rainy darkness. They passed a handful of country turn-offs, one of them with flashing "Road Closed" signs, likely due to flooding.

Keeping his eyes wisely on the road, Sam asked, "Did you hear at all from Checkmate today?"

"Briefly," she replied. "He offered to coach me through my interview with Portermann, but I turned him down."

"He?"

"It was Peter Leko's voice. So for now, I'm going with 'he.'"

Sam chuckled. "I can relate. Why'd you turn him down?"

"Because I wanted to conduct the interview myself. Not that it went very well."

"So you said. And he never got in touch again?"

"Not so far."

"Well... Listen, don't get mad. But maybe you should take that as a sign."

"A sign?"

"That you should back away from this. Lay low again tomorrow and meet with the governor on Thursday. Then write your article for Dag. But leave it at that. No more spy stuff with your mysterious new buddy."

"Buddy?"

"Or whatever. Nobody would blame you if you just walked away."

Cheryl didn't have a ready reply. After all, everyone seemed to be saying the same thing, including Checkmate.

"Just forget it, honey."

"You're playing with fire."

"Just go home."

She knew Sam meant well. But everyone's conviction that she was either too young or too naïve to handle all this was starting to piss her off. True, the People in Gray had frightened her badly. But what would it say about her if she just—ran? For as long as she could remember, she'd wanted a career in investigative journalism. How could she hold onto that ambition if she took everyone's advice and called it quits now?

She opened her mouth to say just that, but never got the chance.

Sam muttered, "Damn."

"What?"

"Road's closed."

Cheryl peered through the windshield. Several hundred yards ahead of them, state troopers had blocked both the west and eastbound lanes. The lights of at least two New Jersey police cruisers were flashing in the rainy gloom.

"What is it?" Cheryl asked. "An accident? More flooding?"

"I can't tell in all this mess," Sam groused. "But it looks like another detour."

"Life in the Garden State," Cheryl quipped.

"Always a party."

As Sam made the indicated turn, the rain began pelting down more heavily, forcing the car's wipers to work harder. The Prius' lights shone down a steep decline, a narrow, unnamed road with muddy ditches on either side.

Sam lowered their speed, his brow furrowing as he peered through the windshield. The road was very dark and there were zero cars, none in front and none behind. Somewhere along the way, they'd lost their fellow detour travelers and were now alone out here.

"I'm not liking this," he finally said.

"Me neither. But take it slow and we'll be fine."

"It's not that. It's..." His words trailed off.

"What?"

"Those were state police."

"Yeah. So?"

"Since when do state troopers manage traffic in the sticks? Where are the local cops? Or the county sheriff? I'm not even sure if this is Hunterdon County or Mercer."

"Still Hunterdon, I think," Cheryl said. "But why are you worried—"

She gasped as Sam suddenly hit the brakes. The Prius slammed to a halt hard enough to shove her forward against her seatbelt.

"What? What's wrong?" she asked.

"Look."

Cheryl did.

A black sedan blocked the road just fifty feet ahead of them, having come into view as they'd rounded a sharp bend. Cheryl couldn't see anyone either inside or around it. "Broken down?" she wondered aloud.

Sam shook his head.

A moment later, the sedan's doors opened. A man and a woman climbed out. Despite the poor light, Cheryl could tell they were both dressed in gray. "Oh my God."

"Let's get out of here," Samuel whispered.

"Can you turn around?"

"No room. But I can sure as hell back up."

He shifted the Prius into reverse and swiveled his upper body all the way around, putting one arm behind Cheryl's headrest and hitting the accelerator harder than she would have liked.

"Can you see?" she asked.

"Well enough."

The car continued backward, Sam's left hand deftly working the wheel as if he reversed going twenty mph all the time. He cursed as another sedan cut out of a private road about a hundred feet behind them, boxing them in.

Cheryl's heart jumped into hyperspeed.

"They were waiting for us," Sam whispered.

Ahead, the People in Gray started forward. Each carried an open umbrella. They were moving slowly but deliberately.

Somewhere behind them in the darkness, two more car doors opened and closed.

"Check your Cuff," Sam said. "Got a signal?"

Cheryl lifted her wrist. Her hand was shaking. "Nothing," she said, her mouth dry. Dead zones were rare in New Jersey, but this stretch of road was apparently one of them.

"They certainly know what they're doing," Sam mused.

With an effort, Cheryl forced herself to think. These people were scary, yes. But, so far, they hadn't overtly threatened her. Last night, they'd said they only wanted to talk. And maybe all this—theater—was just more of the same. Maybe she wasn't in real danger at all.

Except her lizard brain kept screaming that she was kidding herself, and that the danger was plenty real.

But it's my danger. And mine alone.

"I'm going to get out," she said.

She expected him to look at her in horror. But instead, he simply replied, "No."

"They don't want you, just me. It'll be fine."

"We stay together."

"Sam, listen to me. There's no getting out of whatever this is. They've got us."

As his eyes darted back and forth between the rear window and windshield, there was an expression on his face that she'd never seen before. Determination? Confidence? Or maybe "clarity" was a better word.

He faced forward and put both his hands on the steering wheel. "I want you to brace yourself against the dash and side window. Then I want you to try to keep your head back."

"What are you going to do?"

"Trust me."

"Sam, please! Just let me out. It'll—"

She was startled when he yelled, his voice loud and uncharacteristically deep. *"Not a chance in hell!"*

He shifted into drive and hit the accelerator—hard.

Cheryl stared in horror as the first black sedan seemed to rush toward them through the curtain of rain. Between here and there, the People in Gray froze and then, with alarmed expressions, all but dove out of the way.

"Sam!" Cheryl screamed as the car they were speeding toward filled her field of view.

"Brace!" He yelled. "Now!"

Gasping, she did so, stiff-arming the dash with her left hand and jamming her right forearm against the side window. All she could think of was how short the Prius' hood looked, and how immovable the sedan seemed as they barreled down on it.

Without warning, Sam cut the wheel hard to the left, at the same time slamming the car into neutral and pulling the parking brake.

The Prius' back end spun around in a half-circle, the rear bumper missing the side of the sedan by inches. Cheryl tried to scream, but all she managed was a terrified croak as her body was slammed first forward and then to the right by her rapidly shifting center of gravity. As she fought to catch her breath, Sam released the parking brake and the car hurtled forward, this time heading back the way they'd come. As it did, Cheryl saw them catch a puddle and spray both the man and woman in a geyser of muddy water that sent their umbrellas flying.

"Jesus!" she exclaimed. "Sam, how the hell did you —?"

"Keep bracing!" he commanded as they shot up the sloping road toward the second car. Two more People in Gray flanked it, both men this time, and both with things in their hands that looked a lot like guns. Cheryl's heart, already slamming inside her chest, seemed to freeze solid.

Her lizard brain whispered a told-you-so.

Meanwhile, the Prius closed the distance at almost forty mph. It seemed as if Sam was heading straight for the sedan's rear passenger fender and, once again, the thrill of impending impact made Cheryl's head go light. But then he turned the wheel toward the side of the road, where a narrow, shallow ditch gave way to a sharp incline.

"Get ready! This time we're going to clip them!"

Unable to help herself, Cheryl started chanting, "Oh my God. Oh my God. Oh my God!" as the Prius jumped the ditch and hit the incline, tilting the car precariously for a moment before skirting them around the sedan's rear end. As they did, fender met fender and a grind of metal, loud and viciously grating, filled her ears.

Abruptly, they were in the clear.

Sam pulled the wheel hard to the right. The car lurched as one of its rear wheels cleared the narrow ditch and tried to gain purchase. For a second or two, the world bounced crazily. Then they were back on the road, this time with both sedans in their rearview mirror.

"Jesus..." Cheryl muttered.

"Take a few slow, deep breaths," Sam said. He hit the accelerator, sending them up the narrow sloping road, back toward the site of the detour. "That's the adrenaline."

"Are we clear?" Cheryl gasped.

"I don't—" He glanced in the rearview mirror. His eyes narrowed. "Nope. Not yet."

Twisting in her seat, Cheryl looked out the Prius' back window. Some distance behind them, the lights of first one black sedan and another took up pursuit. Their high beams were on, the bouncing glare almost blinding.

"They want you bad, kiddo," Sam remarked.

"Oh, God. What are we going to do? Do you think we can outrun them?"

"Doubt it. But I might have another idea."

They reached the end of the road, only to find the detour no longer there. No state troopers. No cruiser. Nothing.

So, it really was a trap, Cheryl thought, her mouth going dry. *A real trap. Real danger.*

And they weren't out of it yet.

To her surprise, Sam turned left, heading back toward Flemington.

"Where are you going?" she asked, trying to keep the panic out of her voice.

"Not sure yet. Remember that closed road?"

"What?"

"We passed it before we came across the detour. It was on the right, now our left. Do you remember how far back it was?"

Cheryl wracked her brain, though she had zero idea why Sam cared. "I'm not sure. Maybe a mile?"

"Less, I hope."

Behind them, the lights of the sedans grew brighter. The People in Gray were gaining.

"Should we call the police?" she asked.

"They had two state cops set up to detour us," Sam said. "How sure are you the same thing won't happen again?"

"I… I don't know." Cheryl felt her eyes well up, but she blinked, forcing back the pressure. "Are you sure they were real cops?"

"You can fake cop uniforms," he said, "but a cruiser with 'New Jersey State Police' emblazoned on it and genuine rooftop flashers is something else. My guess is they were real troopers who got bribed to send us down that road and split the minute we were in the snare."

"Jesus." No, they couldn't risk the cops. "I'll call my father instead."

"If you think it'll help."

Cheryl raised her wrist to her lips but hesitated. Suddenly, she was thinking about Senator McAvoy. Checkmate believed that the senator's wife had been murdered by the cabal to send a message: "Cooperate or lose the people you love." If that was true, what would happen if she involved her father in this?

Then again, what if he was *already* involved?

Cheryl let out a terrified squeak as the car lurched when one of the sedans bumped it from behind. The Prius swerved wildly, and for a moment, Cheryl thought they'd lose the road. But Sam fought the wheel valiantly and somehow kept control.

"Hang on," she heard him mutter. "We're there."

It took her a second to grasp what he meant by "there." Then she saw the Road Closed sign looming through the curtain of rain on their left—and gasped when, at the last possible second, Sam cut the wheel and sent them down that side road.

"What are you going to do?" she asked.

"Something really, really stupid."

Both sedans, bigger and less maneuverable than the Prius, screeched and swerved on the slick road as they tried to follow. The turn had bought them a little breathing room, but just a little.

"What if the road's flooded?" Cheryl asked, gasping.

"I don't think that's it. The grade is going up. More likely it's construction."

"Are you hoping the road's passable after all?"

"Just the opposite."

"*What?*"

They cleared a rise as their pursuers closed in on them again. Ahead, appearing through the shroud of rain, a large earth mover stood beside a mound of dirt as big as a tractor-trailer. Apparently, an entire section of road had been torn up for some reason. The site stood deserted, the construction workers having escaped the bad weather. Although Cheryl couldn't make out too many details in the dark, she saw this much with bitter clarity: There would be no getting around it.

"Sam..."

"I see it."

"Sam!"

"I see it!"

"Sam!"

"Brace yourself!" he instructed. "Just like before. But when I tell you, I want you to lean hard toward me. Hard! Got it?"

"What? Why?"

"Cheryl!" he said, his voice like granite. "Got it?"

"Got it." she whispered.

Behind them, the nearest sedan closed in, nearly slamming their bumper. Sam ignored it. Fighting to keep the wheel steady, he pointed the Prius' front end at the edge of the road, where a narrow gap stood between the sloping mound of dirt and the ten-ton bulldozer.

"You'll never get through there!" Cheryl cried.

"One of us won't," Sam said. "Lean over! Now!"

With her heart in her throat, she did so, all but throwing herself at Sam, who cut the wheel hard, pressing himself against the driver's side window. The little car hit the sharply sloped edge of the dirt mound at an angle. A precise angle. A deliberate angle.

The Prius tilted to its right, going up on two tires.

Cheryl screamed again.

Sam kept both his hands locked on the wheel, his mouth a tight line. At any moment, Cheryl expected them to flip right over, landing on the Prius' roof.

Somehow, the car stayed up, balancing precariously as its driver's side wheels slipped past the earthmover. One second ticked by. Two. Three.

Then they were clear.

Sam kind of "tapped" the wheel and the car dropped back, bouncing on its tires and groaning like an old man.

Behind them rose a resounding crash as the final sedan bumped heads with the bulldozer and lost.

"It's okay," Sam said. "We're safe."

Cheryl pushed off him, moving as if in slow motion. Sweat stung her eyes and her hands wouldn't stop shaking. She looked behind them but saw nothing. The rain shrouded their failed pursuers. She turned to Samuel, her friend, her roommate, the person she thought she knew — or, at least, had been coming to know.

"That was —" she began.

"Terrifying?" he said. "Yeah, it was. I swear I vomited up my heart and lungs somewhere along the line."

Except he hadn't seemed terrified.

He'd seemed — capable.

"Sam?"

"What?"

"How the holy hell did you do that?"

He grinned a shaky grin. "I used to date a stunt driver."

"What?"

"Yeah. It didn't last long, but he showed me a few tricks."

Cheryl tried to think of a response, but all that came out was another, slightly more hysterical, *"What?!"*

CHAPTER EIGHTEEN

THE MAN IN THE DINER

BLACK KNIGHT TAKES KNIGHT AT QUEEN'S BISHOP THREE

Wednesday, July 9, 2048

THEY DIDN'T GO HOME.

Neither of them wanted to risk it. Instead, they limped through Trenton without stopping, crossed the bridge into Pennsylvania, and paid cash for a room at a cheap motel just off Route 1. For some reason, they both felt they'd sleep better outside of Jersey, if only for the night.

The room was a single, so they shared the bed, sleeping side-by-side under a musty blanket and atop sheets that Cheryl tried hard not to think about. Her rest was fitful and plagued by dreams about Checkmate, chases, and People in Gray.

She got up around 6 a.m., roused by morning light blazing through ancient drapes. Sam still slept beside her, looking enviously peaceful. For a moment, Cheryl just studied him—and it was still "him" until she was told otherwise.

How much do I really know about you?

Usually, Sam Reshevsky was an easy read. Regardless of the day's gender, she or he was open, straightforward, and kindhearted. But there was steel there as well, the kind tempered on an orphan's forge. The very idea made Cheryl shudder. As difficult as her parents could be, the thought of losing them chilled her to the bone. No wonder Sam so easily stood up to E.J., determined to be who he was regardless of the social consequences.

Careful not to wake him, Cheryl sat on the edge of the bed. Her head ached and she was still wearing last night's dress. Blearily, she eyed the cheap coffee machine that stood on the cheap dresser, then with equal suspicion, the earbud that she'd placed on the nightstand before trying to sleep.

After a brief debate, she picked it up and slipped it into her right ear. There was a beep of activation followed by silence.

She went into the bathroom, washed her face, and ran her fingers through the rat's nest on her head. Of course, she had no brush, neither of the hair nor teeth variety. They hadn't left the house yesterday afternoon anticipating a late-night, rain-soaked car chase through rural Jersey.

There was a bruise on her cheek. She had no idea when it had happened, probably in the car during Samuel's automotive acrobatics. It didn't seem swollen, at least not much, and it didn't hurt, though she noticed for the first time that side of her face felt a bit numb.

My first war wound, she told herself bitterly.

She and Sam would have to head home, of course. Coming here last night had been a knee-jerk reaction. Or would it be safer to hide out here, where Antonov's people couldn't—probably—find them, at least until after her interview with the governor tomorrow morning?

It struck Cheryl that she'd never been on the run before, and she thought: *I don't know how to do it.*

But I know someone who does.

Steeling herself, she tapped the earpiece and waited.

Nothing.

She tapped it again. Her mind's eye conjured up a brief, darkly ironic image of a sleepy Monika or Peter rudely awakened by the beep of an incoming call.

Then, without warning: *"Hey, honey."*

Despite having initiated this, Cheryl gasped. She clamped a hand over her mouth; Samuel was still sleeping just outside the closed bathroom door.

"Sorry if I startled you," Monika said into her ear.

"Where are you? I can barely hear you."

"I know you're not alone in there, so just listen. There's a place called the Sunrise Diner right next to your motel. Get dressed as quietly as you can and go there. Get a booth by the window and order whatever you want. I'll join you."

"But—" Cheryl began.

The connection broke.

Fighting a fresh bout of shakes, she looked at the closed bathroom door. Sam was out there. Fast asleep, but out there.

I should tell him.

The idea was so resolute that she reached for the knob to go out and do just that before suddenly stopping.

If she did, Sam would insist on coming along to the diner, on meeting Checkmate, perhaps even grilling the vigilante. The People in Gray on Monday evening had been bad enough. But last night's stock car race had haunted her nightmares like a demon. Yet, each time she'd snapped awake, sweating and sometimes crying, she'd found Samuel sleeping blissfully beside her. His presence had been supremely comforting, and once she'd kind of snuggled up against him. He hadn't woken up, but he hadn't pulled away or rolled over, either.

Even in his sleep, he'd been there for her.

But there could be no denying that dangerous things were afoot, and she'd be damned if she dragged someone she cared about into it, or at least further into it than she already had.

Bottom line: No Sam.

Dear God, I'm not cut out for this.

Cheryl took a deep, cleansing breath, then slipped out of the bathroom. Sam was still sleeping, "dead to the world," as her mother often said. Getting dressed wasn't a problem since, except for her shoes, she already *was* dressed. She focused instead on silently tying back her bedhead, finger-brushing her teeth in the bathroom sink, and slipping out without him so much as stirring.

I'm so sorry, Sam.

The Sunrise Diner turned out to be a small, clean place, and about a quarter full. Cheryl asked for a window booth, settling into it as comfortably as a cat on a griddle. Her hands shook, so much so that the waitress, a heavy-set woman of about fifty, regarded her with concern.

"You all right, sweetie?"

Cheryl managed a smile. "I'm fine. Can I get coffee?"

"You want decaf?" the woman asked, again eyeing Cheryl's hands.

"God, no. And some yogurt?"

"Sure thing. You want fruit with that?"

"Strawberries?"

"We got 'em fresh. Sit tight, I'll get your coffee."

Cheryl sat tight.

When the waitress returned with the promised fair ten minutes later, she wordlessly slid into the booth across from her. Her nameplate, Cheryl saw, read "Monica."

"Sweetie," the waitress said, her voice low and her tone—careful. "You want to tell me about last night?"

Cheryl stared at the woman. "Are you kidding me?"

The waitress said nothing.

Inwardly, Cheryl chided herself. She should have seen this coming. "The nameplate's a little on the nose," she said.

The other woman blinked. "Sorry?"

"How do you know about last night?"

"I know scared when I see it," Monica replied. "And forgive my saying so, but it's pretty clear that you slept in those clothes. Are you in trouble? Because if you are, I've kind of been there myself and maybe I can help."

"Look," Cheryl said, feeling suddenly close to tears and not sure why. "I don't have the energy for these games right now. I don't care what you're calling yourself this time. All I know is somebody came after us really hard last night and my friend got dragged into it."

"Sweetie, eat something."

Cheryl looked down at the bowl of yogurt. The strawberries did look fresh. "I don't know if I can now."

"Try. Go on. It'll help."

She took up a spoonful. It was good, cold and creamy, and the instant it hit her belly she wanted more. The coffee nearly forgotten, she cleaned that bowl in under a minute, all under Monica's watchful eye. When she'd finished, she looked up at the woman across from her. "What happens now?"

"Now you tell me about your troubles. I can put you in touch with a battered woman's shelter I know. That bruise on your cheek isn't bad, but sometimes the smart ones do their worst work where it doesn't show."

Cheryl blinked. "What?"

An old man at the next booth cleared his throat. The waitress ignored him. He cleared it again. Finally Monica rolled her eyes, slid off the bench seat, and went to stand by the man's booth. He looked to be in his seventies, at least, with an expensive if dated suit and a thin matt of white hair atop a wrinkled face. Beside him, Cheryl could see an ebony cane propped up on the bench.

"What can I get you?" Monica asked, a little impatiently.

"Nothing, miss," the old man replied in a voice like sandpaper. "I'm just here to pick up my granddaughter."

The fellow stood, collected his cane and straw fedora, excused himself past a speechless Monica, and dropped onto the bench she'd just vacated, the one right across from Cheryl. "Hello, my dear," he said, offering her a wink.

Cheryl gaped at him.

"This is your gramps?" the waitress asked her.

Cheryl looked from her to the old man and back again. Maybe it was the lack of coffee, but her brain was having trouble catching up. Finally, clearing her throat as he had, she replied, "I... I didn't see him come in."

Monica sighed and nodded. "As long as you're okay."

"I'm okay."

She left them, "grandfather" and "granddaughter," with the former looking amused and the latter feeling almost dizzy with confusion.

"But I thought she—" Cheryl began.

"I know," he replied. "It was amusing. Good morning, Ms. Walker."

For several interminable seconds, she didn't, couldn't, say anything more. He waited patiently, his cane across his lap.

At last, she asked, "Who are you?"

"Well, the name on my driver's license is Ivan Saric. But you've known me by others. Monika. Peter. And, of course, Howard Staunton. Though we never met under that name, did we?"

"Prove it," she said.

"Well, I could take your drink order, honey," Monika's voice replied, bubbling inexplicably out of that weathered face. Then Peter Leko added, "Or we could catch the sights around the Trenton State House."

It was surreal, just this side of magic.

"Um, okay," Cheryl muttered. "But why did the waitress sit—"

"She's obviously either been the victim of abuse or knows someone who was. She saw your shaking hands and your bruised face and made an assumption. Frankly, I admire her for caring. In my experience, Good Samaritans are a rare commodity."

Then Ivan Saric smiled.

He looked like an old man, not somebody in make-up, not even good theatrical make-up, but a genuine old man. His left hand rested on the tabletop, a thin gold ring around its third finger. For a long moment, Cheryl stared hard at that hand. Feeling ridiculous, she reached out and touched it.

Saric didn't move.

The only grandfather Cheryl had been close to passed away quietly in his sleep at the age of eighty-one when she'd been twelve. She'd loved him dearly, often walking with him along the grounds of his nursing home. His hand had felt like this one, dry and kind of rough, a bit like old leather.

"How do you do this?" she whispered.

"Trade secret," the old man whispered back.

"It's incredible."

Saric merely shrugged.

"How many faces do you have?"

His eyebrows rose, which Cheryl found amazing in itself. If those worn, septuagenarian features were a mask, it was the most realistic mask she'd ever heard of, much less seen. To be honest, she didn't expect him to respond to her question.

But he did, albeit with another question. "Are you asking as a journalist or a friend?"

"What difference does it make?"

"If you're asking as a friend, I might just tell you. But if you're asking as a journalist, I have nothing to say."

"That's not fair!" she protested, a bit more loudly than she should have. "Shouldn't truth be truth?"

"You're not that naïve."

"Fine. Forget it."

Saric nodded. "So you *were* asking as a journalist."

"Well, we're not exactly friends, are we?"

Did his expression change? Did this faux old man look a little bit hurt?

Cheryl rubbed her face. "Look, give me a break. It's been a hell of a few days since I met you."

"I imagine so. It's probably why I have no discernable social life."

That statement, meant as a dry quip, sparked in her a sudden realization. Running through it now in her mind, it seemed obvious—crazy, but obvious.

She said, "You don't have a network, do you?"

"A network?"

"Bourbon wanted me to write this second story in the hopes that I'd get your attention and be invited to join your network of... Spies, I guess. Except you don't have one. A network, I mean."

"No, I don't." No evasion, but a simple statement of fact.

"So, your sources of information, they're all just… You."

"Just me."

"You work completely alone."

"I did until you came along."

"All I've done is meet with Bourbon and blow interviews with Cooker and Portermann. Now, because of that, I've got these people after me. Last night, my roommate and I were ambushed on the road back from my parents' house!"

"I'm aware. That's why I wanted to talk to you this morning."

"What do you mean you're aware. How?"

"Not important. What *is* important is you've… we've…scared someone pretty badly."

"Great. Are you going to tell me yet again that I should walk away from all this while I still can?"

"No, Ms. Walker. I'm afraid that option is no longer on the table."

Cheryl felt a stab in her gut, as cold and real as any blade. "What? Why not?"

"Because of Argo."

"Goddamned Argo," Cheryl muttered, struggling to keep her voice calm. "And we still don't know what it is."

"No, we don't," Saric replied. "But Victor Cardellini and Michael Bourbon do. Justice Cooker, too. What's more, the chief justice is frightened, and she's making mistakes."

"What mistakes?" Cheryl asked.

"Antonov is careful. He stages accidents, muggings, fires. Always circumspect. But that car chase last night was big and noisy. Nevermind those two state troopers who were involved, all the activity most definitely drew the attention of local law enforcement. It's possible a couple of Antonov's people ended up in the hospital. Some of them may even have been arrested and hard questions raised."

"Are you sure they were Antonov's people?"

"As sure as I can be."

"And you think Cooker… what, borrowed them… to come after Sam and me?"

"Mostly you. But that's my working theory."

"But that implies that Cooker is working with Antonov, closely enough to know some of his soldiers."

"Yes."

"The chief justice of the New Jersey Supreme Court in bed with a Russian mobster."

Ivan smiled slyly. "It'll make titilating reading, won't it?"

And of course it would, assuming she lived long enough to write the story. "Maybe, but right now I wish to God you never sent me that pawn."

Saric's smile vanished. "So, do I. I shouldn't have involved you."

"Why did you? If you've been going it alone all this time, why invite me into this at all?"

The old man hesitated, then shook his head. "That's for later. We have bigger things to worry about right now. I want you to go home." He waggled a wrinkled finger at her. "Not to NC-22 this time, but really home, and I want you to stay there. Lock the doors, hunker down, and wait."

"Great," Cheryl said. "For how long?"

"That depends. Tonight, I'm going to pay the chief justice a visit at her private residence."

"To look for Argo?"

"Partly. But also to hopefully draw attention away from you and onto me. I plan to commit this burglary 'loudly,' leave enough footprints to let Sally know I've been there. Hopefully, that'll get her to forget you and focus on the 'real prize.'"

"You."

Saric nodded.

"What if the police catch you?"

"That would be unfortunate."

"What if Antonov catches you?"

"Still more unfortunate."

"Wouldn't it be safer to go in quietly and hopefully get what you want and be gone before anyone knows you were there?"

"Obviously."

Cheryl stared at him. "So why aren't you?"

Saric met her eyes. "For you."

Cheryl stared at the man, if this even was a man. Monika, after all, had been convincing—very convincing. But right now, none of that mattered, not in light of what he'd just said.

"I can't figure you out," Cheryl said, shaking her head.

The old man didn't reply.

"What kind of 'footprints' do you intend to leave?" she asked.

"Better you don't know. Just promise me you'll stay safe and wait for me to contact you tomorrow morning. Then we'll plan our next move."

"No," she said.

"What?"

"I said no. You'll call me as soon as you're away from Cooker's place."

"It'll be late."

"I won't be sleeping anyhow. If I'm in this, I'm in it all the way."

"A sensible attitude, I suppose," Saric said. "So?"

"So you're right. There *is* a cabal, and it involves Cardellini and Cooker and probably Bourbon, too. Whatever its goals, it's big, scary, and immoral as hell. Well, I'm done letting these assholes screw with my state. My grandfather used to have this saying: 'Be in it to win it.' Well, that's me, as of right now."

For most of a minute, Saric just sat there, looking down at the tabletop. Cheryl waited, watching him closely and wondering what he was thinking.

Finally he raised his head and nodded. "All right, Cheryl Walker. I'll call you as soon as I'm finished with tonight's business." Saric took a long, old-fashioned leather wallet from his inside jacket pocket and dropped twenty dollars on the tabletop. "Let me leave first," he told her. "Wait ten minutes and leave yourself."

"Nope," Cheryl said, standing. "I left my roomate at the motel. I need to get back there. I'm leaving first." Before he could reply, she stuck out her palm, "Let's go get 'em. You and me, partner."

Checkmate stared at her for a long moment. Then with surprising gravitas, the old man shook her hand. "Partner," he said.

As Cheryl headed back to the motel, she considered Ivan Saric's expression during that handshake, and wondered, *Were there tears in his eyes?*

CHAPTER NINETEEN

SALLY'S DILEMMA

WHITE PAWN TAKES PAWN AT QUEEN FIVE/
BLACK PAWN TAKES PAWN AT QUEEN FOUR

Wednesday, July 9, 2048

SALLY COOKER HADN'T SLEPT WELL IN A LONG TIME, AND THE NEWS she was now receiving firmed up her conviction that tonight would be no different. She sat alone in her office, the door not merely shut but locked. Mindy rarely came in here and never without knocking. But Harrison was a different story. On "good" days — if such a term could be said to apply — when he was unusually mobile, he occasionally wandered the house. At such times, Sally liked to imagine he searched for her, that some spark of the man he'd been then and the love they'd shared still dwelt inside his battered brain. But during less sentimental moments, she knew better.

Harrison, or what was left of him, simply grew restless.

So just in case, this morning she'd locked the door.

Now, dressed in a robe, her gray hair hastily brushed and a half-drunk cup of coffee beside her, she stared in bitter dismay at her Cuff as Cable recounted last night's events.

"The trap was well put-together," the woman said, sounding sheepish. *"Not the kind of thing Mr. Antonov would have gone for, but completely doable. It should have worked. But I've never seen driving like that before, especially in an old Prius!"*

"Where did they go?" Sally demanded, rubbing her temple with her free hand.

"We... Well, we don't know. But they just showed up back at the Reshevsky place. Storch and I are watching them now. Looks like they stopped at the market and the hardware store. They're bringing a lot of stuff inside."

"Can't you..." The word caught in Sally's throat. She cleared it and tried again, hating herself. "Can't you take care of them right now?"

"It's eight in the morning," Cable replied patiently. *"Folks are leaving for work. There's too many people out and about. Too many witnesses."*

But weren't there drive-by shootings? Didn't seemingly random people on the sidewalk occasionally get gunned down from a speeding car? Didn't that happen, especially in cities like Trenton? The chief justice of the New Jersey Supreme Court almost argued this point but stopped herself. It wasn't the authorities that Cable was worried about. She was more afraid that, given Proprietor's interest in Cheryl Walker, her boss would look into the nosy young woman's demise and find her. A staged accident on a rainy road was one thing. Even the quiet kidnapping attempt made the night before might have served. But a noisy assault on the open street, with bullets flying and people screaming? No. Most assuredly not.

"Do you want us to stick around here?" Cable asked, sounding hopeful—and, confounded as she was, Sally understood. Antonov was no mastermind, but he hadn't risen as high as he had in his line of work without being suspicious to the point of paranoia. Sooner rather than later, he'd notice that some of his people had been "moonlighting," and start asking questions, or worse, report it to Proprietor.

Who *was* a mastermind.

"No," Sally heard herself say, the single word sounding like a death nell. Walker knew about Argo, information she could only have gotten from Checkmate, who could only have gleaned it from Victor's Cuff backups. The journalist and the vigilante were following the evidence.

They'll come for me next.

So will Proprietor.

Sally's hands closed into fists. She trembled so badly her Cuff flashed a warning that it couldn't maintain her image in the link. On Cable's end, Sally supposed her visage had degraded. It was a common enough happenstance with these world-changing devices, though Cable would no doubt read it for what it was.

"I'm sorry, Justice Cooker," the woman said, sounding sincere. *"I made a deal and let you down."*

If you'd done that to your real employer, your body would probably be in the foundation of whatever new construction project he had going. This was another thing Sally thought but didn't say. Instead, acting more on impulse than anything like a real idea, she replied, "Perhaps you can make it up to me. I'm going to require security in and around my house, at least for the next few days. Is that something you can arrange?"

Cable's Cuff image went thoughtfully silent for a few moments. Then she nodded. *"I can get maybe a half-dozen guys. Any more than that and the boss might notice the unauthorized allocation of resources. I won't be able to be there personally, though. The boss has me in late meetings all week. Something big is coming down the pike, but he won't tell me what it is."*

Argo, Sally thought but, of course, didn't say. As an underling, Cable wouldn't be in the loop where Proprietor's masterstroke was concerned. That information was strictly Siblings-only—another of his many protocols.

"That's fine," Sally heard herself reply.

"It's going to cost, judge."

Money's the least of my worries, Sally thought, her throat closing up. "I'll pay," she croaked. "But they need to be here by this evening. Sooner, if at all possible."

"I can probably have them there by mid-afternoon."

For the first time in this conversation, Sally Cooker felt her heartrate slow. "Good. That would be good. I've already got some surveillance outside the house, but I'll need more. And I'll want at least four people outside and two inside. All night, every night."

"I'll make it happen," Cable said. The woman actually sounded relieved; at least here was another chance for her to square her debt.

Sally quietly envied her. She couldn't remember the last time she'd felt real relief.

"Thank you, Ms. Cable."

The link ended, leaving Sally to slump in her desk chair. For more than a minute, she stared up at the room's high ceiling with its custom crown molding. They'd lived in this house for fourteen years, the last ten of them while enjoying a lifestyle bankrolled by much more than just her judicial salary. For a long time, she told herself the extra income was merely her due, compensation for everything she'd suffered—or, more to the point, Harrison had suffered. But of course, the truth was more insidious than that.

She owed everything she had, everything she was, to the man in the red mask.

And none of it was free.

Perhaps it would be a blessing if Checkmate and the Walker girl came for her. With this new security, maybe they could be—handled. Capturing them alive wouldn't be wise, though. Alive, they could tell people about Argo and Vince's emails.

No, for Harrison's sake and for the sake of their sons, both the vigilante and his new sidekick needed to die. Who knew? Proprietor might even reward her for it.

For the next couple of hours, she tried to work. She truly did. The supreme court was on summer break, of course. But that didn't mean there weren't briefs to be reviewed, and work product from a half-dozen law clerks requiring scrutiny. Focus had always been her strong suit, but this morning, it eluded her. The words blurred on her Cuff, their meaning lost.

It's all unraveling, she thought and, rather to her astonishment, there was a measure of comfort in the idea. Still not relief, not quite. But comfort. That didn't mean, of course, she wouldn't do what needed to be done to protect her family from Checkmate, from Proprietor, from any of them.

Her Cuff chimed a little after eleven. She looked at the caller id and instantly felt the blood drain from her face.

Proprietor. As always, the link was audio only.

Sally mentally prepared herself, willing her voice to steady and her hands not to shake. She tapped the contact.

"Delta." The voice was electronic, the speaker sounding neither male nor female. Not for the first time, Sally wondered why she'd always assumed that her tormentor/benefactor was male. Could it be a woman under that red mask?

For some reason she could never fully pinpoint, she didn't think it was.

"Proprietor," she said. It was the standard greeting.

"I trust you're well this morning." This was a statement, not a question.

"Yes. Thank you."

"And Harrison?"

Sally's jaw clenched. A tear squeezed out from one corner of her eye. "As well as can be expected," she said judiciously, the irony not lost on her.

"I'm glad to hear it. I'm calling about Zeta." Without waiting for a reply, the electronic voice went on. *"He's being a bit more vocal than we'd like. I haven't spoken to him directly for obvious reasons, but we have communicated through legal intermediaries. He has pled not guilty to all charges."*

This much Sally had heard, though she hadn't spoken to the disgraced speaker since his arrest either. She and Vince Cardellini had never been "friends," but over the years of their shared — "fealty" felt like the right word — they'd established a rapport. Still, it wouldn't do for the state's chief justice to be visiting its most high-profile defendant, especially in prison. "I would have thought he'd have made bail by now," she remarked.

"I've made arrangements for bail to be denied. Right now, for the good of Argo, we need him right where he is."

Sally's mouth went dry. It usually did whenever Proprietor hinted at the scope of his reach. How does one "arrange" for bail to be denied? It would sound simple enough in a political thriller, but in real life it involved circumventing a long-established process and, unless done with tremendous skill and finesse, raising several eyebrows.

Yet, Vincent Cardellini sits in a prison cell just north of Trenton, simply because Proprietor wills it so.

Sally's soul, if she still had any of it left, withered a little more.

"He's not happy about it, of course," Proprietor went on, speaking conversationally, as if discussing a sporting event with a friend instead of state-wide corruption with a co-conspirator. *"But I've also arranged to keep him out of the general population, for his safety, of course."*

"Of course," Sally heard herself answer.

"But that's not why I called. I've made some decisions regarding your Fall docket. I'll send them to your Cuff."

"All right."

A moment later, the device on her wrist chirped, and a small heads-up message displayed: FILE RECEIVED.

"I have it," she reported tonelessly.

"Good. Let's go over it together, shall we?"

That simple. No need to ask the state's ranking jurist if she had the time to talk. After all, one didn't ask a dog if it felt like working.

Over the next half-hour, Proprietor walked Sally through the list of cases that would come before her bench during the next session, starting on the first Monday in October. For each, he laid out exactly how he wanted the court to rule. It was Sally's task, of course, to ensure that this happened. To do otherwise risked punishment, and Sally knew full well what form that punishment would take.

Nevertheless, as soon as the litany of judicial malfeasance had concluded, he asked, *"How are your sons?"*

A knot of cold terror closed Sally's throat. She had to force her answer past it. "They're fine. Thank you."

"I'm pleased to hear it. Steady on, Delta. We're close. Very soon, together, we're going to change everything."

And Sally knew, with terrible certainty, that it was true.

THE RESHEVSKY DEFENSE

Wednesday, July 9, 2048

"CHERYL, IT'S DAG. CHECKING IN. WHERE ARE YOU WITH THE interviews?"

"Bourbon's had me talking to Sally Cooker and Edgar Portermann. They went well enough. Oh, and by the way, you know this is a Cuff-call, right? You don't have to identify yourself."

"Save it, wise ass. You coming into the office today?"

"Okay if I don't?"

"Sure. The only thing on your plate is this story."

"Thanks."

"Cheryl, seriously. Are you doing all right?"

"Of course."

"So... There's nothing you're not telling me?"

Tons, she thought but didn't say. "I'm good. Bourbon's really come through. I'm interviewing the damned governor tomorrow and I'm even hoping to see Victor Cardellini in the next few days."

"Now that would be a coup. He's been turning down media requests since his arrest. You land that interview and you'll be the talk of the town! We might even have to make that a special piece, separate from the Checkmate deep-dive, get it out before anybody else manages to wring something out of either the guy or his family."

"It must be a nightmare for Ms. Cardellini."

"The press is camped out on her lawn. And not just the locals like the Trentonian and, well, us. The Times is there. So's the Inquirer. And just this morning I heard that a CNN van showed up."

"It's a circus."

"It's Checkmate. If it weren't for that connection, Cardellini would be just one more disgraced politician, forgotten with the next news cycle. But as

things are, the family's lawyers are running defense, blocking calls, getting injunctions."

"Jesus."

"Yeah. So, let me know the minute... and I mean the minute... that Cardellini interview gets scheduled."

"I will."

"Good. I gotta go."

"Wait a sec. Dag, mind if I ask you a question?"

"Sure. What's up?"

"Why me?"

"Why you?

"Why did you pick me for this story? I'm not trying to shoot myself in the foot here, or look a gift horse in the mouth, or cliché another cliché. But you've got a stable full of experienced journalists. Why give me the Fourth of July Gala story in the first place, never mind this in-depth piece that's putting me in front of every mover-and-shaker in town?"

For a few beats, her editor remained silent. Then he said, *"I'm not supposed to tell you, Cheryl, but I will. Fair warning, though. You're not going to like it."*

"Okay..."

"Look, I hired you on my own. I want you to understand that. There were fifty applicants. But you had, no lie, the most impressive resume of any kid right out of college that I'd ever seen. You're a solid journalist and a great writer."

"Thank you, Dag," Cheryl replied, meaning it.

"Don't thank me, yet. Your Hume piece on Checkmate was nothing short of stellar. And your work since coming on board has been strong. That said, I probably wouldn't have given you the Drumthwacket story."

"Why not?"

"First, it was an easy write, just prosing out the official press release. Anybody could've done it. Frankly, I'd have preferred to have assigned you something more your caliber."

"Oh. Well, that's flattering!"

"Shut it. The thing is, on Saturday morning two weird things happened. The first is I got a call from Brenda Kaganoff."

"The owner of NC22? That Brenda Kaganoff?"

"Nobody 'owns' NC22. It's a cooperative. But she's been general manager since we started up. And, of course, she's my boss. Hell, she's my boss's boss."

"We've never met," Cheryl said. "I wouldn't even know her if we rode the same elevator."

"Well, she sure as shit knows you. When she called, it was early Saturday. Word about Cardellini's arrest had just hit the news cycle. Brenda wanted a coverage piece right away, and she wanted you to write it."

"Me?"

"You, specifically. But there's more. She instructed me to assign you every Checkmate story that crossed my desk. Called you our 'resident Checkmate expert.' Seemed to think that was somehow funny."

"I don't understand."

"I figured she'd read your Princeton article, was as impressed as everyone else, and decided your professional celebrity could do us some good if we used you right. Or at least that was what I thought until Bourbon showed up. He and that cop waltzed into my office just after 8 a.m., less than an hour after I talked to Brenda. No Cuffcall, no appointment, no nothing. He told me he'd spent the night stewing over 'the Checkmate situation' and had decided on a course of action."

"Use the writing of the second story to make contact with him. Warn him."

"Yeah. Honestly, it seemed like a half-baked plan, and I sensed there was a lot he wasn't telling me. But when somebody like Mike Bourbon shows up at your door with something this interesting, you don't say no."

"How did I come into it?"

"Bourbon asked who on my staff could do justice to his article. Frankly, Omar had been after me for weeks to give him something Checkmate-related, and I knew he had the chops. But after what Brenda Kaganoff said..." The editor's voice trailed off.

"You gave it to me."

"Yeah, and Bourbon jumped on it. He wanted to meet you so that he could 'size you up' for the job. But I got the funny feeling that he had you in mind from the get-go."

Cheryl felt herself go cold. She hadn't told Dag about either the cabal or Argo, not one word. Checkmate had warned her, as they had with Sam, her father, and everyone else, that doing so would put him in danger.

The same kind of danger I'm in.

"Still there?" Dag asked.

"Yeah."

"I told you that you wouldn't like it. But for what it's worth, I'm glad you ended up with the assignment."

And Cheryl thought, *I wonder if I am.*

"Really?" she asked aloud.

"Yeah, really. Look, you're not as seasoned as most of the full-timers, but you're still idealistic enough to put the story ahead of your career path. Brenda aside, I think it was the right call. Omar, most of them, would have used this story to get close to Bourbon or one of the interviewees in the hopes of landing a speech-writing or press-secretary gig. But that's not you. The truth is that you remind me of me."

"Dag..."

"I started out as a newbie newshound with the Trentonian. Did you know that?"

"No," Cheryl admitted.

"Yep. I was a solid writer and, over time, I earned some cred. Eventually, a number of politicos offered me cushy jobs making them look good in the press. I turned down every one of them. You know why? Because in my heart, I'm an old-fashioned journalist. I believe in the Fourth Estate and its role in society, especially regarding politics. We're the watchdogs, Cheryl. The Truth Police. We have to be because, if we're anything else, we end up becoming the very thing we're supposed to be policing."

This was all very "not-Dag," at least in Cheryl's admittedly limited experience. Dag Roman wasn't a speechmaker. He was an editor, impatient and frequently callous. To hear him wax all philosophical was a real surprise, and maybe a little bit jarring.

"And you think I'm like that? Like you?"

"Yeah, I do. And, at the end of the day, that's really why you got the story. Satisfied?"

"Not especially, no."

"Good. A journalist should never be satisfied. Listen, gotta go. Get back to work. And make sure you call me when you hear about Cardellini."

"I got you, chief," Cheryl replied with a grin.

"Shut it, 'Lois.' Talk to you later."

He ended the call.

Cheryl sat back on her bed. She was bone tired, despite it being just after ten in the morning. But in all fairness, it had been a harrowing twelve hours.

After leaving the Sunrise Diner, Cheryl had returned to the motel expecting to find Sam still asleep. Instead, she'd discovered their room empty except for a note that read, "Went out to scrounge up breakfast. Meet you at the car. Samantha." Cheryl had cleared out of the room, checked them both out at the front desk, and gone to the car.

But Sam wasn't there.

Trying not to be worried, she'd called on her Cuff.

"Hey, kiddo."

"Where are you?"

"Denny's getting breakfast. Where'd you go?"

"The diner next door."

"There's a diner next door?"

"Yeah. It's called the Sunrise. You didn't see it?"

"I'm worthless before I've had coffee. You know that. I just staggered out, looked up the street, and spied a Denny's. Anyway, are you at the car?"

"Yeah. We're all checked out and good to go."

"Thanks for that. Be there in five. I'm just about to pay the bill."

True to her word, Samantha strolled down the road just five minutes later, blinking in the morning sunshine. She wore no wig of course. But delicate hoops dangled from her ears, which made her short dark hair look edgy and interesting. Her mother's locket was at her throat, and she had on canvas flats and a yellow blouse over last night's jeans. Seeing her, Cheryl could only shake her head. Sam had gone to bed as a man, had woken up as a woman in man's clothes, and still managed to look better than Cheryl did.

"All good?" Sam asked.

"Where'd you get the make-up and a blouse?" Cheryl demanded. "And the shoes!"

"I keep a travel bag with me," she replied, hoisting a large canvas backpack from over her shoulder and tossing it into the Prius' trunk. "One never knows, does one?"

"You could've offered me some makeup."

"If you'd been there when I woke up, I would have. I guess you've had breakfast. Ugh! I wish I'd spotted that diner. I like diner food."

"Sorry. Yeah, I've eaten. But I wasn't alone."

"What? What's that mean?"

Cheryl told her about Ivan Saric. Sam listened, obviously trying to hide her alarm.

"Well, I think the old man's right," she said when Cheryl had finished. "You need to hole up for a few days."

"I can't. I've got that interview at Drumthwacket tomorrow."

"Fine. I'll drive you to that. In the meantime, we're going to keep you off the streets."

"Don't worry about me," Cheryl said. "As soon as we get home, I'm packing a bag and finding a hotel." She glanced at their lodging. "A better hotel. Closer to Trenton, too."

"No, you're not."

"Sam—"

Sam raised a finger to shush her. "Forget it. You're not moving to some fleabag crash pad. If you're doing this, if you're 'in' like you told him, I'm 'in' right along with you."

"Sam, this is my problem, my risk to take. I don't want—"

Again the silencing finger. "What you want doesn't enter into it. If you're taking on these assholes, then every time you look beside you, you're going to see me there. Got it?"

Cheryl refused to let her eyes well up. "I don't know what I'd do without you."

"First sensible thing you've said. Now we're going to stop at the supermarket and the hardware store on the way home."

"The hardware store?"

"You'd better believe it. We need better security than we've got if we're going to keep the Big Bad Wolves safely outside. Now, get it the car, Rapunzel. Your tower awaits!"

As mixed and somewhat wonky metaphors went, it had been a nice one.

All that had been just two hours ago. Now, with Sam busily battening down the hatches, Cheryl was alone in her room, fretting over what Dag had just told her.

Brenda Kaganoff and Michael Bourbon.

Had this whole thing been a setup from the beginning? Had powerful people arranged for Cheryl to be a honey pot? Maybe. Or maybe Kaganoff honestly liked what Cheryl brought to the assignment and Dag was reading too much into it.

Jesus, where's a signed confession when you need one? Does everything in this shitshow have to be shades of gray?

Right now, Sam was upgrading the locks on their apartment entrances, and adding electronic deadbolts that she swore would foil the People in Gray if they tried to kick their way in. She couldn't do the same to the street door, at least not without alerting her tenants about recent events. So for now they'd settle for high-security locks on all the first-floor windows, a bracing bar on the door, and cameras to watch the street, the vestibule, and the adjacent alley twenty-four-seven. All these things were on Sam's to-do list this morning, and Cheryl could hear her right now, drilling away like a madwoman.

I did this to her, to her life.

Samantha, of course, would hear none of it. "We're in this together," she'd said when they'd stopped first at the hardware store and then at Best Buy on the way home. Still, listening to her roommate turn their little two-bedroom apartment into a fortress, at least insofar as she could, Cheryl couldn't help feeling sick with guilt.

"Can you talk?"

Cheryl almost screamed before realizing who it was. She'd put in Checkmate's earbud when she'd slipped into the bathroom back at the motel and had forgotten it was there. Thank God she hadn't showered yet.

Catching herself, she listened for Sam. The drilling had stopped, but there were footsteps on the creaky boards in the living room. On to the next item on the list, Cheryl supposed.

"Yes," she said.

"Are you all right?" This time the voice belonged to Monika.

"Does it matter?" she asked.

"It matters to me, honey."

"I'm fine."

"Glad to hear it. Are you hunkering down, like I suggested?"

"Ordered is more like it," Cheryl replied, a little petulantly. When the vigilante didn't respond to that, she added in a more pragmatic tone. "My roommate's turning her house into a fortress as we speak. New locks. Window and door sensors. Video. You name it."

"Sounds like at least one of you is taking this seriously. We don't even know for sure who's after you."

"The cabal?"

"Not necessarily."

"You still think it's Cooker, borrowing Antonov's People in Gray?"

"That's my working theory. But Antonov's still in the mix. I keep thinking about how quickly his people found you after your meeting with Bourbon."

It struck Cheryl that there might be some truth in that. After all, the People in Gray had been on her from the moment she'd left the State House. How had they known to do that? "You think Bourbon tipped off Antonov?"

"I can't think of another way it could have gone."

"So, we have the speaker of the state assembly, the senate president, and the chief justice of the state Supreme Court, all in cahoots with the biggest crime boss in the state. What about Portermann?"

"Maybe him, too."

"That's a big web," Cheryl said. "But which one's the spider?"

"Wrong question. The real question is why? What's the purpose of this conspiracy?"

"Money, of course."

"For Cardellini, maybe. For Antonov, certainly. But Bourbon? He's one of the richest people in the country. He doesn't need money, especially money that carries such a high level of risk. I mean, why bother?"

"I don't know."

"I think maybe I do. I think Argo's at the center of this thing."

"But what is it? The name of the cabal maybe?"

"I get the impression it's more like something the cabal is doing. A plot. A scheme. A plan. Take your pick." After a pause, Checkmate added, *"I'm sorry, Cheryl."*

"For what?"

"For all of this. For the fear. You sound so tired."

"I am."

"Then get some rest."

"What are you? My mother? Or is it my father?"

"Just your friend."

"Friendship's about trust. I don't even know your name."

"Would it make you feel better if you did?"

"Of course, it would."

"Would you include it in the piece you're writing?"

Cheryl felt her face redden. She supposed she could say no. But, if she did, and Checkmate turned out to be somebody who was—well—somebody, what would she do then? Would she break her word and publish that identity anyhow?

Was that what Dag would do?

"Fine," she finally said. "Forget it. So, what's next?"

"For you? Nothing. For me, I'm going to wait until after midnight. And then I'm going to pay a visit to Sally Cooker."

"How do you plan to get in?"

"I'll figure it out."

"More trade secrets?"

"If you like."

"Do a lot of break-ins, do you?"

"Yes."

"Really?"

"Really. But this isn't the White House we're talking about, or even the governor's mansion. I imagine she has rudimentary security, but not much beyond that. Should be a cake walk."

"If you say so," Cheryl muttered. She found herself picturing Monika's face, Peter's face, Ivan's face, and wondering which of any of them was real. "Just… be careful tonight, will you? I don't think I can get through this alone."

She expected a flippant answer. What she got instead was a very serious, *"And you'll never have to."*

Then Checkmate was gone.

Cheryl blew out a long sigh, left her bedroom, and went looking for Samantha. She found her roommate in the dining room, screwing something onto the window sashes.

"How's it going?" she asked.

"Getting there," Samantha replied. She was wearing her brunette wig, a sweet little bob so lovingly coiffed that it fell around her ears just so, but somehow still didn't get in the way. Cheryl envied the look. Her own hair, mousier in color, though at least her own, always seemed wildly awry in comparison.

"Kind of looks like overkill," she remarked.

Samantha gave her a pointed look. "Think so?"

"Well… maybe not. But no matter how good the locks on the doors and windows are, if they want in, they're going to get in."

"Perhaps. But they're going to make a ton of noise doing it. And from everything you've told me, these People in Gray prefer things low-key. Even that business on the road last night would have been pretty quiet if we hadn't slipped the net."

"Twice," Cheryl pointed out.

"Anyway, figuring that, I'm not going the 'silent alarm' route. Every door and window will scream bloody murder if forced. So call all this a deterrent."

"If you say so. How close are you to being finished?"

"Almost there. Just have your bedroom windows to do. That means I'm going to have to go in there."

"Sam, that's more your rule than mine. Go ahead in my room if you need to."

"Okay, but it makes me feel funny."

"I understand. You're a private person. Don't worry, your space is still sacrosanct."

"You think I'm a weirdo," Samantha said.

"What else is new?"

It pleased her when her roommate laughed. "Okay, then I'll need about an hour in there. How do you feel about bars?"

"Are you kidding?"

"Yes and no. The problem with bars is that they work both ways. Sure, they can keep the bad guys out. But if those bad guys then get in another way, they keep you in. In fact, the more I think about it, no bars."

"Whatever you say. I find it a little scary that you know so much about all this."

"I once dated the owner of a security company."

"And he… what? Taught you everything about his business?"

"She, and not exactly everything. Call it pillow talk."

"TMI."

Samantha laughed again as she put down the screwdriver. "It's break time anyway. Hey, how about a game of chess?"

"What?"

"Chess. Sitting alone in the Denny's this morning, it occurred to me that we've never played. Given all this Checkmate business, that seems a little odd."

"I didn't know you played chess."

"It's been a while. I'm sure you'll kick my ass. But while I was running the cables for the CCTV, I came across my old set. It's no great shakes, but all the pieces are there. You up for a game?"

Cheryl almost said no, but then she glanced at her Cuff and saw that it wasn't yet lunchtime. What else was she going to do with herself for the rest of the day?

"Sure," she finally replied.

"It's in the hall closet. Fetch it while I put my tools away."

She did. It turned out to be a cheap boxed set, just a weathered board of folding card stock and plastic pieces. A child's set. Some of the pieces, all standard Staunton style, had their weighted felt bottoms. Others didn't. Just handling them as she lined up the white and black ranks made her smile. Growing up, her father had taught her the game using his own custom-made board, with hand-carved pieces from Spain. But when playing with Megan or E.J., she'd always used a set pretty much just like this.

And she'd always won.

She set up the board on the coffee table in the front room, with the sofa on one side and one of the womb chairs on the other. Samantha joined her a minute later, wordlessly dropping onto the sofa opposite Cheryl. Then she snatched up one white pawn and one black pawn, juggled them behind her back for a moment, and offered her closed fists to Cheryl.

"Pawn draw," she said.

Cheryl tapped the left fist and was rewarded with the white pawn.

"Good," Samantha declared, carefully turning the board around. "Let's do this. Do you want to use a chess clock?"

"Do you have one?"

"No."

"Like you said... weirdo."

Cheryl pushed her king's pawn two spaces. The classic opening.

Sam reacted by advancing her queen's bishop pawn.

"The Sicilian Defense," Cheryl said, surprised.

"Is that what it's called? My mother called it the 'Reshevsky defense.'"

"Your mom taught you?"

Sam nodded. "My dad hated board games, all board games. He was funny like that. My mom used to joke about it, saying that calling chess a board game was like calling a Rolls Royce a golf cart."

"My father would concur," Cheryl said, making it sound like a bench ruling. She moved out her king's knight to further control the middle of the board. As she expected, Sam pushed her queen's pawn up one space, forming the makings of a pawn wall.

And so it went.

At first, Cheryl felt pretty confident. Samantha played a classic variation of the Open Sicilian style, one which Cheryl had learned at her father's knee. But about ten moves in, Sam's strategy seemed to go off the rails and Cheryl quickly realized that her confidence had been not merely misplaced, but manipulated.

Samantha shifted into a bold blitz attack on Cheryl's queenside that forced her into a defensive posture. She threw up every roadblock she knew, but Sam just kept coming, relentless as a cat after a mouse. Gradually, Cheryl found herself outplayed, losing first a pawn, then a knight, and then a rook to her roommate's ever more complex traps.

Finally, on the thirty-seventh move, she tipped over her king, signaling defeat.

"You're full of surprises," she told a smiling Samantha.

"Well, I hope so!" Sam replied brightly.

"Your mother taught you how to play like that?"

"She taught me the basics. The rest I picked up."

"From where?"

"More of a who than a where."

Cheryl couldn't help laughing. "Let me guess. You once dated a chess master."

"'Dating' is probably a little strong. We had a few rendezvous."

"Man or woman?"

Sam offered a dismissive wave. "I don't remember noticing. Another game?"

"Maybe later. I want to organize my notes and draft some questions for tomorrow's interview with the governor."

"Look at the big shot. Okay, but do it here. I need to set up the security measures in your bedroom."

Cheryl did so, opening her Cuff and losing herself in the work. Playing Sam had been interesting and oddly disconcerting. When was the last time she'd lost a game of chess that badly? Probably when she'd been twelve, playing against her father.

She spent the next couple of hours typing up notes from her meetings with Cooker and Portermann, brief though they'd both been. Then she looked up the definition of the word "Argo," and found nothing that seemed remotely relevant. It had been the ship that Jason and the Argonauts had used while searching for the Golden Fleece. But what did that mean? A ship was a conveyance, a way to get from Point A to Point B. If that metaphor somehow applied to Argo in the current context, then that implied a means to an end. But what end?

That day turned into one of the longest that Cheryl could remember. Samantha, bless her heart, did her level best to offer distractions. They watched a movie together, one of the old '90s films that Sam liked. They ate an excellent meal of mushroom risotto and shared a bottle of cabernet, though neither of them had more than one glass. Cheryl didn't want to get drunk, or even tipsy, not with security cameras watching the street for the People in Gray who had designs on her.

She and Sam played chess two more times, and both times Cheryl found herself soundly defeated. Finally, throwing up her hands, she declared, "You need to be playing against my father, not me."

"I'm not sure either of us would enjoy that experience," Sam remarked.

"He's not a bad guy. Set in his ways, I guess. I know the dinner was a disaster, but—"

Samantha interjected, "That was more my fault than his. I really shouldn't have gone as Samuel. We could have skated through the evening with barely a ruffled feather."

Cheryl scoffed, "My brother might have hit on you."

Sam shrugged. "The price of beauty."

The laughter they shared felt good. It would be the last time that Cheryl laughed for quite a while.

As evening turned to night, Samantha retired to bed, leaving Cheryl alone in the parlor. She spent some more time on her Cuff, researching, reviewing, and thinking—a lot of thinking. It nagged at her that she'd forgotten or overlooked something, though she couldn't on her life have said what it was. She'd simply been too preoccupied with Checkmate and his midnight burglary of the Cooker residence. It was now just past eleven, and Cheryl decided then and there that she wasn't going to even try to sleep until they got in touch.

But midnight came and went and her earbud remained silent.

While she hadn't said so to Samantha, the idea of the vigilante putting themselves in danger for her troubled her conscience. It seemed she had too many protectors for a grown woman, too many people determined to keep her safe after she'd willfully exposed herself to Antonov and the rest of the cabal.

Checkmate had promised to call her once the burglary was completed. But what if they didn't? What if, tomorrow morning, she read about Checkmate's capture or, worse, their death? What if Argo remained a mystery, right up until the moment that Cooker, Bourbon, Cardellini, and the rest realized whatever goal they'd cooked up. What was a conspiracy, after all, without some evil intrigue?

It's almost one o'clock in the morning, now.

And still nothing from Monika, Peter, or Ivan.

How long did a burglary take?

More than once, she opened the Cuffapp that Samantha had given her, the one lending access to the video feed from the cameras outside the house. The street, now that it was full dark, looked empty, though Sam's Prius stood parked at the curb, just steps from the front door. It operated solely off its owner's Cuff—most cars did these days—but Cheryl knew there was a fob that could be used in emergencies.

What's more, she knew where Sam kept it.

Cheryl didn't make a plan, exactly. It was more lizard brain than that. One minute, she was sitting in one of the parlor's wing chairs, and the next she was up and moving. Fishing Sam's fob out of the server drawer, she opened first the front door and then the street door.

As she did so, she asked herself: *What the hell am I doing?*

And answered: *I'm taking care of myself for a change.*

With a cautious—very cautious—glance up and down the empty street, Cheryl went to her roommate's Prius, and effectively stole it.

CHAPTER TWENTY-ONE

A NIGHT IN GLEN AFTON

WHITE QUEEN TO QUEEN'S BISHOP TWO

Thursday, July 10, 2048

As CHERYL BROUGHT THE "BORROWED" PRIUS TO A HUMMING STOP at the curb in north Trenton's Glen Afton neighborhood, she had to take a minute to will her heartrate to slow. She'd seen few cars on the road between home and here — and none of them, as far as she'd been able to tell, had been following her. Whatever had been behind the two attempts on her made by the People in Gray, their campaign seemed at least to have been paused.

That seemed like a good thing except for her pounding heart.

What am I even doing here?

The question had nagged almost from the moment she'd taken Sam's spare key fob, and the rather spurious argument that she was "taking charge of her own destiny," now felt both frighteningly and hilariously thin. Yet, she hadn't turned around, she hadn't given it up. Instead, here she was, parked in the shadow of a big oak in the middle of the night, around the corner from Sally Cooker's private residence — and without the slightest idea of what to do now.

With a long, painful sigh, Cheryl opened the car door and stepped out into the sultry summer night. Crickets chirped all around her. Every house was dark.

She started walking, trying to look purposeful and — hopefully — unsuspicious.

Unlike its neighbors, there were lights on in the Cooker house, though only on the first floor. Did that mean people were up at this hour? Or was it simply that the chief justice liked to leave some lamps lit downstairs when she went to bed? Cheryl's mother did that, claiming it made her feel safer if the house wasn't in complete darkness.

A wrought-iron fence, maybe six feet tall, marked the property's perimeter. Through it she could see trees and thick foliage, no doubt planted there for the privacy they offered. She followed the sidewalk, holding her breath and unsure why, until she turned the corner and spotted the break in the fence that she and Omar had driven through on Monday evening.

As Cheryl reached the foot of the long driveway, she paused, scanning the front porch and its surrounding foliage for signs of movement. There were none. Either Checkmate hadn't arrived yet or, more likely given the late hour, was already in the house.

Turn around and go home, that voice in her head told her. It sounded like her father.

Once again, she ignored it, instead starting up the drive toward the house. Cheryl did her best to stick to the shadows and to minimize the thump of her shoes on the paving stones, but she still felt dangerously exposed.

Her plan, such as it was, involved circling the residence. Checkmate, she reasoned, wouldn't have gone in the front door. No, they'd have opted for a window, where the home security would be easier to circumvent. All Cheryl had to do was look for one that was partly open. And when she found it—well, then she'd think up Step Two.

But when she was barely halfway up the drive, someone grabbed her from behind and turned her plan-adjacent agenda on its ear.

She tried to scream, but a gloved hand closed over her mouth. Instinctively, she kicked and clawed, but the figure held her fast.

"It's me!" Peter Leko whispered in her ear.

She stopped.

"I'm going to let you go. For pity's sake, don't scream. Nod if you understand."

Cheryl, her heart now doing its beating entirely in her throat, nodded.

The hands fell away. She staggered, gasping, and spun around.

The figure before her was dressed in black, except for the chessboard mask that covered their entire head. She stared at them—*him?*—for three seconds and then shoved the vigilante with all she had, sending him staggering several steps back. She opened her mouth to say something, to vent some of the shock that was coursing through her, turning into anger.

But Checkmate put a gloved finger to his lips, or at least the part of the chessboard where the lips would be. "Don't say a word," Peter Leko whispered. "You need to leave, right now."

In that instant, the driveway lit up brighter than a noonday sun.

Before Cheryl could even fully register the change, Checkmate leapt forward and literally tackled her. The assault, though sudden, seemed deliberate enough to land them both in the foliage that lined the driveway, bathing them in shadow. For a moment, the vigilante laid atop her, pinning her, his masked face cocked at a listening angle.

Cheryl heard footsteps on the drive. They didn't run, but instead approached slowly, deliberately. Murmured voices accompanied them.

"Stay still," Peter whispered. "Don't move a muscle."

Checkmate rolled off of her and then kept rolling across on the manicured lawn, moving more or less parallel to the drive in the direction of the house. Once he reached a spot behind a large rhododendron, the vigilante came smoothly up to a crouch.

Cheryl didn't move.

The footsteps and the voices, both male, came closer.

"Nothing here," one of them said, and something in his cadence made her think he was speaking into his Cuff. An electronic voice responded, though the response was of course encrypted to any ear but his. "Roger that." Then he addressed his partner. "Spread out. They got a 'blur.' It's probably a raccoon."

"They carry rabies," the other one pointed out.

"You go right. I'll go left."

"Fine. Okay."

At that moment, Checkmate, positioned maybe ten feet from where Cheryl still lay on her back, rattled the rhododendron bush.

Both men were instantly alerted. "Over there," the first one hissed. Together, they stepped off the driveway and onto the lawn, approaching Checkmate's hiding place. As they did, Cheryl saw that both wore suits and, while she couldn't swear it in the juxtaposition of light and shadow that filled the front yard, she'd have bet a week's salary those suits were gray.

The rhododendron was a big one, easily eight feet wide and half that high, its large green leaves looking black in the stark spotlight from the porch. Even from Cheryl's vantage point, it was hard to see the vigilante's form huddled behind it. But the two men surely would, now that they were skirting around the plant, slowly approaching from either side.

Checkmate stood at the last possible second, popping up as abruptly as a jack-in-the-box. Seeing them, the guards were startled — only for a moment — but that moment proved enough.

The vigilante raised both his black-clad arms and closed his fists.

The men gasped and crumpled, hitting the grass at almost exactly the same time.

Wordlessly, Checkmate bent over them and removed their Cuffs. Then he went to Cheryl and pulled her to her feet. "Come on," Peter Leko said — and, for the first time since she'd met Monika the "waitress" in the State Street Pub, the vigilante sounded pissed.

Moving together and keeping low, they left the driveway and cut across the lawn. Every dozen or so feet, Checkmate would stop and listen. Without a word, he'd set off again, holding Cheryl's hand in a grip that, while not quite painful, made it crystal clear that she was expected to follow and keep quiet.

So she did.

They finally reached the back corner of a two-car garage. There were no windows here, nor spotlights or cameras, at least none that Cheryl could see.

Again, the vigilante paused, listening furiously. Finally, Cheryl's hand was released, and Checkmate faced her again.

"What in God's name convinced you that coming here was in any way a good idea?" As before, the voice was Peter Leko's.

Cheryl replied in a heated whisper, "I'm sick as hell of everybody thinking they need to take care of me. You're doing it. My father's doing it. Even my roommate's doing it. Well, if my future, maybe even my life, depends on what happens in that house tonight, I want to be involved!" She'd prepared this little speech in the Prius on her way up from the city, the same Prius that she'd taken from her roommate without permission.

Yes, the whole thing was rife with rationalizations. She knew that. Of course, she did.

Though the chessboard mask gave away nothing, Cheryl could sense the scowl beneath it. "Well, it's too late now, I guess. You'd never make it back to the street, not after this. So, looks like you're involved."

"What do we do?" she asked, annoyed at the sudden quaver in her voice. "Those were People in Gray."

"Yeah, I noticed that, too. Looks like Antonov loaned Sally some muscle. If I needed more proof that she was in this up to her judicial neck, I don't anymore."

"Do you think there are more of them?"

Checkmate nodded. "That guy was talking to somebody. There are probably a few inside and likely a couple more out here. We're going to have to move fast and quiet, and you're going to have to do everything I tell you the instant I tell it. Got that?"

Despite everything, Cheryl bristled. She'd never liked taking orders.

Before she could respond, Checkmate reached into their left sleeve, worried at something there, and produced a strapped cylinder about four inches long. "Give me your arm," he said. "Your right arm."

"Why?"

The chessboard masked just looked at her. With a sigh, Cheryl held up her arm. It was a warm night, and she was wearing the same t-shirt and jeans she'd had on all day. She watched as the vigilante fastened the cylinder to the inside of her wrist using Velcro straps. At one end of the cylinder was a thin wire ending in the leather ring that fit over her middle finger. "You point your wrist at the target and do a Spider-man. Know what I mean by that?"

She nodded. "This is sevoflurane, isn't it?"

"It sure is. You've got enough left in there for five or six doses. Here." Checkmate produced a pair of small white plugs. "Put these in your nose. They won't completely block the atomized spray, but they'll help. But for Heaven's sake, keep it pointed away from your face."

"What do you expect me to do with this?" she asked, feeling the weight of the cylinder and holding the plugs in her palm.

"Nothing, hopefully. It's just for emergencies."

"Those guys back there had guns," Cheryl pointed out.

"I don't do guns."

"But you took their Cuffs."

"Right! Thanks for the reminder." These Checkmate pulled from a pocket and threw out over the privacy fence and onto the street beyond. "Cuffs can't be tracked, but they can make noise when someone tries to call them, and I don't want those two found right away. Come on. We've been out here too long."

"How do we get in?" she asked.

"I'll let you know as soon as I figure that out."

"Great," Cheryl muttered. But when Checkmate turned and followed the exterior wall behind the garage in the direction of the rear of the house, she dutifully followed.

After all, what else could she do?

CHAPTER TWENTY-TWO

INFILTRATORS

BLACK ROOK TO QUEEN'S BISHOP ONE

Thursday, July 10, 2048

THEY CONTINUED FOLLOWING THE EXTERIOR WALL WITH CHECKMATE pausing every few yards to listen. Cheryl stayed close behind, wrestling with her nerves and more than once wishing she'd stayed home and gone to bed. The idea she'd had of seizing the reins of her own fate and following her new "friend" into danger had seemed, if not sensible, then at least noble.

However, the reality was proving to be downright ridiculous.

I'm a journalist, she told herself, *not a burglar.*

I'm an idiot.

Light shone up ahead from around a corner that seemed to lead to the rear of the house. Checkmate stopped there, reacting to a faint sound that carried in the still night air.

A woman's voice.

For a moment, Cheryl thought it might be the chief justice herself, out on her back porch in the middle of the night for some reason. But the cadence was wrong, too young. And the clipped, professional tone suggested another guard, another Person in Gray.

"My partner's taking a leak, Control," she was saying, almost certainly into her Cuff. "But it's all quiet back here. Anything on the cameras?"

The response was, of course, encrypted.

"Here's hoping," the woman replied. "How about Ziggy and Edwards?"

More gibberish, shorter this time.

"Maybe they chased somebody down to the street," she offered.

Now the response was longer.

"Roger that, Control."

The woman sighed and broke the link. As she did, Checkmate pulled Cheryl close and whispered in her ear. "Stay right here."

"What are you going to do?" Cheryl asked.

Instead of replying, the vigilante drew a small flashlight from a pocket, switched it on, and stepped smoothly around the corner. Cheryl didn't think she dared risk peeking, but then she did so anyhow.

The backyard was large and well-manicured, with a spacious deck and built-in gazebo. A sliding door stood at one corner of the deck, lit by a pair of outdoor sconces. As she watched, Checkmate's flashlight washed over a female guard, who stood alone on a raised wooden deck attached to the rear of the house.

"That you, Gorksy?" she exclaimed. "Jeez, get that out of my eyes, will you?"

"It's me," Peter Leko said amiably. "Sorry. Forgot to pull my fly."

"Classy as always," the woman muttered, but Cheryl thought there might be a smile behind the words. For no reason whatsoever, she suddenly wondered if the Woman in Gray and Gorsky were an item.

Just as the vigilante stepped onto the deck and raised his arm, the woman uttered an exclamation, partway between a word and a scream.

Then she collapsed.

"We're clear," Checkmate said.

Swallowing dryly, Cheryl stepped around the corner of the house. As she did, the vigilante shut off his flashlight, took the unconscious woman by the wrists, and dragged her unceremoniously off the deck and toward the heavily landscaped property line.

"Follow me," he told Cheryl.

She dutifully trailed along, watching as the unfortunate guard was dumped in a patch of deep ivy. As before, Checkmate removed her Cuff and threw it over the fence.

"I'm going in," Peter said.

"Me, too."

"No."

"Yes!"

Checkmate took her hand, the black glove warm against Cheryl's bare skin. "You're brave as hell to have come here. But going into that house blind isn't brave. It's stupid."

"You're doing it!"

"It's my job to do it."

Cheryl pulled her hand free. "And it's not mine?"

"Okay, please listen. I don't have much time. This person's partner will be back any minute and I need to be inside before that happens. So this has to be quick. No, Cheryl. Performing burglaries on jurists is *not* your job. Your job is to write about *me* doing it. Your job is to expose Cooker and Argo and the rest. Stay here, no matter what happens. Hopefully, I get in and out without a problem. But even if I don't, I'll Cuffcall 911 and have every cop in town here within ten minutes. Once that happens, you'll either be able to slip away, or you'll get arrested. If it's the latter, then call your father and your editor."

"What about you?" Cheryl demanded, a little desperately.

"I'll figure something out."

"We're supposed to be partners, damn it!"

"And we are. I've never said that before to anyone. Ever. But we are. And that partnership means leaning on our individual strengths. Tonight, I'm a burglar. You're a journalist. Be a journalist. Now, I've got to go. Promise me you'll stay here."

Cheryl didn't want to. She also didn't want to go into that house, not with all those armed thugs running around. But the idea of just cowering—

Then she remembered her family. She remembered Sam. A lone vigilante might have nothing to lose. But she had plenty.

"I promise."

With a nod, Checkmate left her there. Cheryl watched him return to the deck and try the sliding door. When it opened without a problem, the chessboard mask spared one more moment to look around and, apparently satisfied, slipped into the house—

—leaving an unhappy Cheryl to settle herself down beside the unconscious guard to wait.

She didn't have to wait long. Within a minute, a figure emerged from around the far side of the house. From the size and gait, it was a man, and as he stepped up onto the deck and into the range of the porch light, Cheryl recognized his gray suit. Apparently, the unconscious woman's small-bladdered partner had finally finished his business, though whether he'd done so in the bushes or had gone into the house through a different door, Cheryl didn't care to know.

For a moment, the guy looked left and right. He raised his wrist and spoke into it, the words carrying. "Lampert. Where are you? Why'd you leave your post?"

Of course there was no reply as Lampert, presumably the woman at Cheryl's feet, was in no position to offer one. Besides, her Cuff was somewhere in the neighborhood behind the house.

After perhaps half-a-minute, the Man in Gray uttered a low curse and raised his Cuff again. "Control. This is Gorsky. Did Lampert check in? She's not at her post."

The response didn't seem to please him. As Cheryl watched from the shadows at the edge of the property, the fellow turned to the sliding door. Scowling, he opened it and went inside.

Shit, Cheryl thought, thinking furiously.

Checkmate had known the partner would return. But had he expected the Man in Gray to follow him inside like this?

She touched her ear and whispered, "Can you hear me?"

When no reply was forthcoming, she straightened and looked around. The house and its yard, at least what she could see of it, seemed empty and quiet.

Cheryl chided herself. *Checkmate can handle this! This is what he does, for God's sake!*

But, almost against her will, she stepped out of the ivy and began moving toward the deck, the gazebo, and the sliding glass door. Every step, especially the ones on the wooden deck, sounded insanely loud to her own ears, making her feel clumsy and exposed.

Don't do this! Checkmate's right. It isn't your job!

By the time she stopped beside the sliding door, her heart had begun pounding again and she had to fight a rising nausea. Vomiting was not an option.

I have to, she thought, and that was that.

She tried the handle. It opened easily. Inside was a spacious family room, lit by a low-wattage antique floor lamp that stood in one corner. Cheryl peered into every shadow, trying to go still and listen the way the vigilante had.

She saw nothing and heard nothing.

Slowly, painfully so, she stepped off the deck and onto a hardwood floor. It didn't creak. She considered leaving the door open at her back, thinking of a quick escape. But, if spotted, it might alert the People in Gray to her presence—so, feeling conflicted, she closed it. Then she crossed the family room to an archway.

Beyond it lay a narrow hall that seemed to lead toward the front of the house. There she stopped again, listening as Checkmate had. Again, there was nothing.

She stepped tentatively into the corridor.

And that was where he grabbed her.

He came from an open doorway on her right, a hulking figure that caught her hair in one ham-sized fist. She screamed and clawed at his thick wrist, all thoughts of stealth gone like the nonsense they'd been. "Gotcha," she heard him say, not even wincing as she dug her nails into his skin. "Been hoping you'd show up."

"Let me go!" she exclaimed, kicking his shin—hard. That one he evidently felt, because he cursed and threw her like a ragdoll through the archway and back into the family room. She stumbled and went down hard, slamming her hip and shoulder against the floor. Pain lashed her entire left side, but she ignored it and scrambled to her feet— suddenly wishing to God she'd left the back door open after all.

He was on her in two great strides, spinning her around. As he did, she suddenly and terrifyingly recognized him. He'd been one of the two on the street outside Sam's house, when they'd tried to bluff her into their car. He'd also been on the road the following evening, during the car chase.

"Get away from—" she started to yell.

He slapped her across the face, rattling her teeth and making her taste blood. She tried to kick him again, but he was ready for it this time, shoving her into a bookshelf hard enough to rain titles down around her.

"You're going to die tonight, missy," he said, and the grin that came with his pronouncement frightened her on a level she hadn't known existed. Before she realized what she was doing, Cheryl started throwing books at him, one after another, screaming her head off the entire time. He batted them away, actually laughing at her desperate terror.

Then he came at her again, charging like a bull.

A thought, completely unbidden, popped into her mind.

Spider-man.

With a moan, she raised her right arm toward him, toward his face, and—just as his own hands reached for her—she pressed her middle finger to her palm.

She heard nothing. Felt nothing. But her attacker stopped in mid-step, blinking at her with something akin to wonder.

Then he fell, toppling over backward like a lumberjack's tree. The big man landed on his back with enough force to shake the floor.

Lying there, he twitched a few times, and then went still.

Cheryl stared down at him, swaying on her feet, her thoughts reeling.

A familiar voice said, "You really do suck at the whole 'stay put' thing, don't you?"

She looked blearily up at the archway. Checkmate stood there, leaning against the threshold, arms folded across his chest. At the sight of him, Cheryl felt her shock and resolve collapse. As she sobbed and staggered forward, the vigilante rushed up and, to Cheryl's no small surprise, pulled her into a fierce hug.

"It's okay," Peter Leko said, his voice catching. "I got the rest of them. He was the last."

"He…" she stammered, pulling back. "…was one of the ones from last night."

"I know. I avoided him a few minutes ago when he stepped out of the chief justice's office. After he went by, I peeked inside and saw that they'd turned it into a command center. Two more guys were in there. I put them both to sleep. I figure this last guy went out to investigate when they lost touch with their foot soldiers."

"Did you find what you were looking for in Cooker's office?" Cheryl asked, having to force herself to stay on task. "Did you find Argo?"

The chessboard mask shook. "I found a few interesting things in the desk drawers but had to stop when somebody started screaming." The vigilante took her by the shoulders. "I'm so sorry I didn't get here sooner. I'm so sorry you were hurt."

"I'm okay," she replied. And she was, more or less. Her shoulder and hip ached, and her cheek burned where the Thug in Gray had slapped her. By tomorrow, she'd have some new bruises to add to the one already on her cheek.

Did all that qualify as "okay"?

She decided that, for now, it did.

"Let's go back there," she told Checkmate. "I'll help you search."

"Too risky. If I heard you scream, the whole house did."

"But you said all the People in Gray are out of commission."

"They are," Checkmate replied. "But that doesn't mean—"

Cheryl heard a sound. It was one that, in her twenty-three years of life, had never before reached her ears. But she recognized it anyway. Any American who'd seen an action flick would.

It was the sound of a gun hammer drawing back.

She started as Checkmate spun around.

Sally Cooker, the chief justice of the New Jersey Supreme Court stood in the corridor archway, looking small and surprisingly frail. She wore a thin robe over a simple knee-length nightgown. On her feet were fuzzy slippers.

And in her hand was a revolver.

Chapter Twenty-Three

PROPRIETOR

WHITE QUEEN TO KING'S BISHOP SIX

Thursday, July 10, 2048

BEFORE ANYTHING ELSE HAPPENED, CHECKMATE MOVED, PLACING himself between Cheryl and Cooker. It was an oddly chivalrous action, and one that annoyed her as much as touched her. She felt a sharp urge to remark, "You know, the bullet would go right through you and hit me anyway."

But she didn't. This wasn't the time.

The chief justice spoke first. Her voice sounded thin, as if she were at the very edge of crying—or screaming. "Take your mask off."

For several seconds, neither Cheryl nor the vigilante moved.

Finally Checkmate asked in a surprisingly conversational tone, "Why?"

Cooker actually bared her teeth. "Because I want to see the face of the person who's caused all this trouble!"

"Trouble," the vigilante echoed. "You mean like the deaths of Martin Sadler and his family, Catlin McAvoy, and Joseph and Elizabeth Manning. That sort of trouble?"

"How do you—" the woman began, only to stop herself and raise the revolver higher. "The mask. Take it off. Now."

"Do it," Cheryl said to Checkmate. "It's okay."

"Yeah," Peter Leko replied. "I guess it is." He reached up with a gloved hand and gently lifted the chessboard mask away. The hair underneath was long and dark, the face feminine, though without makeup.

"There you go," Monika said.

Cheryl stared at her, her aching body and even Cooker's gun momentarily forgotten. She started to say something, but the chief justice beat her to it.

"You're a woman."

"I'm a woman," Checkmate replied.

"A moment ago, you had a man's voice." Cooker sounded confused, though her gun never wavered.

"Yeah, I do that."

"What's your name?" the chief justice demanded. "Your real name."

Despite everything else that was going on, Cheryl's ears pricked up.

The vigilante smiled. "Monika Soćko."

The name struck a chord of memory, though Cheryl couldn't, in the heat of the moment, place it. Oddly, an image of her father's study came to mind.

Cooker's eyes narrowed. "There's a chess grandmaster called Monika Soćko."

"Is there?" Checkmate said.

"I have a book of her games in my office!" the chief justice declared, making it sound like an accusation.

"Huh. Go figure."

And Cheryl thought, *Yes!* Her father had a book of her games as well. Cheryl had even read it, or some of it. Monika Soćko was a Polish woman in her sixties who had won the women's chess championship on at least a half-dozen occasions. And on the heels of that realization came another. Just two words this time.

Howard Staunton.

And another.

Peter Leko. Ivan Saric.

I'll be damned...

But then Cooker said, "You're the one who catfished Steven Woolsey."

Cheryl had no idea who Steven Woolsey might be, and so was a bit surprised when Monika replied, "Yep. That was me."

"And stole Victor Cardellini's Cuff backups."

"Also me."

Cooker seemed to need a moment to process this information. Nevertheless, her revolver remained leveled at Monika's chest. "And you were in my office just now, searching my desk."

"Started but didn't finish," Checkmate replied. She glanced back at Cheryl. "Got sidetracked."

Cooker ignored this. "You must have found my gun. This gun."

"I did."

"But you didn't touch it."

"I touched it," Monika corrected. "I just didn't take it. I don't do guns."

The chief justice visibly swallowed. "Neither do I. Or didn't, before now. But I have to use it. I have to kill you both."

"Why?" Cheryl asked. To her own ears she sounded calm enough, though the chief justice's words made her feel as if the floor had just dropped out from beneath her feet. For a moment, she swayed, but steadied herself.

Like vomiting, fainting was not an option.

Cooker's answer was both immediate and hard with conviction. "To protect the people I love."

"From who?" Checkmate asked.

"The police," Cheryl guessed.

But Cooker's head shook vehemently. "The police? The police are nothing in this city. They may as well be blind for everything they understand about how things really work here. No one's called them and no one's going to."

"What's their name, Sally?" Monika asked, her tone steady, almost tender.

"W — what?"

"The person or persons that you're so afraid of. What's their name?"

"I..." But the word trailed off and she shook her head again. "What difference does it make? I meant it when I said I have to kill you both."

"Then there's no reason not to tell us," Monika replied easily.

"I can't. I won't," Cooker insisted, her lower lip trembling. "I'm truly sorry."

She pulled the trigger.

The hammer fell with an empty, metallic click that made Cheryl jump.

The chief justice blinked. She fired again, and a third time.

Checkmate raised one gloved hand and opened it. A half-dozen small brass bullets clattered to the hardwood floor at her feet. "I told you, Sally. I touched your gun."

The woman in the archway seemed to shrink before Cheryl's eyes. Her look of conviction, no doubt honed over the course of a long judicial career, vanished in an instant. The gun fell from her grasp, landing much more loudly than its bullets had. Cooker sagged against the threshold and buried her face in her hands.

"Let's get out of here," Cheryl whispered.

But Monika ignored her. Instead, she walked up to the chief justice, her steps slow and her hands up, as if she were approaching a frightened child instead of a woman of letters who'd just actively tried to kill them.

"Talk to us, Sally. We can help you."

Cooker lowered her hands and laughed bitterly. "You don't have the slightest idea what you're dealing with."

"Maybe the slightest," Monika replied with a bit of a crooked smile. "You're... I'm not sure what the right word is. Beholden? To an entity that has been a cancer in this state for more than fifteen years. It's caused, or ordered, the deaths of innocent people, some because they asked too many questions, and others because they needed leverage against someone else. In your case, I think you were leveraged and, given your husband's condition, I can guess how."

If all this clever deduction impressed the woman, she offered up no sign. Instead, her shoulders slumping, she nodded and replied, "Eleven years ago this November, I received a Cuffcall from someone calling themselves "Proprietor." Their voice was electronically disguised. I couldn't even tell if it was a woman or a man. They informed me, very matter-of-factly, that I would be asked to push my court in certain directions on particular cases. And they warned me, if I failed to comply even once, for any reason, that someone I loved would suffer.

"At first, I was furious. I assumed it was a prank of some sort. After all, I was Sarah Edwina Cooker, and no one threatened me. So, I told this Proprietor what they could do with their demands and threats. I told them I would bring all of the might of my office to bear on finding them and seeing them arrested for this harassment."

She fell silent.

Monika waited. So did Cheryl, though her eyes kept straying to the bullets that lay scattered across the floor. *She pulled the trigger. She was going to kill me, kill us both.*

It didn't seem—real.

Cooker continued. "Two nights later, Harrison was attacked on the street. They beat him nearly to death. Sometimes, a part of me wishes they had, because the man I married, the man I loved, is forever gone. In his place is a drooling, empty shell." When she looked up at Monika, there were tears in her eyes. "He used to play chess. Used to love the game. Now he just sits and sits."

"I'm guessing the next time this Proprietor called you, you said yes," Checkmate remarked.

"Not immediately. First, I railed at them, cursed them, used words that hadn't passed my lips since law school. But then they told me where my sons were at that moment, which colleges, which dorms. They said that, if I ever disobeyed again, they'd do to one of them what they'd done to Harrison. Except they wouldn't stop with just a crippling beating. They'd kill one of my boys."

"I'm sorry, Sally," Monika said, sounding absolutely sincere. "Come over here. Sit down."

She took the woman's hands. The chief justice came willingly. Cheryl watched as together the vigilante and the jurist went to a nearby sofa and settled onto it. As they did, Checkmate caught Cheryl's eye and motioned toward the fallen gun. Wordlessly, Cheryl walked over and picked it up. It wasn't the first gun she'd ever held, but it still felt heavier than she'd expected, even empty.

She looked questioningly at Monika, who gestured vaguely toward the bullets, and then went back to consoling the broken woman.

"Tell us about Argo," she said, holding the older woman's hands.

Cooker looked at her. "You found that in Victor's backups."

"Yes, I did. But only references in emails… to you."

"He shouldn't have done that. It was a dire breach of Proprietor's protocols. Siblings aren't supposed to use proper names or other specifics in emails or Cuffcalls."

"Siblings?" Cheryl asked.

The chief justice actually rolled her eyes. "That's what Proprietor calls us. Siblings. As if we're all some kind of twisted family. The whole arrangement is wrapped up in ridiculous ritual."

Checkmate leaned closer. "What sort of ritual?"

The woman seemed to need a moment before answering. In a small voice, she said, "I'm signing my death warrant, telling you all this."

The vigilante didn't reply. Cheryl took the cue and did the same.

Finally, with a shuddering sigh, Cooker said, "Proprietor operates by finding what you want and offering it to you. If you don't immediately acquiesce, they threaten what you love. It's how he gets people under his sway,"

"Carrot and stick," Cheryl heard herself mutter. She collected the bullets and shoved them deep into one of her pockets. No way would she be loading the gun.

"They used Harrison and your sons against you," Checkmate said. "But what did they offer you? What was the carrot?"

"In my case, there wasn't one. Not at first. I'd already been on my bench for a year before Proprietor's call came, at the pinnacle of my profession. He promised to make sure I stayed there for life. I don't know whether you know this or not, but New Jersey Supreme Court justices have seven-year terms and must be reappointed. Proprietor guaranteed my reappointment, said he needed me right where I was."

"And all it cost you was your husband," Monika said, not without pity.

Cooker nodded.

"What about Victor Cardellini? Did he get the carrot, or just the stick, like you?"

"I don't know," the chief justice replied, sounding spent and empty. "We all keep Proprietor's leverage over us close to our chest."

"All? You mean the Siblings?"

Cooker nodded.

"Do you know who they are?"

"At the rituals, Proprietor insists that we wear masks. Instead of names, each of us is given a Greek letter. I'm not certain, but I believe these are assigned based on the order of recruitment."

"Which one are you?" Cheryl asked.

"Delta."

"Fourth," Checkmate said. "But who are Alpha, Beta, and Gamma?"

The woman shook her head. "I... I can't."

"Okay, Sally. It's okay. Tell us about Argo then. What is it? A person? A project?"

"It's a—"

What happened next was one of those moments that Cheryl had only ever heard about in the movies. It was so sudden and so completely unexpected that, for precious seconds, her mind couldn't quite process what her senses were telling her. It started with a crash, loud but somewhat distant—a front door being forced open, or perhaps "kicked in" was more accurate. Then footsteps, a lot of them, spilled across hardwood floors. Someone shouted "fan out" in a deep, heavily accented voice. And fan out they did, a lot of them judging by the ruckus they made, and Cheryl suddenly understood two terrible truths. First, the owners of those feet were wearing gray suits, and second, those same feet would find their way in here in very short order indeed.

She and Monika swapped looks of alarm. But before either of them could say anything, Sally Cooker, who'd been frightened and contrite only a second ago, now leapt to her feet and screamed, "Here! They're back here! Kill them! Kill them both!"

"Well, that's disappointing," Cheryl heard Checkmate mutter. She stood and went to stand in front of Cheryl as she had when the chief justice had ambushed them. "Be ready to run," she whispered.

"Run... where?" Cheryl heard herself ask, her heart now firmly lodged in her throat.

"As soon as I know, I'll tell you."

Armed men and women spilled into the family room, first four, then eight, then ten. They were all dressed the same, just as Cheryl had supposed. Furthermore, each carried a silenced pistol and an expression that contained all the warmth of a jagged cliff face. In front of them, the only one not dressed in the odd gray uniform, stood a mountain of a man. He looked to be in his early sixties, but powerful and vital despite his age. His suit was black, his hair thin and combed back, his eyes dark and blazing. He held a pistol of his own, a big one, and he raised it as he took in the three people before him.

"That's Checkmate!" Sally Cooker cried, pointing like a child at a playground bully. "And the Walker girl."

Despite her fear, Cheryl felt her hackles raise at the term 'girl.'

"I know," the big man replied. He had one of the deepest voices Cheryl had ever heard, even deeper than her father's.

"Hi, Vlad," Monika remarked with a grin. "Welcome to the party!"

And Cheryl thought, *Vlad? As in Vladimir Antonov?*

That thought did absolutely nothing to ease her throat's heart-lodging.

"If either of them moves, shoot them," Antonov told his soldiers.

They immediately fanned out, filling the room and encircling Checkmate and Cheryl. As they did, Cooker started talking again, gesticulating wildly. She hastily described first the invasion of her home and then the incapacitation of her guards. At this latter, Antonov glared at her, the force of his gaze almost physical in its power and menace.

"You mean the guards you took from me? Are those the guards you're talking about, Delta?"

Sally Cooker's eyes went wide. "What? I—"

Antonov, however, was having none of it. He seized the chief justice's arm, squeezing hard enough to make her cry out, and threw her back down on the sofa. She landed there, staring up at him in mounting horror, making Cheryl suppose that Siblings weren't supposed to treat each other so roughly.

Clearly the situation had changed.

"Let me guess," Monika said conversationally. "Proprietor wants us alive for... What? Interrogation?"

"Yes," the gangster replied. "But I'll kill you if you resist in any way." He addressed his nearest cronies, barking orders to have all three of the prisoners restrained.

"What?" Cooker cried. "No! I'm a Sibling! My husband—"

Antonov dismissed this. "You discussed matters with Zeta that you shouldn't have. You knew the rules and you broke them."

The chief justice's mouth snapped shut with an audible click, her bloodshot eyes as round as twin moons. "I..." she sputtered. "How..."

Antonov said nothing, so Checkmate answered for him. "He has you under surveillance, Sally. I'm guessing he watches all the Siblings. For Proprietor."

Cooker's already pale face went so white that Cheryl thought the woman might faint.

For his part, Vladimir Antonov turned his back to her and raised his wrist, activating a Cuffcall. When the recipient answered, he said, "I have them."

The response was naturally incomprehensible to everyone but Antonov, himself. The big man nodded. "Both of them, yes. Checkmate and the Walker girl. They broke into Delta's home." A pause followed. Antonov said, "I don't know exactly what they were looking for... yet. But I will." Another pause followed, longer this time.

While all this was going on, Monika glanced at Cheryl and offered her a small wink. The gesture, clearly meant to reassure, should have struck her as nothing more than courage in the face of—well—"doom" didn't feel like too strong a word. But somehow Cheryl felt the knot of terror that seemed to have taken up permanent residence in her gut loosen, just a little.

Checkmate has a plan, she told herself, praying for all she was worth that this was true.

Antonov scowled. "There's no need for that. I'll bring them to you." Another pause, the longest yet. Finally, the big man sighed. "As you say, Proprietor."

He reached into one pocket and drew out a small black disk. Cheryl recognized it, though this was the first time she'd seen one.

Portable holographic projectors were new tech, only recently released by Michael Bourbon and the good folks at Cufflink. More compact and more expensive than the larger systems like the one in Drumthwacket, these were used mainly by federal types and the ridiculously rich.

And gangsters, apparently.

She watched with as much interest as her fear would allow as Antonov moved into the open space between them and their execution squad and placed the projector on the floor. He stepped back, tapped his Cuff, and told the prisoners. "Do not be disrespectful."

Checkmate, grinning in a way that Cheryl hoped to God wasn't all bravado, replied, "Wouldn't dream of it, Vlad."

An instant later, an image shimmered into existence before them, slightly larger than lifelike. It was of a human head, draped in a red robe and wearing a featureless mask of the same color. For a moment, the image eyed them both, its eyes, the only visible part of its face, moving slowly between them. Then it settled on Monika and spoke, the voice so electronically disguised that Cheryl could tell absolutely nothing about it.

"*Checkmate.*"

"Proprietor," Monika replied with a nod.

"*By now, you must realize how completely outmaneuvered you've been.*"

"Can we maybe do this without you sounding like the bad guy in a Bond movie?"

Behind the image, partially obscured by the projection, Antonov uttered a noise rather like the growl of a bear. From another man, it might have sounded comic, or at least silly. But coming from him, Cheryl felt her fear, only barely in check, threaten to blossom into panic.

"*I wanted us to meet.*"

"And now we have. What happens next?"

"*I'm merely paying my respects. We both know I have no choice but to kill you.*"

"I thought Vlad wanted to interrogate us first."

"*Ms. Walker will serve well enough for that. You present too many risks. You're too slippery, Checkmate. And I don't like taking chances.*"

"Please..." Cheryl heard herself say. "You don't have to do this."

The masked image turned toward her. *"Everything I've done, and everything coming, is all for the greater good, Ms. Walker. I don't expect you to understand that. But it's true."*

"In all my days," Monika said, but this time in Ivan Saric's "old man" voice. "I've never met a villain who didn't believe themselves a hero."

The mask actually laughed at that.

Apparently bolstered by the response, the vigilante pushed it further, this time as Peter Leko. "Since I'm dead anyhow, what's say you show me your face. You can see mine. Seems only fair."

"Fair is a skin tone and nothing more. I don't bargain, Checkmate, and I offer neither concessions nor mercy. In a moment, I'm going to order Beta to take Ms. Walker into his custody and shoot you in the head. This exchange is simply a rare self-indulgence. I wanted to know what you looked like."

Monika actually struck a pose, turning slightly and putting her left hand on her hip. As she did, Cheryl saw her slide something out of a rear pants pocket and into her gloved palm, the motion as smooth as a magic trick.

"And what's your opinion?" she cooed, giving the words an over-the-top coquettish purr.

"Ordinary," the mask replied dryly.

The vigilante feigned a pout. "I'm hurt. But you can make it up to me. Since you won't show me your pretty face, how about satisfying my admittedly insatiable curiosity on just one point."

Proprietor paused before answering. Then the electronic voice replied, *"One question."*

"What do you want with Argo?"

Still standing with his soldiers behind the projection, Antonov's face darkened. He whirled on Sally Cooker, who shrank away from his glare as if it radiated heat. "What have you said to them?"

"I—" she began.

He slapped her—hard. The woman shrieked and fell onto her side, clutching one cheek. Cheryl, who'd been slapped like that herself just a few minutes ago, could almost sympathize.

"Enough, Beta," Proprietor said. Turning back to Checkmate, the mask replied, *"I'm not, in fact, a 'Bond bad guy,' as you so colorfully put it. And I don't see any practical value in answering that question. Beta, it's time. Make sure the body is never found."*

"Yes, Proprietor," Antonov said, drawing a silenced pistol from inside his jacket.

Monika raised both her gloved hands. "Wait a minute." Her tone was steady, but there could be no mistaking the urgency behind the words. "You don't even know my real name."

"Then that makes us even. Good-bye, Checkmate."

The vigilante's face lost all expression. "See you soon," she said to the holoimage.

She opened her right fist and something small and round fell to the floor at her feet.

A lot of things happened seemingly all at once.

The thing she'd dropped exploded in a burst of billowing white smoke that filled the family room just this side of instantly. At the same time, Cheryl was seized around the waist and literally tackled to the floor. She landed hard, too stunned to cry out. Before she could so much as struggle, Monika whispered. "Back door."

As she said this, bullets started flying.

"Keep low," the vigilante commanded softly, so softly, into her ear. Then the weight was off of her, leaving her flat on her belly on the hardwood. The smoke was insanely thick; Cheryl couldn't see anything around her. The blindness was so disorienting that, for a moment or two, she couldn't make herself move.

She heard glass shatter, a lot of it.

The sliding door to the back deck had just been shot out.

That broke her paralysis—hard. With a gasp, she struggled to her feet and staggered forward, bent almost double at the waist and headed in what she hoped was the right direction. Behind her, Antonov was shouting something, making her realize that, while the smoke was certainly thick, it didn't seem to be gagging anyone. Yet the mobster's words were—garbled, somehow—almost as if she'd heard them through someone else's Cuff.

How can that be?

A bullet whizzed past her ear, and her lizard brain insisted it didn't matter.

Cheryl felt glass crunch beneath her feet. In a thrill of panic and a cry that was partly a sob, she all but hurled herself forward, certain she'd be cut to ribbons on whatever remained of the room's only viable exit.

She wasn't. Call it the luck of the foolish, but Cheryl found herself all but tripping across the house's back deck, completely unscathed.

Around her, the smoke billowed outward, staying close to the ground and not dissipating. She considered turning and yelling for Checkmate's benefit that their exit was clear, but another bullet passed her, so close that she actually felt its heat, and suddenly she was sprinting.

The house's rear grounds weren't as extensive as those in the front, with the six-foot wrought iron fence just fifty feet or so from the back deck. Navigating around the house to leave the way she'd come in didn't seem like a smart move just now. Instead, Cheryl made for that fence, running for all she was worth, her breath coming in ragged gasps. From behind her, still inside the house, she heard shouts and crashes and more gunshots.

She pushed through the line of bushes and reached the fence, where she first tried to squeeze through the bars, only to find them too tightly spaced. Instead, her hand gripped a crossbar that ran near the top of the fence at a height of about six feet. To her right was an oak tree, all but invisible in the darkness. Almost without thinking, she jumped and pressed one sneakered foot against a knot that protruded from its trunk at about waist level.

Lifting herself up this way was awkward, so much so that she'd never have attempted it if not for the adrenaline hammering at her senses. As a result, and despite her best efforts, she found herself tilted at a precarious angle, without the leverage or upper body strength to clear the top of the fence.

That was when two hands grabbed her buttocks.

Cheryl screamed. But before she could respond further, the hands shoved her up and over the crossbar, until her own momentum and shifting center of gravity sent her tumbling down onto the grounds outside the property. Luckily, she hit soft summer grass rather than the concrete sidewalk.

Even so, the impact was enough to knock the wind out of her.

She lay there gasping like a landed fish, her eyes wide and her mind numb with shock.

A figure all in black dropped down beside her and unceremoniously pulled her to her feet. Monika said something, but it sounded wrong, unintelligible, the way Antonov's voice had when the shooting started. When Cheryl just stared helplessly at her, the vigilante cupped her hands over Cheryl's ears and said directly into her face, "It will pass," forming the words slowly and deliberately so that Cheryl could read her lips.

With some effort, Cheryl nodded.

Checkmate smiled, took her hand, and together the two of them ran across the street and into the Trenton night.

CHAPTER TWENTY-FOUR

TOMORROW

BLACK KING TO KING'S BISHOP TWO

Thursday, July 10, 2048

TEN MINUTES AND SIX BLOCKS LATER, WITH THE TWO OF THEM walking quickly side-by-side along a narrow street within sight of the river, Cheryl's hearing finally cleared. Her heartrate and breathing had also steadied, thank God, so that she no longer felt on the verge of either throwing up or fainting.

I was shot at tonight! Last night I was almost run off the road and tonight they shot at me.

This is my life now.

It was a dismal thought.

"I don't hear any sirens," she remarked. Her voice seemed steady, and her hands only shook a little.

"Nope," Monika replied.

"Somebody must have heard the shots."

"The guns were silenced. Yes, they still made noise, but from any distance at all the sound is easily mistaken for something else. And certainly nobody in that house is calling 911, not with the infamous Vladimir Antonov on the guest list."

"I was worried they'd be coming after us."

The vigilante nodded. "They would be, but my little surprise is slowing them down."

"There was something in the smoke," Cheryl said.

"Yep."

"Some kind of drug."

"A homemade mixture of some drugs with really long names. I wasn't planning on using it. It was just for emergencies."

"Were you expecting Vladimir Antonov to show up?"

"Nope. Hence the emergency. I'm sorry you were affected. I'd hoped the nose plugs would spare you. They did with me, but then, I made them custom. I'll do the same for you."

That last statement unnerved Cheryl on a very deep level, though it took her a few moments to puzzle out why. "You expect me to be nearby the next time you're throwing toxic chemicals around?"

"Effective, not toxic," Checkmate corrected without rancor. "And yes, probably. You're a part of this now, honey. Antonov knows you. So does whoever's holding his leash."

Cheryl hugged herself and said, "Maybe we should call the cops."

"And tell them what?"

"That I was nearly murdered, for starters! So were you!"

"It was what we in the biz call a 'close one.'"

"That's not funny, damn it!"

"No, honey. It's not. But it happened and it's not going to unhappen. If you decide to call 911, let's consider the likely order of events. They'll register your Cuff ID. Then they'll investigate the Cooker house. They'll probably find something. Vlad's pretty good at covering his tracks, but bullet holes and a shot out glass door are hard to quickly hide. Regardless, though, they're going to come knocking on your door next. There'll be a lot of questions, some of which you're going to have a very hard time answering. How are you figuring on explaining what you were doing in the chief justice's private residence in the middle of the night? You could tell them about your association with me, I suppose. But if you do that, they're liable to hit you with an accessory after the fact charge. I'm a wanted felon, remember? At least as far as Rhona Jackson and the state police are concerned."

It was quite a speech—and, for the life of her, Cheryl couldn't conjure up any way to refute it. "So I'm stuck."

"I did warn you."

And, of course, Checkmate *had* warned her, as Ivan Saric in the diner yesterday.

And I told him I'm in.

They walked on in silence for another block.

Finally Cheryl looked pointedly at the other woman, if she really was a woman, and remarked, "Monika Soćko is a chess grandmaster."

Monika's reply was—reserved. "So Sally said. Funny, that."

"At Drumthwacket last Friday night, you posed as a state police sergeant named Staunton. Howard Staunton."

This time, the vigilante didn't reply at all.

Cheryl kept going. "Also a grandmaster. In fact, the standard chess pieces we use on most boards are named for him."

"What's your point?" Monika asked, stopping on the sidewalk and folding her arms.

Cheryl met her level gaze, holding up her left wrist. "If I were to do a quick Cuff search for Peter Leko and Ivan Saric, I'd find out they were chess masters too, wouldn't I?"

"Maybe. So what?"

"That's a hell of a risk, isn't it? Naming all your aliases after great chess players. Couldn't that pattern end up biting you in the ass?"

Checkmate shrugged. "Monika and Howard are probably blown. But the only person who's heard of Ivan or Peter is you. And I trust you."

"Do you?"

"You came for me tonight, honey. It was stupid, and frankly dangerous as hell, but you did it. Yeah, I trust you. At least insofar as I trust anybody."

That sentiment was both touching and a bit sad. How long had it been since this person, man or woman or whatever, had felt close enough to someone to give them their trust? For a moment, standing there on the roadside, the two continued looking at each other. Cheryl felt a sudden, surprisingly strong urge to offer this "wanted felon" a good old-fashioned hug.

She didn't.

Instead, she sighed wearily and said, "Fine then, Monika Soćko, what do we do now?"

"For starters, we get you safely home."

"How? I left my roommate's Prius on the side street beside the Cooker place. I don't think doubling back for it would be a good idea."

"No, it wouldn't," the vigilante agreed. "Fortunately, I too have a mode of transportation. What, did you think we were walking these streets after midnight aimlessly?"

Cheryl looked quizzically at her before scanning the road. No one lived along this particular stretch, and absolutely nothing was parked within view. "Where is it?" she asked.

Checkmate smiled and touched her Cuff. Instantly, about halfway down the block, an electric engine hummed to life. A moment later, a single LED headlight flashed twice.

"There," Monika said, and something in her tone made Cheryl think she might be bragging.

It was a motorcycle, painted so completely black that it had been all but invisible in the gloom. As Cheryl watched in wonderment, it shifted into gear, left the curb, and came buzzing over to them.

Now, self-driving cars had been commonplace for more than ten years. But she'd never heard of the technology finding its way to motorcycles, or any other two-wheeled conveyance for that matter. She looked from the idling bike to Monika, who wore a pleased, even prideful expression.

"Not bad, huh?" the vigilante said.

And it suddenly struck Cheryl that this person, whoever they were, had never before had the opportunity to share even some of their more impressive secrets with anyone. All this time, throughout their crusade against state-wide corruption, they'd been alone — until now.

Until me.

Dear God. Maybe we are *friends.*

"I… didn't think they made AI-drive bikes," she heard herself say.

Checkmate replied, "They don't, at least not yet. This is a Harley Davidson LiveWire 3. It's got 110 horses and 82 pound-feet of torque. But I added the self-drive tech myself."

"So, you have…what? A Checkmatecycle? You *are* Batman."

Monika waved her hand in an extravagant, dismissive gesture. "Batman wishes he was me."

Cheryl had to fight a smile as she examined the bike more closely. "Well, I have to admit this is pretty amazing," she finally declared. "You should patent the technology and get rich."

"Maybe someday. Right now, it's useful for getting around town, even in heavy traffic."

"So, you always ride a motorcycle?" Cheryl asked.

"That's kind of the point of it."

"No matter…" Her words trailed off as she tried to figure out the right way to say this. "…who you're wearing?"

At that, Monika laughed so hard she had to cover her mouth. "I never thought about it that way, but yeah."

"So… Ivan Saric rides around on a Harley?"

To her shock, the old man's voice came out of the waitress' mouth. "Now, my dear, that sounds a bit like ageism to me. Age is only a number, you know."

Cheryl had to fight a giggle, afraid of how it might sound given the night she'd had. "Okay. Sure," she said finally. "Why not?"

"Hop on," the vigilante told her, switching back to Monika as smoothly as blinking her eyes. She went around to a wide storage box that had been mounted onto the bike's rear fender. Opening it with her Cuff, she withdrew a bulky black helmet. "Put this on."

"What about you?" Cheryl asked.

"Only have the one," Checkmate replied. "Until now, that's all I've ever needed. But don't worry. I've got these." From the same storage box she took what looked like a pair of oversized sunglasses. These she fit over her face and activated. "Night vision. Heads-up display. I'll be fine. Now come on, we have to get off this street."

As she donned the helmet, finding it heavier than she'd expected, it suddenly occurred to Cheryl that she'd completely forgotten about her date with Omar. She checked her Cuff, found no messages from her would-be suitor, and figured that maybe he'd forgotten, too.

I got shot at tonight, she thought, feeling a bizarre mix of emotions. *I wonder what his excuse will be?*

But that was for tomorrow.

Aloud she asked Checkmate, "What about tomorrow?"

"What about it?"

"They're going to be coming after us," Cheryl said, and just uttering the words made her want to crawl into a hole and hide.

"I know. But we had us a big win tonight."

"We did? I didn't think you got the evidence you wanted on Cooker."

The vigilante shrugged. "Well, no… Though something tells me the chief justice is in hotter water now than anything the courts might fire up under her. But that's not what I mean. Honey, we met the enemy tonight. We now know exactly what we're up against, and that's the first step in fighting it."

Optimistic words. Cheryl wondered if Monika really believed them. "Okay," she heard herself say. "So what are we going to do about it?"

Checkmate's expression hardened, her face half hidden by the big glasses. "We're going to find Proprietor," she said. "We're going to rip that stupid mask right off their smug, murdering face. And then we're going to shut them the fuck down!"

The conviction—the righteous anger—helped push back some of Cheryl's fear, letting a few of her more mundane anxieties peek through. Proprietor and conspiracies aside, she had Sam to consider.

Poor Sam, who would wake up in the morning to find her car gone. Cheryl needed to decide how much of the truth to share with her roommate. Up until now, she'd held back almost nothing. But Sam had a protective streak, and if last night's rural debacle had proven anything, aside from Samuel's heretofore unsuspected skills as a stunt driver, it was that the person Cheryl lived with would go to dangerous lengths to protect her.

How might her dear friend, her best friend, react to a stolen car, a midnight burglary, guns, and beatings?

I'm going to be a mass of bruises. I'll have to conjure up some way to explain them.

"But that's for tomorrow," Checkmate said, and it took Cheryl a moment to understand that the vigilante was talking about finding this Proprietor person rather than reading her mind about Sam. "For, as an iconic character once said, 'Tomorrow is another day.'"

Cheryl, who'd read the novel *Gone with the Wind* in high school but had never seen the movie, mounted the bike, wrapped her arms around the vigilante's waist, and remarked wryly, "You're a lot of things, and I probably don't know half of them, but you're no Scarlett O'Hara."

Her partner, protector, and—yes—her friend, twisted around, lowered her sunglasses, and offered Cheryl a wry, conspiratorial wink. "Scarlett O'Hara wishes she was me."

Together the two of them rode back into the city, heading east, toward the dawn.

Toward tomorrow.

CHAPTER TWENTY-FIVE

THE INITIATE

WHITE QUEEN TO KING'S BISHOP SEVEN / CHECKMATE

Thursday, July 10, 2048

"YOU CAN'T DO THIS! ANTONOV! GODDAMN YOU, LISTEN TO ME!"

Former New Jersey State Trooper Jake Merryman fidgeted with his tie. He disliked suits, but had been warned, in no uncertain terms, that his former side gig and now full-time gig required it. The boss, more than one of his new colleagues had cautioned, paid extremely well but would interpret any slip in the dress code as a personal insult.

And insulting Vladimir Antonov tended to invite severe consequences.

Nevertheless, gray had never been Jake's color.

"Merryman!" Antonov called from the other room. "Get in here!"

He actually jumped. Christ, but that man had a booming voice! More than that, upon meeting him face-to-face for the first time, Jake had found himself more intimidated than at any other point in his life. The crime lord had eyed him as if he were a suspicious cut of beef, only to finally grunt something that one of the others had assured Jake translated to "You're hired."

It made him miss the state police, and Colonel Johnson's gruff demeanor — a little.

But the fiasco at the governor's mansion, added as it had been to his other "transgressions" as a state trooper, had effectively ended Jacob Merryman's career in law enforcement.

Well, never mind. Crime, as it turned out, paid a lot better.

"Antonov! Please! I'm a Sibling! Like you!"

Jake hadn't been here when everything went down. Instead, he'd been called in at the last minute, apparently because a number of Antonov's other soldiers had suffered a bad reaction to some kind of drug Checkmate had released. Jake, who remembered all too well his run in with the disguised son of a bitch outside the governor's mansion, could sympathize.

One day, I'll get even with him for that.

But for now, he had a job to do — and, apparently, a test to pass.

The guy who had picked him up from his home had warned him about this as well. "Antonov likes to make sure his people will do as their told, no hesitation, no second-guessing."

Jake had been instructed on the Cuffcall that he shouldn't take his own car, that Antonov would send someone to fetch him. Something about security. It didn't make much sense to Jake, but then any reservations he might have had disappeared when a top-of-the-line sports car pulled up in front of his apartment building. The driver turned out to be a good-looking guy who seemed too young to have a ride like this one.

"This your car?" Jake had asked him as he'd climbed into the shotgun seat.

The guy had nodded, which Jake took as proof he'd made the right call with this change of professions.

Clearly, there was serious money to be made here.

"Thanks for the pick-up," Jake said.

"I do as I'm told."

"No plans for the night?" It was just small talk — and, yes, maybe a way to distract himself from his nervousness. He'd been warned about what would be expected of him.

The guy replied, a little resignedly, "Actually, I was supposed to have a date tonight. An important one."

"Sorry, man."

The driver shrugged. They drove through the night for a few minutes in silence. Finally, again mostly out of angst, Jake asked, "So, you work for Mr. Antonov?"

The guy replied evenly, "I work with him. Let's just say he and I have the same boss."

"Vladimir Antonov has a boss?" Jake had asked with an incredulous laugh. "Who? The Devil, himself?"

But the driver didn't so much as crack a smile. "Forget it. Just believe me when I tell you: don't disappoint Mr. Antonov tonight. Do your job and say as little as possible. And for God's sake, don't ask him about his boss."

"Okay. Fine," Jake had said as the car pulled up in front of the ritzy Glen Afton house. "Thanks for the tip… uh… what's your name?"

When the driver replied, Jake inwardly scowled. The name sounded foreign.

And he didn't like foreigners.

Now as he stepped from the foyer of the fancy house and into what he took to be a small office of some kind, he found the chief justice of the state Supreme Court seated in a heavy wooden chair that looked like it had been borrowed from the dining room. Her hands were lashed to the armrests with zip ties, as were her ankles to the chair's sturdy front legs. She could struggle all she wanted and, at best, all she would do is topple the chair and herself to the hardwood floor. Instead, she'd opted to sit more or less still and express herself verbally.

Jake, who knew the woman only by reputation, was nonetheless amused to see someone so powerful laid low so completely.

Antonov was over by a fancy chess set that stood beneath one of the office windows. As Jake watched, the big gangster pulled the blinds shut and stepped back. Looking around, Jake realized that all the blinds had been closed. The thought of that, and its implications, washed away whatever amusement he might have been feeling.

"I'm here, Mr. Antonov," he said, annoyed at how his voice cracked.

Antonov glanced at him and nodded. Then he went to Cooker, who stared up at him, red-faced and teary-eyed.

"You and Zeta shared emails in which Argo was mentioned," Antonov said. "You both knew this was against protocol."

Cooker licked her lips and spoke again, the words spilling out of her. "That was Victor, not me! He liked to show off. You know that. He mentioned it. I never did. Not once."

"And you didn't report it to Proprietor, either. But that's only part of it, Delta." Antonov leaned close. "You used my people to try to kill the Walker girl, not once but twice. On top of that, when I arrived here, I found no less than a half-dozen of them hired on as private security. Forget the fact that Proprietor wanted, and still wants, Cheryl Walker alive, I take poaching of my employees, even temporarily, as a personal insult."

The woman in the chair stared up at him, her eyes, already blood-shot as hell, widening as it dawned on her, really and truly dawned on her, where this was going.

"Please," she said, not yelling this time but almost whisper quiet. "Please don't."

Antonov ignored her, turning instead to Merryman. "Everybody else has cleared out. It's just you and me. This is where we find out just how well you're going to work out in this job."

Jake, who'd never seen anyone killed before, nevertheless stiffened his spine and replied, "I understand, Mr. Antonov."

The boss grunted, which Jake supposed meant his response had proven acceptable.

"Here's how this is going to work," he said to Cooker. "You'll be found in the morning by someone. I don't know who, though I'm sure Proprietor does. The security camera feeds have been doctored to remove myself and my people from the scene. We've even taken out the Walker girl, because Proprietor has other plans for her. But Checkmate's presence has been preserved, even enhanced. It should be enough."

"Enough for what?" the chief justice — former chief justice — asked plaintively.

"For your murder to be tied to her," Antonov replied with almost no inflection.

"Please," Sally Cooker said again, sobbing openly now. "I have my husband. He needs care."

Antonov shook his head. "He'll be found as well. Proprietor thinks, and I agree, that adding his death to the narrative will strengthen public outcry against the vigilante."

"No!" the woman screamed. "You will not touch him! Haven't you done enough to him already?"

Jake's new boss replied calmly, "Everything that's happened to him has been a direct result of your bad judgment."

Jake wondered if there was any irony in that statement. Then he decided it didn't matter.

"Merryman," the crime lord said. "Do it."

"Do what, Mr. Antonov?"

Antonov fixed him with a look that would have melted butter — and suddenly Jake got it. His mouth went dry. "Oh," he said.

"Now. Do it now."

For perhaps five seconds, Jake didn't move. His entire body had gone cold, despite having felt stifled by the gray suit only moments before. Then, through an effort of what felt like monumental will, he stepped deeper into the room and stopped within six feet of the seated, screaming woman.

Cooker wailed, "Please! I'm begging you! You can't do this! You can't!"

Jake looked from her to Antonov, who had returned to the chess set and was studying it as if it were the only thing in the room worth his attention.

This, Jake supposed, was the test.

Refusing to let his hand tremble, he reached inside his suit and drew out the silenced Sig Sauer compact nine-millimeter pistol. Like the suit, the gun had been issued to him at his point of hire. At the time, the weapon had struck him as an upgrade from the bulkier state police standard issue Glock.

At the sight of the gun, Sally Cooker stopped screaming, her mouth snapping shut with an audible click.

Jake wanted to tell her he was sorry, that this wasn't personal. But he didn't dare show that kind of weakness in front of Vladimir Antonov.

He wordlessly leveled the Sig and, with a hand that only shook a little bit, fired a single round into the woman's forehead. Both she and the chair fell over backward, landing with a heavy *thump* that made the floor rattle.

There wasn't much blood.

"Good," Antonov said without turning. "Now, go upstairs and do the same thing to the old man in the bed."

Jake stared down at the corpse. Bile rose in his throat, but he swallowed it back before replying, "Yes, Mr. Antonov."

With that, he left the office, crossed the hall, and climbed the stairs to the second floor.

When he returned less than a minute later, his entire body cold even while sweat stung his brow, he found his employer standing right where he had been. Antonov had an open book in his hands and was flipping through it with obvious interest.

"All done?" the crime lord asked without looking up.

"Yes, sir."

"You play chess, Merryman?"

"No, Mr. Antonov."

"Me neither. My uncle did though. He loved the game."

"Oh," Merryman said, not sure what was expected of him in this odd conversation. "Where's he now?"

"Dead," Antonov replied, off-handedly. "I killed him." He snapped the book closed and slipped it neatly onto a bookshelf beside the chessboard with others of its ilk. "Stay here a minute. I want to give the house a final walkthrough. Don't leave this room."

"I understand, Mr. Antonov."

"You did good work tonight."

"Thanks. Thank you, sir."

Antonov nodded, pushed past him, and headed down the hallway in the direction of the kitchen and family room, leaving Jake alone with one of the two people he'd murdered tonight.

For some reason, he thought of his mother, who lived down in Woodbury. He hadn't seen her since Christmas, hadn't called her since Mother's Day. He resolved to do so tomorrow, just to hear her voice, make sure she was okay. He didn't know why, exactly, but it felt like the right thing to do.

Without realizing he was doing so, Jake wandered over to the chessboard. It was a nice one, with squares of black and white marble and what looked like hand-carved pieces. He knew nothing about the game. The only time he'd ever tried playing it, he'd found the rules too confusing and the gameplay boring as hell. He preferred vid games.

Then his eyes strayed to the bookshelf, where all the titles seemed to be collections of chess games. This was what the boss had been flipping through? He couldn't imagine anything more uninteresting.

But to each his own.

God, my stomach's in knots.

For no other reason than to quell his nerves, Jake scanned some of the titles: *The Best Games of Bobby Fisher*, *Howard Staunton's Top Games*, *Peter Leko's Top Ten Openings*. There were other names, too, lots of them. But most were foreign—Russian or Polish or something—and harder to pronounce.

"Ready, Merryman?"

Jake turned, "Ready, Mr. Antonov."

"Let's get out of here. Leave the office door open."

"Yes, sir."

Jake Merryman followed his new employer out of the room, out of the house, and into the night, where the sports car and its driver were waiting. Antonov, he'd been told, would be dropped off first, delivered either to his home or his office, depending on the big man's mood. Afterward, Jake would be driven back to his apartment. It would be late, but Jake didn't suppose he'd be sleeping much anyhow, not after the night he'd just had — what he'd just done.

Vaguely he wondered if Antonov liked music while in the car, or if he preferred conversation or simply silence.

Though usually a nervous talker, Jake thought he'd be perfectly happy with silence.

He all but forgot the chessboard and the books with their unpronounceable names. Why were so many chess experts commies, anyway?

And commies with stupid names, at that.

After all, what sort of name was Sam Reshevsky?

ABOUT THE AUTHOR

TY DRAGO IS A FULL-TIME WRITER AND THE AUTHOR OF TEN published novels, including his five-book *Undertakers* series (optioned for a feature film), *Dragons,* an SF genre-bender, and *Rags*, an edgy YA horror novel set in Atlantic City. He's also the founder, publisher, and managing editor of ALLEGORY (www.allegoryezine.com), a highly successful online magazine that, for more than twenty years, has featured speculative fiction by new and established authors worldwide.

Ty's horror novel, *St. Damned*, will be released in 2025, as will his historical saga, *The New Americans.* He's just completed *Angelfire*, a modern retelling of the Orpheus legend.

He lives in New Jersey with his ever-patient wife Helene, one needy dog, and three goofy hens.

CHECKMATE'S SUPPORT NETWORK

Abigail Reilly
Alex Jay Berman
Andrew Kaplan
Andy Holman Hunter
Anthony R. Cardno
Aysha Rehm
Bailey A Buchanan
Barry Nove
Benjamin Adler
bill
Bill & Kelley & Kyle
Brendan Coffey
Brian D Lambert
Brian Klueter
Brooks Moses
Buddy Deal
Caitlin Rozakis
Candi O'Rourke
Carla Spence
Carol J. Guess
Carol Jones
Caroline Westra
Cheri Kannarr
Christine Lawrence
Christine Norris
Christopher Bennett
Christopher J. Burke
Coats Family

Colleen Feeney
Craig "Stevo" Stephenson
Crysella
Dale A Russell
Danielle Ackley-McPhail
Danny Chamberlin
Denise and Raphael Sutton
Doniki Boderick-Luckey
Donna Hogg
Duane Warnecke
E.M. Middel
Ef Deal
Ellen Montgomery
Emily Weed Baisch
Erin A.
"filkertom" Tom Smith
Frank Michaels
Gary Phillips
Gav I
GhostCat
GraceAnne Andreassi
    DeCandido
Greg Levick
Ian Harvey
J.E. Taylor
Jack Deal
Jakub Narębski
James Aquilone

Jamie René Peddicord
Jennifer Hindle
Jennifer L. Pierce
Jeremy Bottroff
Joe Gillis
John Keegan
John L. French
John Markley
Jonathan Haar
Judy McClain
Karen Palmer
KC Grifant
Kelly Pierce
Ken Seed
kirbsmilieu
krinsky
Lark Cunningham
LCW Allingham
Lee
Lee Thalblum
Lisa Kruse
Liz DeJesus and Amber Davis
Lorraine J Anderson
Louise Lowenspets
Lynn P.
Maria V Arnold
Marie Devey
Matthew Barr
Michael A. Burstein
Michael Barbour
Morgan Hazelwood
Mustela
Niki Curtis
Paul Ryan
pjk
Rachel A Brune

Raja Thiagarajan
Reckless Pantalones
Rich Gonzalez
Rich Walker
Richard Fine
Richard Novak
Richard O'Shea
Rigel Ailur
Robert Greenberger
Robert Ziegler
Ronald H. Miller
Ruth Ann Orlansky
Scott Schaper
Shawnee M
Shervyn
Sheryl R. Hayes
Sonia Koval
Sonya M.
Steph Parker
Stephen Ballentine
Stephen W. Buchanan
Steven Purcell
Subrata Sircar
Susan Simko
The Creative Fund by BackerKit
Thomas Bull
Thomas P. Tiernan
Tim Tucker
Tom B.
Tracy Popey
Tracy 'Rayhne' Fretwell
Will "scifantasy" Frank
'Will It Work' Dansicker
William C Tracy
wmaddie700

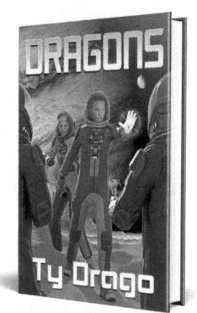

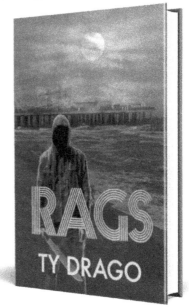

www.ingramcontent.com/pod-product-compliance
Lightning Source LLC
LaVergne TN
LVHW090817080525
810575LV00001B/13